The Torc of Tethera

BOOKS BY MICHAEL LAIRD

The Chronicles of Tethera

The Forged Prince

The Torc of Tethera

The Queen of Deceit (forthcoming)

The Torc of Tethera

Book Two of the Chronicles of Tethera

MICHAEL LAIRD

This one is for my parents, whom my daughters, nieces, nephews, and cousins know as Kay-Kay and Applejack. Besides being all around incredible folks, they read a lot of books and it led to me becoming addicted to the habit at an early age.

CONTENTS

Chapter I

Well Met on the Road

Prince Llew, heir to the mighty kingdom of Gwent and future high king presumptive of all Tethera, had been living in fear for nearly a year now.

It was not the prospect of visiting the kingdom of Gwynedd that had evoked such dread. Indeed, the journey had been fascinating and he would have enjoyed every moment of it were it not for the impending doom that awaited him at its end.

Helgar reined in and looked at the mountains ahead of them. "You know, Llew," the young Northman said, "if we had taken one of my people's ships we would already be there instead of getting blisters on parts of the body not meant to be sat on all day."

"More likely we would be at the bottom of the sea," replied Cymri. "It is never a clever thing to travel on top of the sea when the Fomorii that live under that sea are ruled by a being that hates you."

"Bah," said Helgar, "Northmen ships are not bothered by

the sea people and how would Dylan even know that Llew was on such a ship?"

"Northmen ships are not bothered by sea people—that you know of," she corrected. "How many ships disappear on the voyage to and from your homeland? One in every three is it not? And as for knowing if Llew was aboard, we have to assume Dylan has his informants on land. Certainly he knew precisely where to find Princess Llewellyn when she sailed up here last year."

As Helgar prepared his next response, Llew interjected with, "Peace, please, the both of you. Gower and I are just having a pleasant ride in the countryside and we shall be crossing into Gwynedd very shortly, I am sure."

Helgar snorted. "A pleasant ride he says, two weeks in the saddle, most of it through wilderness, while constantly expecting to be leaped upon by some strange beastie of one sort or another. And he calls it a pleasant ride! We still have a three day ride to the capital when we *do* enter Gwynedd."

Shrugging, Llew said, "It has been pretty pleasant so far." The weather had favored them and allowed them to make good time, passing out of Gwent and skirting the border of Dyfyd, crossing into Ceredigion, and coming right up the coast to Gwynedd, all without significant difficulties. The journey had afforded Llew an opportunity to see more of Tethera. It was a wild and beautiful land and he loved it, even if it was becoming a bit too wild.

Cymri cast her eyes over the uninhabited lands surrounding them. "My father told me that a century ago this trip only took a week, all told, from Caerleon to the north coast of Gwynedd."

"Because of the Wild Growth?" Llew asked.

"Yes, Llew, because of the Wild Growth."

Their travel had been planned in such a way as to stay within civilized lands as much as possible, but that meant little when such lands were clearly both diminished and farther apart than they once were.

The civilized lands were diminished because Man's fortunes were on the wane, and had been since the fall of the great kingdom, over a century earlier. They were farther apart because, due to the strange effects of the Wild Growth, the lands of Tethera were stretching and expanding. Yet this stretching was a subtle thing. It never happened where anyone could see it. Forests, bogs, hills, caves, and ruins were appearing where they never had been before, while some, that had already existed, merely grew larger. The wilderness areas, and even the gaps between towns and villages, were thus increasing in size, although at nothing like a constant rate. In this way, shorter journeys inevitably became longer ones.

It was fortunate that, in most cases, roads were not severed but were, instead, somehow stretched across the expanded areas. Although theories abounded, no one knew why the expansion was occurring, it was generally seen as a curse. It was certainly helping to further isolate the fragmented kingdoms of what had formerly been the Great Kingdom of Tethera. Worse, evil things kept emerging in the wilder places; many of them were like nothing ever seen before.

"Ah, and what is this?" Llew asked. He halted Gower beside a slender stone set upright and just off to the left side of the road. Standing about five feet high, it had large symbols chiseled into the sides. "This would mark the border of Gwynedd if I do not miss my guess."

Cymri regarded the stone a moment. "A very good guess, Llew. What gave it away?"

Llew cocked one eyebrow at her and replied, "The fact that I can hear ten or twenty men and horses hidden just ahead of us. No doubt they are awaiting us so that they may assess our intent in the mighty kingdom of Gwynedd."

"Llew, how do you know they are not bandits instead?" Helgar asked, while he checked his weapons.

"Because, their scouts have been watching us all morning as we approached. I could hear them when they were moving and so could occasionally catch sight of them. They are not bandits."

Flanked by Cymri on one side and Helgar on the other, Llew rode very slowly past the border stone. A voice rang out from ahead, "Hold there!"

A dozen armed warriors rode out from concealment ahead of them and took position on the road about sixty paces away. The one in the best armor called out again, "I am Captain Wogan and my men and I are charged with the safety of Gwynedd. Do nothing rash, I warn you! I have one hundred of the finest bowmen in the kingdom already surrounding you on the slopes above."

Sensing their consternation, Llew sought to allay the concerns of his companions. "They have somewhere between one and two dozen such men unless some of them are being far more quiet than I believe they are capable of."

"You are within the sovereign kingdom of Gwynedd. You are outnumbered and without reinforcement. Lay down your arms peacefully and you may be permitted to leave in the same manner," the captain continued.

Helgar rode a few steps closer and called out, "You ask Prince Llew of Gwent to disarm before you will even deign to treat with us? Outrageous that is! For fifteen years you have known this day would come and this is the welcome you give?"

The captain called back, "Even if your appearance did not give you away, your tongue certainly does. You are a wretched Northman and will find no easy passage here!"

The Northman in question reached for his great axe, perhaps not the best weapon for a mounted man, but daunting all the same. Knowing firsthand what it could do, Llew reacted immediately and cried out, "Hold Helgar! I have no wish to start our visit by butchering the border guard."

Then to the captain, "It is as he says. I am Prince Llew of Gwent, come to," there was a long pause while Llew swallowed deeply, "come to present myself to my betrothed, the Princess Bloddeuwedd of Gwynedd."

Captain Wogan left his men where they were and rode a few paces closer. "If your intention is peaceful, why then do you need an army at your back?"

Llew turned in his saddle and glanced back past his man servant, Addfwyn, at the forty extremely dangerous looking men that had been following him in two mounted columns, then looked back at the captain before answering, "After what happened the last time I rode the length of Tethera? Are you serious? Do you think my father would let me come all this way alone?"

"Hear me, men of Gwynedd," called out a new, higher-pitched voice. "Your courage and devotion is unquestioned and unquestionable, but here and now it is wisdom that is needed. At least some of you must know of me, I am not at all a stranger to Gwynedd. I am Cymri ferch Taliesin. Yes, the chief of all bards is my father and I give you my word this is indeed the Prince of Gwent and, once their marriage is complete, your own ruler as well. Are any of you really thinking to attack him if he declines to lay down his weapons?"

Cymri's voice seem weirdly amplified. Llew glanced to her and saw she had her harp out and was gently plucking at strings—so gently that he could barely even hear music. Oddly, it still seemed to be making everyone feel calmer, despite that those further away could certainly not hear it.

Captain Wogan, his sword sheathed and his lance not leveled, rode right up to them then. Pausing about four horse lengths away he removed his helm, revealing a youngish man with hair still brown and curly. Like most Tetheran men, he was clean-shaven, save for a large but finely groomed moustache that framed his mouth and chin.

Llew was a bit envious. Earlier attempts had made it clear it would still be a while before he could grow himself a moustache worthy of the name. Yet, when nearly every grown man sported one, it made Llew look unreasonably young to be going about completely bare-faced. In contrast, Helgar was already well on the way to growing a full beard in the manner of the Northmen.

The captain saluted, then said, "Taliesin is certainly well known here and I find it easy to credit that this is his daughter. Greetings, Prince Llew, and to you as well, Lady Cymri. A thousand apologies for our introduction, but these are difficult times. As I said, I am Captain Wogan. Your men can certainly keep their weapons. In truth, that is a good thing. These borderlands are poorly settled and there are rumors—and more than rumors—of many strange and terrible things appearing in such sparsely populated places."

He glanced toward Helgar, who was glowering at him in return. "And my apologies to you as well Lord Helgar; if you are in service to Prince Llew then my sentiments were out of place."

"Service?" rumbled Helgar, somewhat ominously.

"Ah, Jarl Helgar of Lindenjal is a friend and ally, captain. Certainly not a—" Llew began.

"Ya, Prince Llew is my drott," explained Helgar.

"Ah, yes," said Captain Wogan, clearly not sure what direction the exchange had moved in. "Your highness, a moment while I give my lieutenant his marching orders and select a detail, then I will personally escort you to Queen Enid."

A few moments was all it took before Llew and his group were again moving up the road. The captain took his place with Llew and his friends, while five of his men ranged ahead and five took up the rear.

"Not afraid that we will overpower you as soon as we are away from the bulk of your men?" Llew asked. "The better to sneak in and assault your capital?"

"Nay, your highness. I already sent a rider on ahead some hours ago when my scouts first spotted you approaching. You will not march on Caer Pyn y Mwd to find it unprepared."

"Just one rider?" asked Llew.

The captain grimaced and said, "Three in fact, at different times and by different routes—just in case."

Llew nodded his understanding.

* * *

The entire trip had been relatively uneventful. They had stayed too far from Pictish lands for any trouble from them and, although the Lord of Death's reach had grown long of late, they had remained sufficiently distant from Annwyn to avoid potential threat from that quarter as well. Likewise, their numbers were great enough that any bandits or war bands sighting them knew better than to get in their path, even without the addition of Captain Wogan and his warriors.

That ended the next day while, as they were traveling higher into the mountains, two of Captain Wogan's forward scouts came riding back at a gallop. Wogan spurred forward to meet them. "Report!" he barked as they reined to a halt in front of him.

The rider to the captain's left wasted no time in replying, "Sir, it is Blevens; he was slain. We found his body just ahead and he has probably been there since yesterday. It looks as if something ate his horse, bones and all, there is not much left of it. Blevens was nearby, but not eaten. Possibly whatever killed him was either satisfied by the horse or else did not like the taste of his chainmail. No one looted him; we found his weapons lying where they fell, apparently unused, and he still had his coin pouch."

Captain Wogan turned a concerned glance on Llew and explained, "Blevens was one of the three men I dispatched to bring word of your coming to the queen."

Alerted, the formation moved down the road to the remains of the unfortunate rider. Captain Wogan and his men spent some time examining the dead man. Then they moved him off to the side of the road and began gathering stones for a cairn.

Captain Wogan rode back to Llew, "My apologies, your highness, but we must take care of this. We also need to look about a bit. We have never seen wounds like his and must know more about what new evil may have come into the wilds. Blevens was a solid warrior, and a capable rider; he would not have been easy prey for any ordinary beast."

Llew called out to his subalterns, "Iau, Trynt, take your squads and assist them with the stones. Cynan, Drym, form a perimeter in case whatever did this is still about." With so many men working at it, the cairn was complete in minutes. The last stone was so large it took two of Llew's warriors to bring it.

When it had been laid to rest on top it was evident that the wolves would not be disturbing this warrior's remains. Captain Wogan ventured closer to that last stone and examined it at length. "This one has carvings on it and is a type of stone that I know is not found anywhere near this place." He looked toward the assembled men. "Which of you brought it?"

Two of the men raised their hands.

"And where did you find it? Show me."

After glancing at Llew and getting a nod, one of the two led Captain Wogan up the slope away from the road. They were accompanied by Llew and Helgar, along with a collection of guardsmen from both kingdoms. They took less than a hundred steps before the trooper pointed toward ruins that had been obscured by the trees.

Captain Wogan swore when he saw it. "By Balor's fangs! I know this area well and that was not here even a few weeks ago."

Llew regarded the ancient lichen covered stones and the ivy that climbed it on one side. "Are you certain? It looks to have been here for ages."

"I am certain, your highness, and I expect we may even find Bleven's killer there. I would seek to investigate it but you should remain at the road with your men it case whatever did this is too much for us."

"Nay, captain. If we are to assume it may be the lair of something dangerous then we should act accordingly. We should either retreat, or be prepared to attack at full strength. Anything else simply invites misfortune." Then, in a sharper voice, Llew added, "No, Helgar, please wait for the rest of us."

Helgar had his axe out in a two-handed grip and looked ready to charge straight up to the ruins. With a sigh, he relented and waited while Llew and Captain Wogan formed up their warriors, leaving a dozen to hold the horses ready down below at the road.

They picked their way up the slope to the ruin. It was obvious why the warriors had found a loose piece downslope. Whatever this was, it was ancient beyond reckoning.

In appearance, it was little more than a level platform built up from large stones that were intricately fitted together with no visible mortar. Many of the stones boasted what once must have been ornate carvings, now difficult to discern due to ages spent in the sun and the rain. Additionally, four huge circular pillars rose from the surface. They were roughly four or five man-heights each, but one was shorter. Apparently the top stone had fallen off in ages past for it was split and lying on the slope nearby.

As they approached, Llew realized the whole thing was bigger than he had initially thought. When they actually reached it, they discovered climbing up on top of it while still in armor was not an easy feat.

Here it could be seen that the four pillars surrounded an enormous well, perhaps two horse-lengths across. Its depths were unknown, lost in inky darkness far below. It was, thought Llew, the single most ominous and frightening thing he had ever seen that was not already actively trying to kill him. Helgar pointed to traces of fresh blood on the edges of the pit. "What say you?" he inquired of Llew. "Shall we lower men on ropes to see what is at the bottom?"

Llew stared at Helgar while Captain Wogan visibly blanched. "Ah no, thank you, Helgar," said Llew, at last. "That might . . . not be in our best interests right now." He looked again into the depths of the well, "Even so, if something dwells at the bottom and slays travelers we should put a stop to that."

"And how would you propose to do that, Prince Llew?" Captain Wogan asked.

"I am thinking the builders of this place offer us a solution ready-made. The rearmost of these pillars is already listing towards the hole. We have the men and the horses it would take to topple it completely. With careful aim we could probably drop most of it into the shaft to plug it. This would be a service to the world if our fears are correct and will do no harm in any case. From what you say, this thing does not properly belong to our world in the first place."

"Unless you brought a good deal of rope and chain this will require some ingenuity," Cymri remarked.

"Cymri! You were supposed to stay with the horses," Llew admonished.

"You never ordered me to do so and I am certain I never announced that to be my intention. Besides, you have some champion horse-holders down there and they certainly do not require my supervision, while you, on the other hand—"

He snorted before saying, "Uh huh, and your plan would be?"

She pointed up the side of the hill. "Fell some trees and brace them sideways on the hill to make a kind of dam up there, then pile more logs behind it—big ones—and carefully roll boulders from above down into it. When you judge it to be enough, break the restraints. With any luck the avalanche will strike with enough force to topple that back pillar and, with a little more luck, at least part of it will go down that shaft. Certainly a lot of the other debris will. It might be enough, if delivered all at once, to really wedge it up proper."

Helgar regarded the hill above them and stroked his beard, then said, "It would take most of the day but I think we can do that, Llew."

Llew looked to Captain Wogan. "Any objections on your part, Captain?"

Wogan sighed and said, "It is going to be a very long day."

* * *

Getting the first logs in place and bracing them was a bit ticklish, but after that it was just a matter of felling and stripping more of the large trees that grew along the slope. While this was going on, a number of boulders were dislodged from up slope and rolled down to fill behind as well.

For all that it was relatively straightforward, it was not easy work. Only the largest trees were worth using and they took the most time to cut, strip of branches, and haul into place. It was too steep here to bring up the horses so it all had to be done with men's muscles. Likewise, many of the boulders did not want to move from their resting places of old.

Even so, as the afternoon wore on, the weight that was creaking against the impromptu dam became so alarming that Llew found himself checking constantly to make sure no one was downslope of it. He did not trust it to hold until they chose to unbrace it.

The shadows were getting longer when Llew started having a problem with his ears. There seemed to be an odd high-pitched thrumming noise in them. He brushed at them but failed to clear the sensation. In fact, it was getting worse.

Around him, he looked at the other men. They, too, were

now apparently having the same problem. A dreadful suspicion arose in his mind. "Helgar! Get to the other side! We have to be ready to release this now!" Helgar looked up from where he had been stripping the limbs on a huge tree trunk and his eyes grew wide as realization dawned on him as well.

The supporting braces had been built with their eventual removal in mind, yet, to hold back the enormous weight, they were built strong. Simply knocking them out of the way was beyond the strength of mortal men. Accordingly, Cymri had suggested a mid-sized log be positioned at each side of the dam. By using these as levers, the supports could be pried out. Or at least that was the plan.

The noise and vibration was rapidly increasing. To Llew, it sounded like nothing so much as a high pitched clicking noise repeating itself so rapidly it was almost one undulating sound. Because of it, he was reduced to hand signals to call men to help employ the log. He saw Helgar was having similar problems on the other side. Captain Wogan was helping by getting men's attention directly and pointing them to Helgar. On Llew's side, Cymri was doing the same for him.

With a dozen or so men on each side, Llew signaled Helgar and both sides lifted their logs and inserted them behind the braces, then strained to pry them out. Nothing happened. They were too stout and the weight squeezing them between the dam and the hill was too great. Llew began to have doubts that this was workable, or that it would be in time, even if it was. Perhaps the logs would be better applied to the braces as battering rams?

The vibrating shriek of a noise reached its crescendo and out of the shaft erupted a monstrous dweller from the darkness below. Llew had expected something more in the way of a dragon or a herd of wolf-sized rats, something—anything—that he could reference in terms of creatures he at least had heard of. What came shooting out was the spawn of some terrible nightmare. Llew could not imagine what cursed world or age of horror it had come from. In form it had legs not unlike a centipede, and it was covered in flexible armored plates, but, aside from that, it was nothing like a centipede. Great pink tentacles of pulpy flesh, each of them easily three man-heights in length and studded with sharp fang-like projections, protruded from between the armored plates. The mouth itself was a horror of four great saber-sized mandibles with more tentacles writhing between them. Of eyes there was no sign at all.

Llew suspected the bulk of its body was still in the well, yet the creature raised itself up nearly as high as the tops of the columns themselves. Its head, if whatever was around that mouth could be said to qualify as such, whipped around in all directions before suddenly turning back to aim straight at them. Llew's heart quailed in his chest. Even without eyes it could sense them! Somehow, too, he felt certain it was possessed of far more than animal intelligence, although he could not say why.

More men had applied themselves to either side now. "Altogether now! Everyone! HEAVE!" Llew cried out. As one, over forty men, many too panicked to even try to run, did as their prince ordered. The braces bulged forward, then shattered under the weight. The dweller from the pit opened its mouth wide, exposing still more tentacles, and made a sound that was, perhaps, part roar, part primal scream. It was good their work was done, for many men now released their grip on their respective log to cover their ears and the others were forced to let go as well. This was fortunate in that the avalanche caught the part of each log that was behind its respective brace and both were snatched away as the dam collapsed and the great mass began to move. That only three men suffered minor injuries from the logs, as they jounced up and down and moved away, was a small miracle.

The avalanche, however, was underway and, although the

titanic monster from the elder depths might match its noise, it could not match its force. Llew watched as the boulders, stones, and logs bounced down the hill gaining speed. The monster visibly hesitated. Retreat, thought Llew, was probably foreign to it nature. Yet it seemed to realize that, even if it might get out of the shaft in time, it would still be unable to get clear of the oncoming wave of destruction. It began to inch its length back down into the depths, but it had waited too late.

Before it was below the lip of the shaft the crashing fury of logs and boulders cascading down the slope hammered into what would have been the head of a more earthly designed creature. An impenetrable wave of dust blasted up and obscured everything near the ground but above it they could see two of the columns come down. A third actually wobbled for a time.

Captain Wogan barked commands at his men and Llew's subalterns did the same with their own. A flurry of weapons were drawn and shields gathered and distributed as they all readied themselves in fighting formation.

Llew had no idea what they thought they were going to do if the great worm proved capable of surviving such an onslaught. Then he understood. By invoking the result of endless training they were being kept too busy to allow them time to consider their fears. As a bonus, if the beast had survived, they would at least be able to go down fighting rather than waiting like sheep for the slaughter.

The dust cleared sufficiently for Llew to see the platform. Actually, it was so covered in broken stone and timber that he would not have known a platform had ever been there save for the remaining two columns. Of the dark well there was no sign; it was thoroughly sealed. Of the worm itself there was nothing to show that it had ever existed.

Llew permitted himself a cautious smile and clapped

Captain Wogan on the back. Helgar let out a great yell and shouted loudly, "The great worm! Dead! Big heroes we all are! Three cheers for my drott, Prince Llew!" And the men cheered.

Llew took it stoically; he was getting better at that, and called out, "Indeed, three cheers for you all! We have injured or killed the beast that slew one of our own and sealed its dark portal into our world. Those who are enemies of Tethera will learn that the time of Men is not yet over. If Tethera, great kingdom of old, has fallen and cannot be restored, why then, we shall build a new one and nothing will be beyond us!" The men cheered again. Llew tried not to let it go to his head. Then his eyes fell on Cymri. "And three cheers for Lady Cymri as well. It was her plan by which the beast was defeated—and so it is by her design that all of us are still alive to see the result."

Llew gave a mental sigh of relief. He suspected that, by remembering to give her the credit she deserved, he had narrowly dodged an arrow. For a moment he thought that Cymri might blush as she accepted their cheers with a quiet dignity and what Llew thought of as 'the royal wave,' but she did not. Aside from musical ability, Llew briefly wondered how much overlap in desirable skills and abilities might exist between bards and royalty. Although . . . she was heir to the kingdom of Ceredigion should she or Taliesin ever desire she should take up that burden, and, therefore, technically a princess in her own right.

Helgar and Captain Wogan crossed the debris to them and Helgar called out, "Did you see, Llew? Some big bad thing from depths of Hel itself and what does it do when it sees us? It tries to run before it even tries to fight."

"Ooh, I know what that means," said Cymri.

In unison, Helgar, Cymri, and Llew all recited: "Scary fellows we be, eh?" Then broke up laughing. Captain Wogan looked at them as though they had all lost their minds and he was too polite to say anything.

"I am noticing, I am, that you like to roll heavy things down upon your enemies," remarked Helgar.

Llew shrugged, "Afaggdu was very emphatic that I should not worry overmuch about honor when fighting creatures that have none themselves. I suspect that worm fell into that category."

"Ya," responded Helgar, "it fell into a big hole, too! I think also maybe Hafgan had the right of it when he said that if your force is not strong enough to do the job you should use more of it."

"Hmm," Llew mused, "that may not be exactly what he meant but it is close enough. Now we already have another issue. It is getting dark. We should camp here and, in the morning, clear the road of any debris that reached it. Gwynedd likely needs that road kept open, eh captain?"

"It certainly does and I appreciate it, your highness," the captain answered. "The job is not over until it is over, eh?"

"That might be true," Llew replied, "but I am starting to find that it is never over. Further, it is what I must begin at this expedition's end that worries me most. Once begun, it will never be over."

Chapter II

Welcome to Gwynedd

Two days later, they were approaching Abergwyngregyn, the capital of Gwynedd, called Aber by most folk, when Captain Wogan offered a suggestion. "Your highness, Aber is a not a large town and this many mounted men moving through it will be a problem. With your permission I would rather skirt the town and lead you around. That will make it easier to approach the palace."

"Send the men around," directed Llew. "I want to ride through and see it." He laughed at Wogan's expression. "Oh do not worry, you can escort me and I will bring Helgar and Cymri as well. I cannot believe we will be in too much danger, or that we four will present a major disruption."

When they entered the town Llew cast his eyes about and found he was disappointed. Calling this a town seemed overgenerous. The home of choice was the simple round house, a single room dwelling with mud and wattle walls and a high thatched roof. Most of these were so primitive they did not even have chimneys; instead they allowed the smoke from the central fire to simply rise up and pass through the thatch. Despite this general backwardness, the town was busy and even moving through it was a challenge at times.

Cymri saw his expression and commented, "You were expecting something more on the scale and sophistication of Caerwent, were you not, Llew? Do not think that this is all there is to Gwynedd. The kingdom has moved its capital many times and all of them ere now boast larger towns than this poor example. Most are on the Isle of Mona."

"Then why do they now have their capital here?" Llew asked.

"When the crown went to Princess Bloddeuwedd's father he brought it here to his own cantref. It does have the advantage of sitting on the approach to the Isle of Mona. At the same time, because it is still on the mainland, it is more accessible for those traveling by land."

Llew spotted a face in the crowd watching them, then lost it and tried to find it again, only to see the man dodge behind a building. "Cymri, Helgar, did either of you see a man in a brown cloak watching us from down that lane to the left?"

Cymri peered that way, "I confess I did not. Where is he now?"

Rather than immediately attempting an answer, Llew urged Gower into as fast a trot as they dared in the little town but, by the time they reached the house the man had vanished behind, there was no trace of him.

Llew's companions had followed him closely and now he pursed his lips and glanced at them. Taking in their questioning looks, he said, "He noticed me looking back at him. Then he spun and disappeared behind this round house."

"It seems probable he had not seen a woman who was also

a bard, as my bright outfit clearly shows me to be, and then you embarrassed him."

"I doubt that is what it was, Cymri," Llew replied, "chances are it is merely that he had never seen a red-headed, left-handed bard before."

"Clearly we will soon have to take a break from history and heraldry and take up the study of humor," she sniffed.

"Sounds like a guilty conscience he might have," boomed Helgar. "Was it someone we might know?"

"Of that I am not certain," Llew replied. "I did feel it was someone I had seen before but I did not get a long enough look at his face."

The young Northman remained stolid. "He is probably not a friend if he hides from us. Of course, if he is an enemy and makes himself known to us he would have to be very foolish. We should ask whoever rules here to keep an eye out for him."

"You are going to ask her to keep an eye out for an ordinary looking man in a brown cloak? I think Queen Enid might need a bit more to go on than that," Llew remarked.

"Queen?" asked Helgar. "I thought this kingdom had a regent?"

"She is the queen of the cantref of Malltraeth; she is not queen of Gwynedd. There is no queen. When Princess Bloddeuwedd weds Llew, then Bloddeuwedd will be queen," Cymri reminded him, "until she passes it to her closest relative in the succession, Queen Enid's grandson. Then Queen Enid will be regent again, until the boy is fourteen and can be crowned."

"That makes no sense," Helgar grumbled, "if the regent is a queen without a king, why cannot a princess become a queen without a king?"

"Because the steward is not expected to produce an heir," Cymri told him.

Helgar's forehead furrowed in perplexity. "But if the heir was a man he would not have to be married before being crowned, no?"

"That is correct," said Cymri, "a male heir could be crowned upon turning fourteen."

"Can he be married at that age?" Helgar inquired. "Llew is fifteen now—almost sixteen—and he is not permitted to marry."

"No, Helgar," Llew broke in, "in the days of the Roaming Empire, the age was only twelve but—"

"A moment, Llew," Helgar interrupted. "Why is it you say Roaming Empire when you speak of the Roman Empire? Several times I have heard you do this."

Completely perplexed, Llew asked, "What? Why would anyone call it the Roman Empire?"

"My fault," said Cymri to Helgar. "When he was much younger and I was tutoring him, I tried several times to get him to say it the right way, but he insisted on calling it the Roaming Empire. I knew he would eventually learn better and it was not hurting anything—it was even somewhat cute—so I let it go."

"What!" exclaimed an outraged Llew.

"Ho, ho!" laughed Helgar.

Captain Wogan bit his lip but otherwise gave no indication he was listening.

"See?" Cymri continued. Then to Llew she said, "And now

you know better and it did no harm."

"Other than making me sound like a half-wit in front of anyone that ever heard me say it? Well, no, I guess not," Llew complained bitterly. "Any other little gaps in my education we should clear up right now?"

"Really, Llew, other than being illiterate, you are exceedingly well educated for your age. Do please continue with what you were saying about required ages for marriage."

Llew gave her quick glare. "As I was saying, Helgar, when the *Roman*," he said, placing an exaggerated emphasis on the word, "Empire ruled these lands, the age for marriage was only twelve but High Queen Boudicca, with no less than two daughters of her own, felt this was much too young. She decreed that no one, neither woman nor man, would marry before their seventeenth birthday, and so it remains, although it has been over a century since the fall of the great kingdom."

"It seems unfair that women must wait three years longer to take power than men," Helgar rumbled.

"Why Helgar," Cymri said, "I think that is the most enlightened thing I have ever heard you say."

They came out of the town on the opposite side and the warriors of Llew's guard were still approaching from their right, having had further to come. Llew spared them little attention, his focus was on the structure before him.

"That is it?" he exclaimed in disbelief. "That is Caer Pyn y Mwd?"

It shocked Llew to his core to find the capital fortification of Gwynedd so much more vulnerable than Caerleon. Gwynedd was a powerful kingdom, comparable in many respects to Gwent itself, yet the main fortification of its capital was built of wood, resting on top of a large flattened clay mound. Although it stood very close to the river it had no moat at all, only a protective ditch that encircled it.

An enormous mansion and its outlying buildings lay just southeast of the fort and this was clearly where the royal family dwelt and held court. Llew shook his head in disbelief upon seeing it. Did these people not know there were barrow warriors and shape-changers and other things running loose in the world?

It suggested to him that Gwynedd, well situated for defense against human foes, and guarded by its mighty armies, felt there was no power that could or would attack it here. Llew cast his eyes to the coast that was only a few hundred feet away. He had never heard of the Fomorii attacking anything bigger than a village but there could always be a first time, especially if the people of the sea were now led by Dylan, a being with a virulent hatred of Tetheran royalty. If they came out of the sea they could be at the palace before the royal family could even reach refuge in their wooden fort.

Bypassing the wooden fort, Llew's contingent went directly to the palace. A small army of servants had assembled there and was waiting to meet them. No apparent dignitaries waited with them, for which Llew was grateful. He really needed some time before what he knew was coming. He needed time not just to clean up but to come to grips with the dread that had been growing in him this past year.

A well-dressed servant boy tried to take his reins as he dismounted. Gower, although better trained than in the past, made an ominous snort at this and Llew had to act quickly to introduce the two. He first checked his pockets and, realizing he had none of the small apples left, palmed a piece of dried meat to the lad, then indicated it was to be offered to the steed. The boy looked askance at this but did as he was bid and watched in disbelief as the huge horse snapped it up, then panted for a moment. Llew patted Gower's side affectionately and passed the reins to the boy without further incident.

After his men and horses had been seen to, Llew followed another servant to his rooms for a much needed cleanup. Fifteen days in the rain and the sun and the dust and the mud had done him few favors. It was a shame, he thought, that the Roman—he grimaced anew at the corrected name—Empire had never gotten around to building any of their incredible baths here. He had first encountered them in Caerwent and would have scoffed at the very idea had he heard of them in advance of that. Time and usage in Gwent had changed his mind.

Once Addfwyn had everything in place, including a large tub of steaming water, Llew shooed his retainer out.

"Are you certain, my lord? You may need additional water or . . . or something. This is what I do! I have not even begun to unpack your things yet."

"Heh, you are about as filthy as I am, Addfwyn. By royal decree I command you to go get cleaned up yourself. Take your time, my audience with Queen Enid is not for hours yet."

"Oh, I will be back long before that, my lord. We have much to do."

After Addfwyn left, Llew found himself wondering, not for the first time, how a simple crofter from the wilds of fallen Powys could know so much about being the personal manservant of a prince.

Eventually, the cooling water forced him out of the tub. He briefly considered calling for more hot water but the general muddiness of the used bathwater easily convinced him that he did not want to reenter it. After what was barely sufficient time to draw on some simple woolen breeches and a soft linen shirt, there came a knock at his door.

He opened it to find the boy from the stable, the one who had taken Gower, standing there holding a tray of what had to be food. The boy looked to be around ten or eleven years old and not especially big for his age. He was still wearing fine clothing and now wore a big smile as well.

"Greetings, your highness!" he chirped. "Welcome to Gwynedd. I have brought some light snacks that might help tide you over until dinner. It is still seven hours away and you will otherwise be quite ravenous I should think."

"Oh, thank you," replied Llew, somewhat amazed by the boy's verve and enthusiasm. He gestured to the room behind him, "Please, just put it anywhere."

The boy proceeded to do just that, choosing a small table with two chairs near the fireplace.

"We were all so disappointed when you did not show up last year and then we got word your ship had been lost in a storm and then we heard you had survived and found your way home to Gwent and did you really cross swords with the Lord of Death? And cleave the king of the Picts in two?" he asked breathlessly.

Llew tried to unravel all that in his head before he replied, "Yes, to Lord Arawen, but I did not win the sword portion of the fight, and no to the Pictish war chief. I only poked him in the eye and then rapped on his head until he was unconscious."

Llew went to the table with the food and sat down. Instead of offering to hold his chair or leaving, the boy dropped into the other chair.

Llew was completely nonplussed. "Are you joining me for this meal?" he asked incredulously.

The boy started uncovering the items he had brought. "Certainly, if you do not mind, I brought enough for us both and then some. Ma Cadding even donated one of her best berry pies. Ha! I never could have gotten that loose from the kitchen if I had not said it was for you! Besides, this way you can tell me some more about the many monsters you have vanquished while we eat."

More dumbfounded than before by the boy's sheer effrontery, Llew tried to decide whether he actually admired it or was about to eject him from the room with a swift kick to his backside—or both! Then a thought came to him.

"Have we met?" Llew asked. "Before you took Gower, I mean."

"Oh no, forgive me, your highness. I never even introduced myself. I am Caradog!"

Llew was feeling a bit lost. "Caradog?" he repeated.

"Prince Caradog," the boy added helpfully. "Queen Enid is my grandmother and you are about to marry my cousin, Blod."

"Oh, that Caradog," Llew exclaimed, silently counting his blessings for the fact that he had not yet applied his boot to the seat of the boy's pants. This young fellow was in the direct line of succession for the throne of Gwynedd!

Llew gave a mental shrug and sat down. The young prince was rather annoying but Llew had learned when such things had to be endured. This seemed one of those times.

"I did not expect to find you working as a stable boy," Llew remarked. "Surely that was you that took Gower from me when I arrived?"

"That was just so I could see you right away," explained

Caradog. "I did not regret it. I still cannot get over the fact that you feed your horse meat, and he likes it."

"Gower is a bit different from most steeds in many ways."

"He certainly is!" agreed Caradog. "Tell me about the monsters you have killed?

Llew shrugged and said, "Oh come, there are not that many monsters to my credit. I killed a barrow warrior but I had an assist from my sister and barrow warriors are already dead so that may not count. I did triumph over the war chief of the Picts but I did not slay him. See? I still wear the torc I took from him. That was just before I rescued Helgar and we had to defeat several Pict warriors—that was mostly Helgar's doing. He took down three while I only managed to get one. There were a few bandits but the survivors merely ran away after my sister and Helgar reduced their numbers. Later, I shot another Pict with my bow but that was only due to luck, mainly his bad luck. Then there was a strange chaos beast with endless mouths and eyes that I slew in the caves below Cas-Eiddew, but I am not certain it was real. We killed three hundred barrow warriors at Cas-Eiddew but that was mainly Hafgan's doing, as it turned out, I was just the bait. Hmm, I did defeat Lord Arawen of Annwyn but only because he was running away, he is a much better swordsman than any I have ever seen. And then of course it was not precisely him, he was just occupying another's body. And that," Llew concluded, "was pretty much it."

"How does he possess another man's body?" Caradog inquired. He had to wait for the answer while Llew devoured a large piece of Ma Cadding's best berry pie. It was, Llew admitted to himself, good enough to make up for having to entertain Caradog.

"It is some sort of enchantment he uses. You need not worry. He seems only able to do it to those who have agreed to be in his service. Queen Moriganna knows the same trick but for her it is only used on her shape-shifters, and they are most definitely in her service."

"Oh, right, and what about the shape-shifter in your quarters, the one that appeared to you first as Moriganna?" demanded Caradog.

Llew raised an eyebrow. "Word does get around does it not? I just stuck my dagger in it and pinned its jaws shut for a moment, then ran like a scalded cat. My sister, Llewellyn, took it down and Helgar delivered the killing blow with his axe."

"Yes!" exclaimed Caradog. "I have seen that enormous double-bladed axe he carries. Was it truly a gift from the Spriggan king? And it can split even enormous boulders apart without chipping or even dulling?"

Llew laughed, and said, "Well, it was actually more of a prize but yes, it was from the Spriggan king. It may be something like my sword in that I have never seen Helgar sharpen it but as for splitting boulders? I think Helgar would faint dead away at the suggestion it should be used so."

Now Caradog laughed. "I have wondered about that, my lord—"

"It is Llew, please, Caradog. We are both princes and I hope we will be friends as well as kinsman. When we are not in public, Llew is always fine. I was not taught to stand on ceremony, not initially at least. Growing up working in the stables of a wicked sorceress in a hidden stronghold teaches you not to place overmuch importance on formality for formality's sake alone."

Caradog was speechless for a moment, clearly trying to pick the words from a jumble of emotions and ideas running through his head.

Uh oh, thought Llew, *here it comes.* He braced himself for an outpouring of the spoken word.

Caradog then surprised him yet again by sitting up straight and calmly, and responding with, "Thank you, Llew. I very much wish to be your friend as well."

Perhaps there are hidden depths in this one, Llew thought to himself. *We shall have to keep an eye on him.* Then he wondered why he was referring to himself as 'we' in his own thoughts. Was it some legacy of his speaking with Lord Arawen and Queen Moriganna, both of whom always spoke of themselves in the third person?

Caradog furrowed his brow in puzzlement and asked, "You grew up in Caer Mallcoedwig? The stronghold of Moriganna? I thought that was where she had hidden away Llewellyn?"

Llew sighed. He had bobbled it. Perhaps he could recover the situation. "This is a crown secret that I am entrusting you with, Caradog. You must not repeat it. That was just the story we gave out, actually, it was me that grew up under the thumb of Moriganna. Llewellyn was in Gwent disguised as me, almost from birth."

"But why—" Caradog began. Then it clicked. "Because with only a princess, Gwent's betrothal to my cousin would have been off, and so would the alliance and the eventual merging of our kingdoms. It is a good thing you showed up!"

"That is exactly right, Caradog. Your perception does you great credit."

"What a wedding night that would have been if you had not appeared!"

Llew repressed a grin, "There might have been complications, yes."

29

"Ooh, I guess I am glad your family kept that one so close to the vest. I will tell no one! This way, Blod still gets to be high queen and when she does she will make me king of Gwynedd—after I swear eternal fealty to you and to her—which I am ready to do!"

Llew smiled, "I am glad to hear it, and my apologies, Caradog. I cut you off in mid-sentence. What was it you were wondering about?"

"Cut me off? Ah, it was about Helgar. I have been studying what is known about the Northmen a bit lately and—well—is not Helgar a girl's name?"

Again, Caradog had taken Llew off guard. "I think," Llew replied, in his most serious tone, "that you had better ask him that yourself."

They regarded each other expressionlessly for a moment. Then the room erupted in their uncontrolled laughter as they slapped their sides and pounded the table, barely able to breathe. Caradog actually fell off his chair.

Chapter III

She of the White Flowers

Two hours later, Llew found himself in his full regalia just outside the huge doors leading to the main hall. The ceremony to come had all been scripted to the finest detail.

He had gathered Cymri, Helgar, and half a dozen of his guardsmen to come with him when an overweight and somewhat florid man had come running up, out of breath, as they left their rooms.

"Hullo," he cried, "Prince Llew? I am Lord Prothos; I serve here on your father's behalf."

Llew stopped to meet the newcomer. "Ah, yes, I recall him mentioning your name. You are our envoy? I had thought you might meet us here when we arrived and then, frankly, decided something must have come up and you were no longer in the area."

"Oh yes, your highness, I do apologize for that. I have been watching for you for some days now and simply missed your arrival. My runner eventually came and told me you had come and here I am. You are on your way to meet with Queen Enid are you not?"

"Indeed I am," replied Llew.

"Oh that is excellent," Prothos said, "We worked it out ages ago. You brought a gift for Queen Enid and another for Princess Bloddeuwedd? Of course you did. Now—oh, but where are my manners? Greetings, your highness, you and I are second cousins, once removed. I have been here in Gwynedd these past eleven years. You were only four years of age when I left Gwent. You probably will not recall sitting on my lap and searching my pockets for sweetmeats."

Llew wondered if Llewellyn remembered that. Llew's primary recollection of being four was that it might have been about the age when he had been assigned to mucking out stalls in Queen Moriganna's stables.

"I am afraid I do not, good Prothos, but I harbor no doubt I was pleased with your generosity. Now you mentioned having worked out in advance how this meeting is supposed to proceed? We really do not have much time if I have to master some intricate ceremony while we make our way from here to the great hall."

"It is not that difficult, your highness. You will be announced, proceed to the throne, and make a sweeping bow. Then Queen Enid will rise and come to you to show she does not consider you her inferior. Indeed, her heir, Prince Caradog, will swear fealty to you once she passes the throne to Princess Bloddeuwedd and she, in turn, passes it to him."

"And then she winds up as regent again while waiting for Prince Caradog to reach his majority?"

"It should not come to that but even if it does it will not pose a problem."

And then they were at the doors.

Cymri allowed a palace guardsman to open one side for her and she went in. Llew made to follow but Prothos interposed himself between Llew and the doors and whispered, "Ah, not just yet, please, your highness. Lady Cymri will be playing for us and she will need a moment to get prepared. The guardsmen will let us know when all is in place. Ah, Jarl Helgar, if you would be so good as to remain at Llew's right side and one step back as he approaches the Queen that would be just the right touch. The two of you will be flanked by two of your own guards on each side."

He spared a look at Addfwyn and said, "Your man servant is dressed nicely enough. He can carry your gift and be ready when you call for it. You simply have to give it to her and try to say something polite and flowery if possible."

"What about Princess Bloddeuwedd?" Llew asked, his long-building dread now reaching epic levels.

"She will not be here. After this meeting you will go to the formal gardens and wait and she will join you. Since you have not met her since you were but four years of age, it was deemed wise that you should both be able to do so in a quiet place, with as few other distractions as possible."

"Why, yes," Llew said slowly, enthusiasm for this approach increasing quickly. "That does sound like a nicer way to meet than in front of the entire court."

After that, things went well. The great room was nearly as large as the largest one at Caerleon although not as richly appointed. Cymri was along one side of the hall providing a wordless low melody that conveyed just the proper amounts of formality. The room was mostly empty, with only about thirty prominent citizens of Gwynedd present. Llew realized immediately they must have kept the numbers down, probably with some difficulty, in order to make him feel more comfortable.

Queen Enid turned out to be everything he could have hoped. Although she was of advancing years and even somewhat frail, she was, paradoxically, both tough and strong; Llew could tell at once by her eyes that the spirit that moved her still burned brightly.

She came to him and greeted him warmly saying, "So you are the one my grandson will not stop talking about. I dare say you will set a good example for him." They talked a bit further and she put him completely at ease. So much so that Llew actually caught himself wishing he had a grandmother like her. Llewellyn never spoke of either of their grandmothers and, for the first time, Llew found himself wondering if there was some reason why she did not.

The queen regent accepted her gift graciously. It was a golden birdcage with three bejeweled birds sitting within it. When a crank was turned they looked from side to side, fluttered their wings slightly, and opened and closed their beaks, all while faint tones of music could be heard in a haunting melody.

"This is astounding," she declared. "I believe it to be the nicest thing anyone has ever given me. Is it magic that motivates these small singers?"

"I do not know," Llew answered, "but the family of artisans that makes them does not share their secrets, and they are rumored to have some dealings with the Fae; so who can say with complete certainty?"

"Well," Queen Enid exclaimed, "they are quite remarkable either way. For the first time I feel I can actually put some stock into the old tales concerning the three birds of Rhiannon. These will not fly away if I open the cage door will they?"

"I do not believe they will, your highness, not like High Queen Rhiannon's did in the story," Llew answered seriously.

"Just as well," she declared, "be a shame to have them fly south for the winter after you traveled so far to bring them north.

"Enough. I will not keep you in suspense any longer. I know what must be on your mind above all else. I was going to walk with you to the garden and perhaps talk a bit about our Bloddeuwedd but I think you, and she, deserve the right to learn about yourselves directly, without any of my generation trying to fill your head with ideas that may or may not be accurate.

"Instead I will send my steward, Ffodor, to guide you there. My advice to you is this: Do not see this as a duty. You have duty enough and more will follow. Take what opportunity you have to enjoy your youth, Prince Llew, for youth is in your mind and in your soul, not just your body. When it is gone it will not come again, even if you should live throughout all the remaining ages of the world."

* * *

Ffodor was a short man and, inevitably, was clean-shaven except for an elaborate moustache. Unlike most, he was bald as an egg, without even a fringe of hair around the sides of his head. Nodding politely to Llew as they were introduced, he then led him down a short hall. They exited through an ornate door into what Queen Enid had called a garden.

Despite his pounding heart, Llew noticed at once that, although they called it a garden, no vegetables grew here. They went a short way in and stopped by a large fountain where a mermaid emptied an urn of water that was never ending.

"Here you are, your highness, I am certain the princess will be here shortly," his guide said as he turned to go.

"Wait," called Llew, "will you not be staying to make sure we are chaperoned?"

"Ah, and there is no need, my lord. Some of her handmaidens will accompany her. Not to worry though. They have instructions to hang back as far as possible. You and your betrothed will be able to speak privately."

"But we have not even been introduced yet," Llew objected.

"You will do that yourselves. The queen is quite of the opinion that this is the best way to do it. I am sure it will go fine, my lord. It is certainly not like the two of you just got betrothed yesterday, after all." With that he was gone.

Llew looked around and saw that he really was quite alone. Very odd customs these northerners practice, he thought to himself.

It occurred to him that it might be some sort of trap, but he was wearing his ceremonial armor and it was serviceable enough for most things. He was also armed with Fragaroc, the enchanted sword Taliesin had loaned him and, whether it was fully deserved or not, Llew had developed a reputation for being extremely dangerous with it. It was doubtful that an assassin would care to come upon him thus armed and armored.

He decided he was being overcautious and sat down on the edge of the fountain to wait alone for his betrothed, the fair Princess Bloddeuwedd, she of the white flowers. He was half crazed with apprehension and had been trying desperately for days to think about this meeting as little as possible. Now he had too much time to think about it and it was at the worst possible moment.

The princess was a bit more than two years older than Llew. With him still just fifteen years of age, this was a huge gap and it only served to heighten his dread of what was to come. It put him at even more of a disadvantage, he felt, that their parents had arranged for them to be affianced within a week of his birth, yet she had been given fifteen years to grow used to the idea that they would one day be married; he had only found out about it less than a year before.

The single reason that Llew could think of to explain why he was not lying on the ground, curved in a ball and making weak mewling noises, was that the marriage was not scheduled to occur until he reached his seventeenth birthday, almost a year hence.

And there she was! She approached along a path with two of her handmaidens. Her gown was a rich shade of green, both complementing and accentuating blond hair so pale it was nearly white. Her appearance was such that Llew would have sworn she had just stepped out of a painting. She smiled when she saw him and, in an instant, Llew's fears all fell away in wonder. Had anyone other than Gower ever been that happy to see him? Only with difficulty did he suppress a wild urge to look behind himself and see who she was smiling at.

The fear of what she meant to his future was abruptly transformed into a fear that she might not be part of his future—not if he bungled it here and now. Meeting her for the first time was a delicate matter and he was still terrified he would make a mess of it, but now it was for a completely different reason!

Realizing he was still sitting on the edge of a reflective pool, he quickly jumped to his feet. Despite having spent months trying to think up what he should say at this moment, Llew drew a complete blank. The awkwardness did not stop there. His hands were another problem he realized . . . what should he do with his hands? And his feet? Should he advance to meet her?

He did of course. Moriganna and Cymri's training came to the fore and had him making all the proper moves—and making them automatically—without his even thinking about them. This was fortunate; his ability to think was not at its best in that moment.

She was, he realized, far too magnificent for a stable boy from Caer Mallcoedwig. She was too good for even a future king of Gwent. Were High King Math himself to stride back into the world then he, only he, might be appropriate to take a place at her side . . . maybe.

She spoke to him. The words did not even register, although he heard himself saying something in response. He hoped it was the right response.

Finally, it came to him that, at the very least, he must take charge of his own tongue. She had just asked him something. He searched back through his memory and realized it was about visiting in Gwynedd.

"Up to now, my lady, my visit to Gwynedd has been all I could have hoped for."

"And now?" she inquired in a voice so perfect for her that he wanted nothing so much at that moment than for her to use it again.

"Now it is far more than I ever dared wish for," he heard himself saying.

"You may be young but you seem to know the right things to say," she said approvingly, then showed she was teasing him with a quick grin.

"Oh but I wish that were true, Princess. The truth is I have

THE TORC OF TETHERA

no idea what to say. Should I comment on your eyes, your hair, or complement you on your lovely gown? I simply do not know. All of it seems so obvious you must have already heard it a thousand times before."

Her mouth quirked with amusement before saying, "A woman never tires of hearing these things anew and, as pleasing as they are, they can never have more import than they do when they come from the man to whom her hand is already promised. What more could he hope to gain by them?"

"I will say them," breathed Llew, "I will say them every morning and evening for the rest of our lives if such be your desire."

"I scarcely think that will be necessary, my prince. It is the willingness to do so that matters."

"Llew," he found himself saying, "for you I am but Llew, and that will surely do."

"Ah," she chuckled lightly, "a poet who does not know it. And I am Bloddeuwedd, just Bloddeuwedd, but never Blod. There is only one that gets away with that and if I could cure him of it I would."

"Caradog," murmured Llew, "We have met."

"That is the one," she replied with an exaggerated grimace. "But now is not time to be discussing anyone but ourselves. I am, after all, here with my very own prince in shining armor, the greatest hero in all the land if the tales the bards are singing are even slightly true."

Llew laughed and said, "Hardly the greatest, I suspect. Yet give me time and for you I shall make the effort."

"Look at you," she said reprovingly, "all this and modest,

too. Even as you stand there with your enchanted sword and enchanted armor, fresh from having trodden the width and wilds of Tethera. I have already heard that you slew a great wurm not two days ago! Even that pales beside the tales of how you laid low even the Lord of Death and sent him fleeing from certain doom, while managing to rescue your sister, long believed dead since birth!

"No Llew, even with just the two of us here, you certainly merit the most discussion."

"It is not all as you hear. It was not a wurm at all; we called it a worm because it looked more like one of those than like anything else. In the same vein, this armor is not even enchanted."

"Really?" She made a small frown. "I rather liked the idea that it was."

"This is ceremonial armor," he explained, "I would hate to have to even try to fight in it. It is not at all well-made for that purpose. The enchanted armor that Moriganna gave me is in my room. I suspect Addfwyn, my man servant, is busy removing fifteen days of road dust from it even as we speak."

"So it is impervious to damage but not to dirt? How funny and yet predictable that is." She laughed, then said, "Oh Llew! But you should wear it always! What good is it to have armor in which you are safe from all harm if you are not wearing it?"

"I am hardly safe from all harm when wearing it. There are all manner of means possible by which a man might come to harm, even if a spear or sword cannot be thrust through the middle of his chest."

"How can that be?" she asked confusedly.

"Well, the enchanted parts seem to be only the mail and a helmet. Most weapons will not penetrate even ordinary mail yet it does not confer invulnerability to the wearer!"

"That is true," she mused, "so here I was thinking that only Celtchar's Spear could pose a menace to my future husband, and such is far from the case. Now I will have much more to worry about."

"Celtchar's Spear?" Llew asked, genuinely interested. He had a very wide knowledge of the old stories and yet this sounded like something he should know of but did not.

"It was a fabulous spear and one of the twelve great treasures of Tethera," she explained. "Supposedly made by the gods, it was given to a warrior to do great deeds with, such as slay sea serpents and so forth. Its sovereign power was that it always hit and it always killed."

Llew considered that and said, "That sounds a bit unfair on the part of the gods. So, you think an enchanted unstoppable spear could penetrate enchanted impenetrable armor? If each were as stated, the only possible solution would be that both must fail. Yet that does not appear to be an option with the spear and the armor. There is no middle ground—the spear must either succeed in bursting through or be prevented by the armor and, either way, one would succeed and one would fail."

"It is a silly topic anyway," said Bloddeuwedd, "so far as anyone knows, Celtchar's Spear was taken into Annwyn ages ago and will likely never be seen again." Her eyes suddenly narrowed, "Wait a moment, Moriganna gave you your armor? Why would she do that? How is that even possible?"

Then Llew found himself explaining, not for the first time, that it was not his sister that had been stolen away by Moriganna as a babe, but himself, and that he had to more or less rescue himself before he rescued her.

"So," she said slowly, as he finished the familiar tale, "your family kept me bound in an arranged marriage for over fourteen years without telling me that my husband-to-be was believed dead?"

"Bloddeuwedd," he said earnestly and would have taken her hand in his had her chaperons not still been watching them from the end of the path, "you must keep the greater good in mind. Things did work out and, because they did, even if I were not completely under your spell, the marriage would still have to go forward. Evil is upon Tethera and the hour has grown late indeed; only the restoration of the Great Kingdom can offer hope and only you and I can make that happen in time to turn back the impending doom."

"Your marrying me and giving Gwynedd to Caradog as your sworn man will not remake the Great Kingdom, Llew," she replied softly, eyes downcast.

"No, not by itself, but Gwent already has merged with Glywysing through my parent's marriage. Taliesin will bring us Dyfyd by promising to reclaim the throne of Ceredigion and pledging to it us if they do not themselves rejoin willingly. Dyfyd will rejoin rather than let that happen. That will leave only Clwyd and Ergyng and we will find a way. We must."

She looked up then, a wisp of a smile on her face. "You are completely under my spell you say?"

"I am," Llew averred, and meant it.

"And what would you give for me?"

"Anything," he promised.

She did smile then, "Good! And just so you do not forget—" She leaned forward and gave him a quick kiss on the cheek while she pressed something into his hand.

A pair of matched shrieks emanated from a short distance away. Llew looked to see the handmaidens running at them full tilt. With nary a word to him, they each took one of Bloddeuwedd's arms and rapidly propelled her away. She found time to glance over her shoulder and give him a last parting grin.

Llew continued to stand there for some time after she left, an unfocused smile on his face.

Chapter IV

Driven by Honor

Llew sat back down on the edge of the pool and remained there for some time after she had left. Eventually he looked into his hand and found he was holding an ornate ribbon, possibly for a woman's hair. He sniffed it and discovered it smelled like flowers—like Bloddeuwedd. It was a mark of her favor. He very carefully put it into an empty belt pouch to preserve it. Nothing else, he decided would ever be allowed to share that location, and then he realized the pouch was not empty. He mentally kicked himself then. He had quite forgotten to give her his gift! It was the one King Pendaran had helped him pick out specifically for that moment. Thankfully, there were bound to be more opportunities.

A shrill caw pierced the air next to his ear as a familiar weight manifested itself on his left shoulder.

"Why hello, Cilgwri. It is about time you showed up. You must believe it is dinner time."

"Cilgwri!" the large black bird affirmed, saying his own

name.

"It appears the joke is on you, my gluttonous friend. Had you only stayed closer earlier you could had some of Ma Cadding's famous berry pie, and many other good things as well."

Cilgwri cocked his head and regarded Llew with unblinking eyes.

After many seconds of this, Llew snorted and gave in, extracting a crisp honey-wheat bar from his pocket. "I think maybe you are getting to know me too well," he told Cilgwri. "Alas, this is all I have left of Caradog's midday snack." He got up and began walking, breaking off fragments of the treat and feeding them to the bird as he did so. He wanted to see some more of the gardens. Somehow he had scarcely noticed them before Bloddeuwedd arrived, and had forgotten they were even there at all while he was speaking with her.

The paths were cunningly planned, twisting and curving through as many unique venues as was possible in a large but finite space. For all of its size, the garden was packed with a wide variety of shrubs, some flowering, some cut in pleasing patterns or in the shapes of beasts, men, and Fae. There was also statuary, various pools and fountains, and stone benches interspersed throughout. Llew wandered up and down and about, enjoying some time by himself, something he almost never had anymore.

He had much to think about. He had never imagined, for example, that rather than being a duty, marriage to Bloddeuwedd might actually be something he would find desirable. The truth, he admitted to himself, was that there was nothing he had ever wanted so badly in his life. It was not merely that she was beautiful or even that she, and he admitted it to himself, had sparked baser desires, ones that he had been aware of for some time.

He was heir to the greatest kingdom in the land and, if the plans laid down by his father's father came to pass, he or his son would be high king. He was also, deservedly or not, regarded as one of the greatest heroes in the land. A surprising side effect of this was that he could not enjoy the company of women. While it might not be all of them, he had discovered that too many of them tended to regard him, not as someone whose company they could enjoy, but as a prize to be seized and won through any means whatsoever. This was certainly a disservice to many of them, he knew that, but it meant he could never let his guard down with any of them. With Bloddeuwedd there was none of that. He could be himself and she was happy with that.

This was someone that would be his partner in life, ever there for him as he would be for her. She would be his better half. He shook his head ruefully when he realized he had actually applied that old phrase to her. He had heard it so many times before without even considering that it might have real meaning, yet it was fully applicable. Instead of it all being him and his friends against the world, this would be the two of them, with their friends, against the world. When no one else would listen to him, really listen, she would; and he would always be there for her, no matter what might come.

For the first time he found himself wondering if there was some way to have an exception to Boudicca's Edict so that he could marry before the age of seventeen. The prohibition had been issued to protect young women. It certainly was not men that needed such a rule! Llew kicked a pebble from the path into a reflective pool, scattering the large fish that lived in its shallow waters. A full year, which had formerly seemed more like a short stay of execution, now seemed to be an eternity away.

By chance he came out of the gardens within sight of the side of the palace where work was done. This was where food was brought in, laundry hung to dry, game and farm animals butchered, and myriad other activities were conducted that, while absolutely necessary, were not things that one wanted to show to the world at large. It was, he realized, a decided advantage to live in an open palace like this. In a walled fortress there was no getting away from such things. Here there was that greatest of luxuries, space.

Such a layout ensured room for stables that were not so close you smelled them at every breath, for gardens where one could take reflective walks. Even his assigned room was easily eight times the size of what was available to the lords of most castles.

But the price paid was in lost security during a dangerous time. There were simply too many enemies in the world for him to live in such a way. Llew stopped and looked closely at two men entering what were probably the palace kitchens. Although he was not able to see the first man's face before he passed into the open doorway, Llew did get a good look at the man following him. Something about him jogged his memory. He was nearly certain he had seen the man before and not under happy circumstances.

Llew broke into a run as Cilgwri protested and took flight. He charged right into a kitchen where many servants were at work. The men he sought were not here. He rushed past several open storerooms and workrooms but did not see them there either. A door at the end of the corridor took him into Queen Enid's great hall. Fortunately, court was not in session. A massive table now ran the length of the place and was being set for a feast. Other servants were fetching in chairs and benches to go around it. Llew ran past them, ignoring their startled glances, and into the hall outside, then looked about wildly. There was no trace of them.

He dashed around the corner in the direction of the guest

rooms and ran smack into someone else coming the other way, knocking their slighter frame heavily to the floor. Halting, he looked down, praying he would not discover it was Queen Enid or Princess Bloddeuwedd.

"Caradog! I am so sorry," he exclaimed, extending a hand to help the boy to his feet. "I really should have been more careful."

"So," said the scowling Caradog, "you admit you are to blame for this entire incident?"

"Well, yes, of course and I do apologize." Llew felt himself loathe to explain how he had been pursuing someone he had only glimpsed for a moment and thought he might have known.

"Very well, then," Caradog replied, "but words are of no use. We will settle this thing outside and with swords, at once. Honor must be satisfied."

"What?" Llew asked, amazed at the turn this had taken.

Caradog leaned closer, winked and said, "Practice swords in the training yard, of course. Blod said that if I asked nicely you would probably be happy to give me a lesson. It is still a couple of hours until dinner. Please?"

Confused, Llew said, "I . . . thought I saw someone I might know, but they have eluded me. Bloddeuwedd said? A command performance then! Very well, let me see if my real armor—not this ceremonial stuff—is cleaned and ready to go."

Cilgwri chose that moment to land on Llew's shoulder, a warm fresh roll in his beak. "And if Cilgwri just pilfered the kitchen as we went through we should probably stay well away from there for a bit in any case," he added.

Cilgwri cocked his head and regarded Llew. It was comical

with the big roll still in his beak but Llew favored him in return with a frown. "I warned you about kitchens; do not pretend I did not. 'Six-and-twenty blackbirds, baked into a pie.' Where do you think that song came from, eh? That would *not* be a dainty dish to set before a king."

Caradog laughed.

* * *

There was, Llew thought grimly, such as thing as being too efficient. Of course Addfwyn had his real armor clean, repaired, ready to go, and hanging on a rack in his room. This left Llew no real basis to refuse Caradog's request—which was why he was now standing in a graveled training yard near the stables.

He had been told that Gower and the prince's horse were being saddled and equipped. Apparently the second half of their session was to be mounted combat. That was fine with Llew, at least it meant he could be sitting down for that part.

The practice yard was just that, a medium sized area surrounded by a low stone wall and covered in small river stones. They were quite small and not deep but they could, Llew suspected, be fairly slippery when they were wet. Llew made a note to watch out for that. Falling on his fundament would be rather embarrassing and do nothing for the way in which he tried to present himself.

Caradog, wearing a reasonable assortment of armor, and gripping a wooden practice sword, approached cautiously, then changed tactics and charged in waving his sword above his head and giving out a very loud yell. Llew ignored the yell and did not move a muscle until Caradog closed and began his swing. With a minimum of motion he stepped forward inside the swing, then crouched inward like a coiled spring before he expanded at great speed, using all of the muscles in his frame to smash his shield into

Caradog's. Coming up as he was, the impact actually drove the boy off his feet and sent him flying several paces back to land flat on his back, skidding a bit through the pebbles.

Llew had meant only to show Caradog the futility of such an approach against a superior foe. A few bruises would serve him right for making such a silly attack. Too late, Llew was concerned he might have overdone it and the young princeling could have taken some serious injury. The servants started to move in but, in a flash, Caradog was back on his feet and ready for more. He immediately took a defensive stance behind his shield, until he realized that he no longer had a sword in his hand. Llew had not meant to laugh but the expression on Caradog's face when he realized this was beyond price.

Sheepishly, Caradog retrieved his blade from where it had fallen, then returned to his defensive stance. "I was just testing you," he explained, without rancor, "now you must be prepared!"

Llew gave a short laugh, and replied, "Testing me? Did I pass?"

"Oh, so far so good, but it may be too early to tell," Caradog responded.

"Ah," said Llew, while circling warily, "I do note your stance is good and your grip is well formed."

"Come closer that you might better inspect it," suggested Caradog, with a grin.

"Well, and I would be happy to; just hold still."

"Ha," cried Caradog, "I will be still when I am dead and not before, thank you!"

They skirmished for perhaps a quarter of an hour, Llew periodically pausing the action to show Caradog a few pointers.

This also allowed a few breathers for Caradog, who, despite his high spirits, did not yet have nearly the stamina required for an extended go of it. The armor was heavy, the wooden sword was heavy, the shield was heavy, and the boy was still a boy, not yet come into a man's build so that he might better manage such things.

Llew found his technique, other than that ridiculous first charge, to be quite good for his age and background. Caradog had not spent years training under the exacting and unforgiving tutelage of Afaggdu, as Llew had, but so far as he knew, no one else alive had, with the exception of his sister, Llewellyn. Caradog's enthusiasm for the subject at hand was certainly beyond reproach. Llew decided that, with continuing training, Caradog might be a very dangerous fellow in a few years—if he got the kind of growth he would need. Technique was essential, to be sure, but with heavy weapons and armor, a stronger man of similar skill would beat a weaker one every time. Second place was not good enough against someone trying to kill you.

Caradog set off with his servant to the stables to see if their steeds were ready. Llew took the opportunity to sit and rest while another of the palace staff brought him a cool drink in a silver cup, upon a silver platter.

Screams and yells came from the direction of the palace. Standing and looking towards it, he saw servants and guards pouring out of the doors in considerable agitation. Llew seized his sword from where it rested and ran to see what was the matter. Then he cursed in mild exasperation and ran back to where he had been sitting. Tossing aside the wooden practice sword, he seized up his real weapon, the enchanted blade called Fragaroc.

Halfway to the palace he met an out of breath guard. "What is it, man? Report!" Llew demanded, in his command voice.

The guard was of Gwynedd but he never thought to

question Llew's right to give him an order. "My lord, it is the Princess Bloddeuwedd, she has been taken!"

Llew felt as though a black smith's hammer had struck him on the chest. "She—what?" Seizing hold of himself he demanded, "Where and when? Details!"

"At the outer edge of the royal gardens, just a few minutes ago, my lord. Three men on horseback tore through and seized her."

"What of her guards?" cried Llew.

"My lord, they were on foot and too far away to intervene, her lady's maids were powerless against armed warriors. Please excuse me, the training yard is this way. I must see to the safety of Prince Caradog!"

"He is not there," snapped Llew. "He has gone to the stables." Thinking quickly, Llew added, "I will come with you, let us make haste!"

In moments they were approaching the stables. There was no sign of Caradog outside. Llew drew a small reed from his belt and blew it. No sound emerged yet a moment later the double wooden doors to the building flew open with a crash and Gower, already saddled, came out at a gallop, making a beeline for Llew.

As they met, Llew swung himself up on to the great horse's back. "No rest for the wicked, Gower. We must ride!" To the astonished guardsman, Llew commanded, "Follow your mission; see to Prince Caradog. I am after the princess before the trail can grow cold! Oh! Wait one, which way did they go with her?"

"Your highness, they took the old road to Powys, it forks just past the palace and heads southeast while the other way goes to the kingdom of Clwyd."

Urging Gower into a gallop, Llew circled the palace and headed for the road.

Chapter V

The Horse Race

After passing around the palace, Llew and Gower met the road and continued east for only a few hundred paces before coming to the fork the guardsman had spoken of. Every instinct commanded Llew to continue at a gallop, but he knew from experience that Gower would be all in after only a few miles of that, even were he fully rested—which he was not. It had been barely six hours since they had arrived at the palace. With considerable effort, he restrained his impulses and nudged Gower down to a trot.

He simply had no idea how large the kidnapper's head-start had been. Perhaps he would meet traffic coming from the other direction and be able to gauge the interval separating them. Not knowing that made this an endurance race rather than one based on pure speed. He knew that, to win an endurance race, Gower must travel by alternating between a trot and a canter. Not that it would matter in the long run; Llew was quite certain his steed would overhaul any normal horse in either kind of race. The Prince of Gwent still found it almost unbearable as it meant that much longer his betrothed would remain in the hands of those that had taken her.

Llew enjoyed practice and training. He was not frightened by real combat—well, not overly so, at any rate. Nonetheless, he never enjoyed having to inflict injury. It was not something one talked about but that was actually the part he could do without. However, insofar as these kidnappers went, he felt that might not be true. It was with a trace of guilt that he realized some part of him was secretly hoping they would not immediately surrender. Whether they did or not, he would soon find out.

He was still thinking that as he and Gower traveled under the moonlight. They had met no other traffic coming the other way. With the kingdom of Powys having fallen, there probably was not much moving in either direction. The condition of the road itself was getting worse to the point where, for long stretches, it had grass growing in it. That made him think of something Moriganna had once said: "Now the great kingdoms themselves are collapsing. They will soon all fail and grass will grow in the roads. The lands will be become a single howling wilderness, an unmarked grave for the dreams of man, with all the great castles fallen."

Llew gritted his teeth. This would not come to pass while he reigned!

He thought to wonder then if he was still on the kidnappers' trail. How could he not yet have caught up to them? There was simply no way they had steeds of Gower's capability. Gower was undoubtedly quite unique. Beset by doubts, he eventually stopped, then pulled out the favor Bloddeuwedd had given him and held it under Gower's nose.

"Good Gower," he coaxed. "Get the scent. Find Blod." He made a mental note never to call her that when she could hear him but, for some odd reason, he preferred to use shorter words when speaking to his horse.

Gower sniffed the scrap of ribbon repeatedly in a manner that was most unhorse-like. He then brought his nose close to the ground and sniffed again. His ears flicked and stood up straight. Llew leaped back into the saddle as Gower took off at a canter down the dark road. Llew sighed. He was not off-track then. They had come this way—but how could they still be ahead of him?

He was still thinking on this when the setting moon forced them to stop. It was just too dark to go on. The road was bad enough already and to go on without being able to see it could mean serious injury. Besides, Gower needed a few hours rest, not to mention himself, if he was going to be fighting three men in the morning.

They were moving again before the sun was up. In half an hour's time it became evident how the kidnappers had kept ahead of him. He and Gower came to the body of a dead horse in the road. It was still saddled, but there was no sign of a rider. The cause of death was readily apparent. The dead beast's mouth was covered with dried froth. It had simply been run to death by a rider with no concern for keeping it alive. Llew scowled fiercely and looked ahead down the road. Such a tactic would keep them ahead of him for only a short time; with four people and three horses that must themselves be close unto death, they would soon be walking. He would catch them quickly now.

He kept thinking that for the next half a mile until he came to the ruins of a crude cottage by the road. The building was a shambles, but the small paddock to one side showed signs of recent repair. Three more dead horses lay on the road before the cottage, still wearing saddles. Two had apparently died of overexertion, as the first had. The last had been killed by a sword.

Llew edged Gower over to the paddock's fence. It only took a quick glance to see that several horses, easily four or more, had been kept here until very recently. Llew's heart sank at this. He had been so close! Perhaps if he had—no. He looked at Gower and knew in his heart he could never use the big galoot so harshly as to risk what had happened to these poor animals.

"No," he said to Gower. "They have only delayed the inevitable, they will never evade us."

Forcing himself to take the time, he discovered several large bags of oats in the ruins of the cottage. It looked like an additional member of the kidnappers' band had been camping here, holding fresh mounts ready. That would mean Llew was now facing at least four of them if he caught up to them. When he caught up to them, he corrected himself.

There was a well behind the cottage that had a new bucket attached. With this and the oats he was able to properly feed and water Gower, taking the time to remove his saddle and give him as good a rubdown as he could manage without a brush. They might have a long way to go yet and, as he had once told a certain young prince, it would do no good to move quickly, but fail to arrive at your destination, or even to arrive quickly if you were in no shape to do anything once you did.

They continued onward after less than an hour. Despite the additional weight, Llew had managed to sling about three stones of oats onto the back of Gower's saddle. That was only a two day supply for the huge animal. It was weighty, but would save considerable time in stopping to graze.

The road continued to worsen. Llew found himself passing through forests and valleys that looked as though, with the single exception of the road, they had never seen a human being. He shuddered inwardly, recalling the Wild Growth. It was entirely possible some of these places had never seen a man or even a horse before, save for the kidnappers.

It was even possible, he supposed, that some of these areas had appeared in the time since they had ridden through. Although, when he followed that line of thought it seemed unlikely, as Gower had not yet lost the scent. Would the scent get stretched with the road? It was also possible that those he pursued were much closer now. Having run one set of horses to death, he would bet they were going much more easily on the new ones, both because they might not have any more remounts waiting ahead and because they felt confident no pursuit could now catch them.

Still, Llew thought to himself, if it was possible they were close then he should be on the lookout for potential ambushes. Accordingly, from time to time—not too often—he began reining in Gower while he listened.

Llew's sense of hearing was not as that of other men. He could hear sounds far too faint for anyone else. The Spriggan king, Hafgan, had told him this was because he had a little bit of Coraniaid blood, far back in his family tree. The Coraniaid had been a variety of Fae whose hearing was so incredible that they could reputedly hear any danger approaching in time to avoid it. Llew gathered Hafgan had not really approved of them. All he would say of them was that they no longer existed. They had all been poisoned, that being the one danger they could not hear approaching. Although Llew's own hearing was nowhere near that level, it had still saved him from peril on more than one occasion.

It was nearly midday when he heard the sound of other horses. His hand was already straying to his blade, when, with a start, he realized the noises were behind him. How had he gotten ahead of them? They must have been off the road somewhere. Had they seen him go by?

Llew hastily dismounted and led Gower deep into a clump of nearby alders. He then returned to the road to hide. He had to get a look as they went by and see what he was up against! Not for the first time since setting out on this pursuit, he mourned the powerful war bow he had left in his rooms at Queen Enid's palace. With it he could probably have gotten at least two of them before they could even close with him.

He also considered remaining on Gower and just confronting them. It was difficult to imagine how even four of them could prevail against him on horseback—if it was only four. The sound of horses' hooves got closer. They were moving at a pretty good clip. Then they slowed as they came near. Had he been seen? They stopped. Watching from his vantage point under some bushes he could see a pair of boots hit the road as a rider dismounted. He risked a peek around to one side where the horses had to be and saw them, they were roped together and only two had saddles, both empty.

He looked up at Cilgwri, sitting on the branch of a tree high above them. The bird was watching when he did so and let out a single loud caw. This put a wholly new complexion on things. Assuming the black bird had not regressed in his training then there was indeed only one man out there. In training, the black bird had quite reliably demonstrated he could count as high as ten, and then relay as many caws as he counted.

Had this fellow been the one waiting with the horses? Perhaps he had taken them somewhere and let them off when they no longer needed his services? Llew shook his head, there were just too many unknowns here. It would be necessary to ask questions.

Llew exploded out of the bushes and drove the approaching figure on to its back. He was astride the stranger, one hand on the throat, his other poised holding a downward pointing dagger just inches from the man's left eye socket. Then he spoke, "Do not move if you value your—Caradog?" he finished, in some confusion.

Caradog's breath had been knocked out of him by the impact so it was a moment before he could gaspingly reply, "Good morning, Llew," he finally managed. "I think this is three times in two days you have knocked me down."

Llew hastily let him up and sheathed his dagger. "Caradog, what are you—no, how did you—forget that, why are you here?"

"To help you save Blod, of course. I was worried you would already have it done by now."

Llew sighed and asked, "How did you catch up to us? We were not exactly taking our time."

"Oh, well you are still in Gwynedd, Llew. Had you not left without me I could have shown you the back trails to get here much faster. I also took four horses so I can shift between them and travel faster still."

"I see, and why are the royal guard not with you as well?"

"They are coming but they left before me and I was not invited. That means they will be taking the long route. I doubt they will be along in time to help us. But look, I did not come empty handed. See? I have brought us supplies, some extra clothes, food and drink, even blankets and some things to let us cook with."

"You brought me these things, Caradog, and I appreciate it. I do. But it is time for you to head back now. These things you have brought will surely help but you have done your part and your grandmother will be anxious. Without Bloddeuwedd you are next in line for the throne and Gwynedd can ill afford to lose you both."

"No Llew," Caradog objected, "this is important and she is

my cousin and closest living relative. I have every right to be here. Also, you will need my help managing so many horses and you need the horses so you can switch between them and let them get some relief so we may travel faster."

Llew hesitated, it was bad enough the boy had traveled two days through wilds with all manner of potential dangers. Sending him back alone was asking for as much trouble as taking him forward and, forward, the boy could be of some use, just as he said. All right Caradog, but if the situation changes substantially and I do you send you back I want to go, no excuses, no arguing. Fair enough?"

"That would depend on our joint definition of 'substantially' but, yes, I do agree to your terms, sir."

"Good enough, now please tell me there is something in your saddlebags that I can eat as we ride for I am famished. We left before dinner yesterday and I have quite run out of crisp honey-wheat bars."

A few hours later, Gower led them off the road altogether. The route he chose was an actual path of sorts; it just was not very much of one. Caradog had a hard time understanding that Llew was leaving the road strictly because his horse seemed to smell something more interesting. The trail snaked through a small marsh at the lower end of a lake, then moved upward across rocky ground and eventually brought them to the crest of a ridge surveying a craggy, treeless valley. A mile or two distant, five mounted figures rode swiftly towards the stony hills on the far side.

Llew spoke quickly, "Caradog, follow and bring the horses. Under no circumstances are you to engage these riders. If Bloddeuwedd should get to you on her own, take her and flee. You are not to allow yourself within bow range and, should I fall, retreat and try to find our guardsmen. It will be crucial above all else that someone is told what has happened here. Be sure that Cymri and Helgar know."

Llew's dagger appeared in his hand to cut loose the bags of oats he carried, then he recalled that he had already removed them to one of the other horses Caradog had come with. The dagger vanished and he and Gower plunged down the ridge towards their quarry. They had closed over half the distance separating them when one of the small band noticed his approach and shouted an alarm. Llew could not hear them over the noise of Gower's thundering hooves but the sudden consternation amongst them was clear. After the briefest of delays they broke into a gallop themselves. Llew smiled inwardly; let them fear him! As hard used as he had been these past two days, and despite having just run half a mile, Gower's speed and endurance ensured that no half mile lead would suffice for ordinary equines to escape him.

A mile later their destination became apparent. It was a pair of stone columns. Llew squinted, trying to see better. It was difficult on a racing horse. It was a bridge! His heart felt like it was hammering in pace with Gower's hooves. Did they mean to escape across it and destroy it? Was there some way he could wring an additional bit of speed from Gower? The answer was evident; of course not, the great beast was already giving his all. Llew had never applied a spur or a crop to Gower; there had never been a need and it would serve no purpose if he did. The very idea was foreign to their bond. Then he thought again and hurled away his shield to shed the weight.

The riders dismounted at the columns. This was it then. In less than a minute he would surely be upon them!

He had a moment of exultation when he was close enough to see that, although the end supports still stood, the bridge itself, once spanning a high ravine, had long since broken and fallen into the abyss. No escape for the wicked then, and yet . . . Llew frowned to himself. The closer he came, the better he could see them, and the stranger it got. They appeared to be rapidly working with something at the edge rather than preparing for his impending visit. Abruptly, the smallest of them went sailing over the edge, thrown by two of the others.

Llew raged in fury and despair. They had done the unthinkable! They had thrown the princess to her death rather than chance his defeating them and rescuing her. Fragaroc cleared its sheath in an instant and was over his head before he saw that the figure had not fallen but was now flying across the empty space to the far side of the ravine.

Disbelief warred with superstition for a moment. As he continued to close, it was with a crash of relief that he began to discern ropes stretching across to the other side. The form of what had to be Bloddeuwedd was tied to a small basket that quickly reached the far edge where another figure waited to wrestle her free.

Llew also noted that the ground around their launching point was too covered in rubble for him to ride directly up to his foes. Some long collapsed stone structure had once stood there. Walking on that with hooves would be a feat beyond even Gower, let alone galloping. At thirty paces distant he reined in the great beast and swiftly slid out of the saddle, moving carefully but quickly across the rubble, sword ready.

The largest of the four men remaining, and the only one wearing metal armor rather than boiled leather, whipped a chain up and over the ropes across the chasm, then grasped the other end and proceeded to slide across. Llew swore to himself when he saw this. They were escaping! The men still on his side voiced cries of dismay at their abandonment. The figure holding the chain reached the other side and dropped to the edge. In a single motion he turned and drew his sword. Striking once, then a second time, the ropes were severed.

Two of the remaining men groaned while the third, screamed out, "Cai, you treacherous snake, I will find you in this world or the next, whatever it takes!"

Cai? That could explain much, Llew realized. If this was the same man then he was a deadly enemy of Llew's that had once served Moriganna, more or less.

All three turned and readied swords for Llew's approach. "Steady boys," said the one who had cursed his escaped comrade. "We have no place to run and one such as this would only save us for the headsman, if at all. We stand and fight for all we are worth."

Recognition came to Llew and he called to them. "You all had axes when last we met. You also seemed little inclined to use them, as I recall." Llew threw a look to their leader. "As for you, you are that little would-be bandit named, oh, something-or-other. Milar, perhaps?"

The bandit peered at him then seemed to relax a bit before saying, "Well, boys, it is that little lord we met at that wretched crofter's place last year—just a boy in his father's armor. We owe him a big one and his friends are not here to prevent us from collecting."

Emboldened, the other bandits began to spread out to either side and advanced so as to encircle him. Llew found he had no patience for this. He moved rapidly over the rubble to meet the one to his right, keeping his sword just in front of him with the grip about a foot from his belt and the blade pointed straight up. As he got within range the bandit took a wild swing at Llew with his own sword, using it just as he might attack a tree with an axe.

For those others present, there was just a metallic tink as, barely moving his sword at all, Llew deflected the bandit's blade and sent it flailing to the right. In the same instant, almost too quick to see, there was a sickening noise as Fragaroc flashed forward and down in a single stroke. The bandit dropped, stone dead before he could even cry out. Llew had not even drawn back for a swing, just chopped forward from where he held his weapon upright before him.

Llew did an about face and was on the other bandit, in three steps. He tapped his opponent's sword to one side and ended that encounter with a single stroke as well. This man did scream, but only for a moment. Then Llew turned to the final foe.

"Molar, was it not? Your name, I mean."

The bandit swore, "It is Meilyr, curse you! Come and get what you gave my men!"

"A moment then, Meller," Llew responded. "What are you doing with Cai? He has a very bad record for taking care of his men. And for what reason did he have you take the princess? There is little value in taking her unless it is for ransom and there are surely less dangerous ways to obtain coin than this?"

Meilyr spat, "My name is Meilyr! All of those are questions for Cai. I did not even know he had a record for taking care of men, bad or otherwise. At least when we met him he got us out from in front of that wave of Picts you would have let us blunder right into!"

Llew was flabbergasted. He had done everything he could to prevent that very thing and yet Meilyr had attempted to rob and plunder him for his efforts.

"I cannot help you," the bandit reaffirmed. "If you want to ask Cai, do so."

Meilyr's face then took on a crafty expression, "You probably want to ask him right away and there is no way I can help with that. I will just make my way out while you two are speaking. You will never see me again in these lands."

"A fine try, Miller, but my lands include all of Tethera, or will eventually, and I already have you. Why would I let you go?"

"You are the boy prince?" Meilyr exclaimed, the color draining from his face in an instant. He dropped his sword and tried to sprint away but immediately tripped on the debris and went sprawling.

Moving forward like a mountain goat across the broken stones, Llew seized him by his neck and belt, hoisting him up to his feet. In the process, Meilyr managed to plant one boot and spun, driving a dagger into Llew's solar plexus. It could not penetrate his enchanted armor, but the impact still hurt. There were also many other places on Llew where he was completely vulnerable. Fully cognizant of this, Llew used the man's momentum to whirl both of them in a tight arc and used some of that force to aid him in lifting the bandit bodily over his head. Meilyr yelled with surprise and flailed awkwardly with his knife. Llew never hesitated; all in one motion he finished whirling about to end in a partial crouch with his knees and elbows bent, then, not completely dissimilar from what he had done with Caradog's charge, he used every ounce of strength in his legs, arms, and back to explode forward at an angle to propel Meilyr's body directly into one of the upright stone pillars that had marked the end of the bridge. That would take the fight out of him!

Instead, Llew found his aim was badly off after spinning around. With an odd commingling of distress and satisfaction, he watched Bloddeuwedd's kidnapper miss the pillar entirely and fly far out over the crevasse before falling out of sight, all the while emitting a blood-curdling scream. The scream faded away into distance before it ended.

Whoops, Llew thought to himself. He retrieved Fragaroc, then walked to the edge and looked down. Far, far below, there rushed a river through a rocky gorge. Of Meilyr there was no sign.

There came a clapping noise. Startled, Llew looked up to find it was Cai, about thirty paces away on the far side of the ravine, applauding him. "Nicely done, boy. You are acquiring a certain ruthlessness; it is not entirely a substitute for style yet it serves."

"Cai! You sniveling coward. Come over here and I will show you some style."

Cai smiled and said, "Tut tut, credit where it is due. I had to work very hard to stay beyond your grasp and you, of all people, should appreciate that. Had I let you catch me I would have had to kill you. I think you know I could do it. Youth and vigor is fine but it will only take you so far."

"So why not, Cai?" Llew shouted. "Come get me if you are so confident. You have no reason to keep me alive; neither you nor Moriganna can possibly hope to rule Gwynedd through me any longer."

"Oh please," Cai replied, "that ship has sailed and I have much grander aims now. No, overall it is really for the best; perhaps I should thank you but I do not think I shall, not yet at least. No, Prince Llew, I need you alive. You know I have your princess fair and you can imagine what I will do if I do not receive her ransom."

"Silver and gold," Llew sneered. "How much did you have in mind? I warn you, she had best be unharmed in any way while I gather it."

Cai waved a hand, dismissively. "She is in no danger from

me and mine and will receive only the finest of care—unless you fail to pay what I ask. But Llew—may I call you Llew?—who said anything about precious specie? No, coins will not serve for so fine a treasure as the Princess Bloddeuwedd. I want something only you can bring me. I want the Torc of Tethera. You do not happen to have it on you, do you? No, do not lie. I would have allowed you to catch me and then merely killed you had that been the case.

"The mighty Pyn y Gogarth stands on a peninsula to the east of the river Conwy. You will find a trail marked with small piles of stones. Follow that trail up to the standing stones overlooking the sea. Come alone, on foot, and bring the torc at midday in three weeks' time."

Llew's confusion was near total. "What torc, what are you babbling on about?"

Cai gave him a look that seemed to mix sorrow with distaste. "You really do not know your own history very well, do you, Llew? The High Queen Boudicca, when she allied with the Druids and the Fae to drive out the Roman Empire, received a great golden torc, crafted by the Fae and enchanted by the Druids, as a pledge of their loyalty. Of course, the Fae know little about loyalty, but it was still a very nice torc."

You should talk about loyalty, Llew thought, but kept it to himself.

"In time the torc went to Mathonwy, then to Math who declared it to be the Torc of Tethera and made it a symbol of the realm—sometimes it is referred to as Math's Torc. It is even visible in many illustrations since that time—I best like the one in the Green Book of Ceredigion—you must have at least noticed it when you read it, did you not? You know the one; it shows it being passed from Boudicca to her daughter Aeron in trust for her own son, Mathonwy."

Llew, still quite unable to read despite promises he had made to himself, ground his teeth quietly.

"Through thirteen generations after High King Math it passed from ruler to ruler. When Pwyl met his untimely end after he destroyed the great kingdom, his most trusted cantref king, Bran, took up the throne and tried to hold things together, but he only succeeded in keeping Gwent. You should know this well as he was your great grandfather, or so I am told. This means your father, King Pendaran, must have it now. If he is loath to pass it to you for Bloddeuwedd's ransom, you can remind him how important this impending union is. I doubt you will have to."

"I have never heard mention of this torc you speak of," replied Llew. "I do not believe he has it. What then?"

"Oh Llew," Cai shook his head in mock ruefulness, "that just would not do. I would not believe you and you know what would happen then."

Llew clenched his hands, trying to control his rage. "Wretched villain! High King Pwyl died a century ago. Lord Arawen of Annwyn stole the body. Look to him for your torc."

Cai gave Llew a mocking grin before saying, "No, Llew, I know for a fact that he does not have it, although he would very much like to. You knew I was no longer working with that treacherous hedge witch, Moriganna, did you not?"

"Are you insane!" Llew screamed back. "There is ultimately only one reward for those in the service of the Lord of Death!"

Cai casually turned to go, then looked back and said mildly, "Three weeks, Llew."

"You actually are insane!" cried Llew. "To Caerleon, assuming this torc is even there, it is a fifteen day ride—each way!"

Cai smiled. "Then use a ship, Llew. It will be less than a week each way. Dylan has sworn to leave all Tetheran ships alone for the coming month. Moreover, any flying the royal banner of Gwent will receive only the best of all possible winds." Then he turned his face away and stepped toward the west.

"Show me Bloddeuwedd then, Cai! Prove to me that was really her and this is not some elaborate swindle."

Cai continued walking and out from behind the rocks came two mounted riders and a horse with an empty saddle. The riders were easily recognizable. One was Meirion, Cai's lieutenant, whom Llew knew to be a quiet unassuming man of surpassingly dangerous capabilities, and apparently loyal unto Cai beyond all reason. The other was Bloddeuwedd.

Her hands were bound before her so she could still hold the reins. She cast him one glance, both sorrowful and frightened, then tried to flash a brave smile in its place. Llew found himself desiring nothing more than to be able to leap across the gap between them and carry her away. Again he had to settle for clenching his fists. Cai swung onto the riderless horse, and they all three trotted out of sight.

Llew stared after them for a considerable time.

Chapter VI

The Way Home

"So what do we do now, Llew?" came a voice at his elbow.

"I thought I told you to stay at least one hundred paces back," Llew replied in an empty voice.

"You said bow range and there is no way I could hit them with a bow from here. Look, Llew, I brought your shield."

"So you did and thank you, Caradog."

"Llew?" asked Caradog.

"Yes?"

"That—that really was amazing. I have never seen anything like it. They never had a chance, you were just, well—amazing."

"They never did have a chance, Caradog, they were just poor frightened peasants pretending to be bandits. Someone, Cai probably, had given them armor and swords to replace their axes but they had no training with the swords. They tried to use them like children having mock sword fights with sticks. I could have captured them instead but I was in a hurry and, as Meilyr said, had I done so I would only have exchanged this fate for another on the headsman's block."

"But," and Caradog's voice quivered with emotion, "then their leader tried to stab you after you had both disarmed yourselves and you, you just picked him up and—"

"I was quite angry with him, Caradog. Even so, I did not intend to kill him. I had just spun about and my aim was off. Perhaps if I had better mastered my anger I would have taken more care and he would still be alive and our prisoner. He claimed to know nothing, but he probably had some information we could have used."

"Llew, can you train me? Make me your shield-bearer, perhaps? I will work very hard; I swear it!"

Llew turned a skeptical expression upon the boy and said, "I doubt it would work out in the long run, Caradog, one way or another you have a kingdom to run. But perhaps I can arrange some training with Afaggdu for you."

Caradog's disappointment was obvious as he asked, "Afaggdu? Whoever he is he cannot be nearly as good as you."

"No," Llew replied, and surprised himself by grinning at Caradog's naivety, "he is far more skilled than I am. He is the greatest warrior in all of Tethera and has been for centuries. It was he that trained me, and my sister Llewellyn as well."

Caradog looked skeptical. "Llewellyn is a girl, how much did she learn?"

"Llewellyn? With a sword she is more dangerous than I am! At least I think she is. I have not quite summoned the courage to test myself against her yet. The last thing I need is my little sister beating me repeatedly in the practice yard, for all of Caerleon to see."

Caradog still did not appear to be convinced but said, "Very well, I should like to try training with him, at least. That would mean I could come to Gwent for a time! I should very much like that! I hope we will find a ship already at Aber when we get back. There are fewer and fewer of them still plying the coast these days."

Llew began walking back out of the rubble to where Caradog had left the horses, the young princeling close on his heels.

"Hopefully, that will be the case. But that is not where we are going now."

"What?" asked Caradog. "Why not? Time is of the essence if we are to meet King Gronw's ransom in time."

"I do not believe the torc he wants is in Caerleon, Caradog. I would know something of it ere now if it were—hold a moment," Llew said, stopping abruptly. "Who is King Gronw?"

Caradog looked perplexed as he replied, "You were just talking to him. The insolent fellow who wants the torc. I have never liked him. I am not surprised to see his true colors emerge although he must know it will cost him his crown and possibly his head."

"Now let me get this straight," Llew said slowly, "I was talking to a disgraceful mercenary that I know as Cai. Are you saying that he is someone you know as King Gronw?"

"Yes, he is a wicked snake. He rules a small cantref called Penllyn that was in Powys before it fell. Since then it has been more or less a part of Gwynedd since it is right on the border. He is frequently at court, stirring up trouble as he is wont to do. Between that and whatever else he has been doing it has been said he does not spend two months a year actually in his cantref. That is probably a lucky thing for his subjects."

"Did he see you? And would Bloddeuwedd also recognize him?"

"No, Llew, I hobbled the horses and sneaked up behind the rocks so I could, um, watch. And yes, of course she knows him."

"So either he is giving up his crown, or he intends to kill Bloddeuwedd, and almost certainly me as well, lest we expose his infamy. Caradog, this is important, I know him as mercenary captain, a rather evil one, who worked for Moriganna. Now he has intimated that he is in the employment of Lord Arawen of Annwyn."

"I would presume," remarked Caradog, "that he was tired of working for the lesser of two evils."

"Why would he be a sell-sword at all if he is a king, even if only a cantref king?"

"Well," mused Caradog, "Penllyn is not an especially rich cantref and it is frequently menaced by Picts, and Fae, and even by things that wander in from the Wild Growth. Perhaps he just needs the money. But that would not be in character for him. No, it would have to be part of some greater scheme. As I said, he has caused no dearth of trouble in the court and only my grandmother's quick actions have kept the lid on some things that could have been very much worse than they were. Based on what you have said, I would say someone, probably Arawen, has offered him something he wants dearly in exchange for that torc."

"Or perhaps he thinks it will give him some legitimacy to take Bloddeuwedd as his own bride and claim the throne of

Gwynedd?" Llew asked.

"Well no, that would not work, Llew, because if he got the torc from us he would no longer have Blod and—" Caradog trailed off, clearly feeling foolish.

"He does not really intend to return Blod no matter what we do, does he?" the boy asked.

"I do not think so. As I said, I also do not think the torc is at Caerleon either. If it were, it is most likely my father would be wearing it."

"Llew! What do we do? He may kill or enslave Blod if he does not get it!"

"I am not going back to Caerleon right now," Llew stated flatly. "I will send someone to check and ask if it really is there, and if my father will yield it up, but I have little hope for success with that. Instead I must either find that torc or rescue Blod. I have no idea how to do either at present, but three weeks is time in which to at least try if I do not spend it all on a ship going back and forth. I was going to send you back to Caer Pyn y Mwd—"

"I will not go! Blod is my cousin—"

"—but I have decided I am not letting you out of my sight until this affair is settled," Llew resumed.

Caradog changed course immediately. "Where do we start then, Llew? You said we were not returning to Aber."

Llew stopped and looked at Gower. He was grazing, with friends.

"Caradog?"

"Yes, Llew?"

"Why do we possess a herd of horses?"

"Well, you had Gower, I brought four more, and then those we pursued left their five." Caradog made a protracted performance of counting his fingers. "I come up with ten, Llew."

"Thank you, Caradog."

"Anytime, Llew."

"In answer to your question, Caradog, unless I am totally lost, I rule a small cantref less than a day's ride from here, much closer than Aber. We will—"

"A moment, please, Llew. How is it you rule a cantref in Gwynedd and I, who am supposed to become king of Gwynedd, have never even heard of it?"

"Mind your own business!" snapped Llew. Then he grinned broadly at the growing confusion on Caradog's face while raising his hands placatingly.

"Technically it is only on the outskirts of Gwynedd, Prince Caradog. Further, it is a very small cantref, with but a single keep and village. It is also hidden by magic such that no one can ever find their way to it unless they have been there before."

"You are taking me to Caer Mallcoedwig? Moriganna's stronghold?" Caradog asked excitedly. "I am not complaining, but why there?"

"We need to properly provision ourselves and also to dispatch a messenger to Queen Enid about sending a ship to Caerleon for a torc that is not likely to be there. We can also turn in all these extra animals there and get you a proper horse."

"A proper horse?" Caradog inquired.

"They breed very special horses there; I am something of

an expert."

"Provisions, messenger, horse. Anything else?" Caradog asked.

"Yes. If you behave yourself I will also get you a dog."

"Llew, I already have many hounds."

"They breed very special dogs there."

"I will be on my best behavior, Llew."

"I am glad to hear that," he replied dryly.

* * *

Cutting to the south they continued until they intersected the road to Powys. An hour's travel further along it and Llew found a trail he had recalled seeing on one of Moriganna's maps. It would eventually lead to the very trail he had taken when he had left a year earlier, sent forth with Afaggdu, Cymri, and a company of mercenaries led by their captain, the villain Cai. Llew shook his head. It was difficult to reconcile Cai with someone named King Gronw of Pellyn.

They had just crossed a wide rocky valley where no trees grew when Caradog spoke, "Llew, something is coming across the valley behind us."

Llew turned and looked, then stared in disbelief. It was half a dozen hounds, white with red tipped ears and each one nearly the size of a small pony.

"Are these those special dogs you were telling me about," Caradog asked hopefully.

"I am afraid they are not. These are what some folk call the Hounds of Annwyn—hell hounds! Move!"

They rode at a gallop but at the bottom of the next hill it was clear it was hopeless. The beasts were just too fast for any of their horses but Gower, and even he would be mightily strained to stay ahead of them carrying an armed and armored Llew.

Next best, thought Llew, refusing to give up, would be to find some place highly defensible. Surrounded by barren rocky hills, this valley had a small forest growing within it. The forest could provide no hiding place against creatures that could hunt by scent, as the hounds surely could, but on the other side might be a cave or a crevasse, or at least a cliff face they could get their backs against.

They thundered along the trail between the trees, Llew watching as best he could for potential low hanging limbs or fallen logs. Behind them, they could hear the hell hounds begin a terrible baying as they entered the forest in hot pursuit. The horses needed no encouragement to keep up. Llew momentarily considered sacrificing a horse to distract the pursuers, but then chided himself for even beginning to think the hounds might be this far from Annwyn just because they were looking for food.

As they passed deeper into the forest, a series of roars came from behind them, quite different from the calls of the hounds. The baying abruptly stopped and Llew could hear snarls and fierce growls that sounded like nothing so much as a dogfight on a massive scale. Were they fighting amongst themselves?

From just ahead of him, Caradog cried out and reined in as all the horses came to an abrupt stop, packed into a milling mass and with their eyes still rolling with fear. A large tree that had fallen aslant across the trail. Llew slipped from his saddle and yelled to Caradog, "Keep an eye out!" He ran to the tree and drew Fragaroc. A sword was by no means an axe but, since the blade never dulled, it might serve the need here, especially as he had no intention of chopping through the log itself. Clearing a hole through the branches under it at the higher end would be enough for most of the horses. For Gower he would have to clear the limbs above and to the sides of part of the lower end, then trust his great steed could leap it.

It was tiring but the sword performed well, each branch requiring no more than one or two strokes. Caradog dragged them out of the way as they fell. Llew decided the opening was big enough and sent Caradog through, then drove the rest of the horses through, all save Gower.

"Get to the far side of the wood. Find us a defensible position if possible, otherwise get as far down the trail as you can," Llew instructed. "I am not sure how well they fight individually, but meeting a pack like this in the open would be hopeless!"

Caradog and the horses galloped off. Llew turned to move to the other end of the log just as Cilgwri, perched on one of the fallen tree's extended branches, cawed a warning. Looking behind, Llew froze at what he saw.

A single enormous hell hound, easily as large as a pony, with its head bloody where one of its red ears had been badly savaged, was slowly advancing on them from perhaps fifty paces away. It was very near Gower, growling deep in its throat, and had the big horse's full attention. Llew was almost sick with the fear that flooded through him. Rather than fleeing, Gower was advancing on the hound with his head held low and his stance belligerent, more like a bull preparing to charge than a horse.

Frantic to save Gower, Llew remembered the sword in his hand and started to run. This must have distracted the hell hound for a moment because it glanced in his direction. Gower took the opportunity to attack. With a savage growl, the great horse fairly leaped into the hell hound, bowling it over completely before burying his teeth in the hound's neck. Despite his panic, Llew stopped and stared.

The hell hound remained unmoving, flat on its back with its legs in the air. It whined pleadingly and Llew realized with a start that Gower had not actually bitten the animal, merely seized it by the ruff of its neck with his teeth. Gower lifted his head, mouth still opened, and Llew found himself wondering how it was that Gower had a mouthful of vicious fangs and sharp teeth. This, in turn, made him wonder how Gower had gotten his bridle and bit off.

Llew had never thought of Gower as frightening before, but now? Now he was terrifying. The fanged mouth remained open as the big horse panted and a large pink tongue licked his teeth. The hell hound whimpered a bit.

Then came the biggest blow to Llew's sanity. Gower dipped his head toward the hell hound and expelled air in such a way that it sounded much like, "No, bad!" spoken in a very deep voice. Despite the pitch, in timing and inflection, it sounded just the way Llew himself had spoken those words with a younger Gower, on those rare occasions when it had seemed especially warranted. Llew wondered, somewhat dazedly, if Gower actually understood the words or just the tone.

Gower lifted his head up, then thumped the hell hound in the side with his left front hoof while making another growl that was very nearly a roar. It was, Llew thought, perhaps the most frightening thing he had ever seen . . . certainly it was in the top three.

The hell hound rolled over with alacrity and raced away from the trail and into the forest.

Gower straightened up, turned back to Llew, and trotted over to him.

"What scary fellows we be, eh?" Llew said to Gower, somewhat feebly.

He reached into a pocket and found one of the small carrots Caradog had brought with him. He slowly offered it to Gower and watched as the mouth opened—there was no sign of any fangs—and big flat normal horse teeth took the small root from his hand and chomped it into orange splinters.

Numbly, Llew tried to convince himself that Gower had somehow lost his bridle and that the rest of it was something he had imagined under the influence of all the stress.

The sword in his hand reminded him what still needed doing. He returned to the fallen tree. Quickly removing the offending limbs, he ran back to the waiting horse. He hesitated just a second, then climbed on and took a strong hold on Gower's mane since he had no bridle or reins. After trotting a short distance back, they turned and raced for the log. As anticipated, Gower made the leap without difficulty and continued on at a gallop. They even managed to overtake Caradog before he and the horses exited the forest.

As they emerged from the trees, Llew saw precisely the kind of thing he had been hoping for. A partial cliff face rose not far to their right. Large boulders ringed most of its base, forming a semi-protected place where the entire pack would not be able to reach them at once.

Llew and Caradog rode in, the horses all still following. Though Caradog had managed to cut them loose, they had elected to follow Gower; he had that effect on horses. Several people, upon seeing the way other horses behaved around him, had dubbed Gower "the King of all Horses." Perhaps there was some truth to it. Paradoxically, most dogs, just like the recent hell hound, seemed to regard him as an exceptionally large canine.

"See if you can find anything to make a fire with," Llew commanded. He dismounted and strode to the space between the boulders and the cliff face, prepared to sell his life dearly if it came to that. Providing the beasts did not scrabble over in some way, it might be possible to prevent them from coming in, if he could sufficiently injure the first one or two that tried it.

There they waited, then waited longer. Caradog had been unable to find sufficient wood to make any sort of a lasting fire but it did not matter, no hell hounds came. Llew strained to hear as well as he possibly could but there was nothing, no sound of pursuit whatsoever.

Recalling the fighting he had heard behind them in the trees, he thought about the way the hell hound—surely it had been the pack leader—had been so badly savaged about the head. Was it possible the noise of their passage had drawn something out? Something that then encountered the Hounds of Annwyn? The problem with that as a possible solution was that it meant something worse than half a dozen hell hounds was out there.

He whispered to Caradog, "If we had some way to muffle all these hooves I would be tempted to do so but, even if we had the cloth or leather to wrap them all in, I should still dislike taking so much time. Instead we will just go our way, but quietly."

They had left the valley nearly a mile behind them, and the evening light was beginning to fade, before Caradog ventured to speak. "That was all very strange, Llew."

Llew considered the understatement. Then he started to chuckle, finally laughing a bit. It was too much for the inadvertent humor of Caradog's remark, he realized. It was mostly just because he was so very relieved. By all rights they should have both been ripped apart by the Hounds of Annwyn.

Caradog waited until he settled down, then raised a single

eyebrow at him. He had evidently been watching the way Llew did things with his eyebrows to accentuate his points. "What is so very funny?" he asked.

"It was stranger even than you know. A single hell hound, the pack leader I think, attacked us after you had gone on. Something had already injured it about the head. Gower ran it off."

"You did not kill it?" Caradog exclaimed.

"I never even had a chance to get a swing at it. It was more important to get ourselves hither. Whatever killed his pack and injured him might have been following close behind him."

Caradog shuddered. "Why does a simple ride in the country have to be so very dangerous in these days? I know from reading some of the books in our library that our land was not always so."

Llew noted to himself that even Caradog could read. *When this is over*, he vowed to himself.

"It is all very strange, Caradog. You saw the white fur and red ears? Their tremendous size aside that alone would mark them as Hounds of Annwyn. They serve only the Lord of Death, Arawen himself. They would never be out roaming the countryside, so very far from Annwyn, for no reason whatsoever. They were sent for something, and it looks very much as though they were after me."

"They are intelligent then?" Caradog asked.

"I have not heard that they are great thinkers, any of them, but they can follow instructions nearly as well as a man, or so I am told."

"That they were sent for you makes little sense," Caradog

said. "Did you not say you believe King Gronw—er, Cai—is doing Arawen's bidding in sending you to get the torc for Blod's ransom? How would killing you help you do that? For that matter, would they even have known you are who you are? If we assume that they could be that specific then they could just as easily have been after me. They have Blod already, killing me would leave no clear heir for Gwynedd."

Llew considered this. "There is something in what you say. However, now that you raise the question of whether it was even me they were coming to kill, that opens up another possibility."

"And that would be?"

"Gower."

Caradog blinked, incredulous. "Gower?"

"They could have been on another mission and picked up his scent when they came upon our trail," Llew mused aloud. "They would certainly have had no reason to recognize your odor, or mine either, for that matter. Gower's, on the other hand, is probably quite distinctive to them."

"Llew, why in the name of Auberon would they—"

"Do not swear by the names of the Fae, lest you invoke them," Llew reprimanded, repeating the rote admonition he himself had been given many times while growing up.

"—drop everything to come attack your mount?" Caradog finished. "Sorry. And why would Gower's scent be so special to them if they have never seen or smelt any of us ere now?"

"I do not claim to fully understand any of this, but possibly it is because he is a distinctive beast from Caer Mallcoedwig, recent stronghold of Moriganna. Lord Arawen believes she is his greatest enemy."

"Queen Moriganna is Lord Arawen's greatest enemy?"

"I did not say that; although it is probably what he believes," Llew said darkly. "In time I will inform him that this is no longer the case, but right now it is neither here nor there. When we arrive in Caer Mallcoedwig I will have some questions for Master Oswalt ap Hire."

"And who is he?" Caradog asked.

"He is the fellow who may have a special dog for you."

"Llew, this dog is not going to be a lodestone for hell hounds, is it?"

"That will be one of my questions for Master Oswalt to answer, my young shield-bearer."

Chapter VII

Homecoming

After a cold camp and a dismal breakfast of dried meat and fruit, they came to the lake the next morning and headed around on the same path Llew had taken when he had left home the year before.

He found himself strangely excited about this visit. It was perplexing. He had spent most of his life plotting on how to get away from this place and, now that he had, he was looking forward to coming back.

He mentioned as much to Caradog.

"Well, whatever else it was, it was your home, Llew. Many important things happened to you there and not all of them bad. It is part of who you are now, and it always will be. It will prod memories back into your awareness that you might never again have recalled, and that is not altogether a bad thing.

"Then too, you are probably eager to see how it has fared

in your absence. We all have this tendency to feel that the world stops for a place that we have left and only restarts upon our return. You know this is only a feeling, and that it actually does not stop at all. This makes you anxious, concerned about what parts of your past may have changed beyond recognition, or are gone altogether."

Llew was somewhat taken aback by this. "I am not sure if you are right or wrong in what you say, but I am tremendously impressed that you can vocalize it. Caradog, you have unexpected depths and continue to surprise me."

"Thank you, Llew, I guess all that education my grandmother forces on me is of some good after all, even the philosophy."

Coming around the next curve they could see the stables. Llew gave them his full attention for a moment, then decided that perhaps a year was not enough time for any real changes.

By chance, the first person to spot him was Braen, the stable master who had halfway raised him after his adoptive father, the old stable master, had died. Braen, apparently on his way to the largest stable, stopped and regarded Llew and Caradog suspiciously. Two figures bringing ten horses in to the village must have seemed very odd to him.

Caer Mallcoedwig exported horses to sell, it did not bring in new ones, and it most especially was not visited by strangers. It took a moment for Braen to realize that at least one of the riders was not a stranger at all. Llew knew this had happened when he saw the man's eyes go wide with incredulity.

Braen yelled excitedly and men began appearing from all over. Out of the main stable came Luc, and Seith, who were brothers, followed closely by Cary and Renfrew. From the direction of the paddock Gruffin and Emlyn trotted into view.

Out of the smaller stable emerged Alun, Peredur, and Yorath. Llew knew all of them and three or four more as well. They were the stable hands he had lived and worked with since as far back as he could remember.

Something was different now, however, and it showed in the way they came quickly, then edged up slowly, Braen just slightly ahead of the rest. Llew had seen this behavior before in the past year but it seemed somewhat surreal to experience it here. It was respect, mingled with something that was more than that: awe.

"Greetings, your highness," Braen said, tugging at his forelock and trying to execute something of a bow at the same time. "We are very pleased to see you come again to Caer Mallcoedwig and proud we can be the first to welcome you back."

Llew laughed in delight. It had not always been sweetness and light here. When he was little he had been the victim of many pranks from some of these men.

Renfrew had once hung him by his collar on a wooden peg on the back of the front door of the bachelor's quarters when he was perhaps six. Llew had swung in and out with the door for hours as the rest of them came and went. Were it not that Braen had eventually wanted him for some minor errand, he might still be there.

Peredur, Yorath, and Gruffin had once stood idly by as a pack of boys from the village had come into the stable area to find him and, when they had, they proceeded to thrash him within an inch of his life.

Afterward, it had been Braen who had remonstrated with the stable hands for allowing this to happen to one of their own. He had shamed them sufficiently that, when next the village boys had come looking for him, the stable hands had run them off, both then and every time thereafter.

Llew had taken quite a bit of rough treatment from these fellows back in the days before Moriganna began his slow elevation in society. Nonetheless, he was pleased to see them again and, more than that, happy to find that, confronted with all of them again in the flesh, he honestly held no ill will against any of them. He had certainly got his own back and more when he had secretly taken over much of the direction of the stables, giving his own orders when they had thought he was simply relaying those of Braen.

"You probably all know I have traveled far and seen many wonders in this year past," Llew told them, "but words alone cannot express my pleasure at being here again. I never thought I would ever say that, but it is the absolute truth."

The men seemed to like hearing that and grinned and nodded amongst themselves, no one seeming to have quite enough courage to reply to him directly, other than Braen.

"Will you be staying a bit then, your highness?" Braen asked. "Ever since the queen flew away we have all been hoping to see you again."

"Nay, not this visit, Braen. In fact, we have little time at all, for we are on an urgent mission even now; yet I could not ride past Caer Mallcoedwig and not come in for a tiny bit."

"It is good that you did, my lord," said the man who had once had him mucking out stalls all day, every day, for two full weeks after catching him in the act while he was trying to learn how to stand on the bare back of a moving horse. It is fortunate, too. I believe there are visitors at the castle, and they seemed to be looking for you."

"Really? I cannot wait to see who it is and how they were

able to get here. Ah, but first where are my manners? Everyone! This fellow with me is Prince Caradog, the next king of Gwynedd."

Caradog gave the royal wave, and the men gave him a half-hearted cheer before returning their full attention to Llew.

"Braen, as you can see, we acquired far too many horses. Four of them belong to the royal guardsmen of Gwynedd, I believe, and will need to be returned to Aber when possible. Perhaps it can be done the next time we have a horse and hound merchant going that way. The other five are simply horses I did not want to leave to wander in the wilds. You may do whatever you wish with them, their last owners are not looking for them."

"Most of their last owners will not be looking for anything ever again," Caradog remarked. "Prince Llew was rather annoyed with them after they all decided to attack him, rather than be brought to justice."

That got the attention of the small crowd and there was some low murmuring among them and knowing looks were exchanged. Llew did not bother to try and hear what any of them were saying to each other, but he gave a Caradog a warning look.

"Were they horse thieves, your highness?" Braen asked.

"Nothing like that, although I would not have put it past them. They had certainly done much worse. Ah, Braen, Prince Caradog and myself will be departing soon, perhaps even tomorrow. Our mission is truly urgent. I realize you will not have any more of Gower's breed about but I was hoping you might have the next best thing available for him. It needs to be dependable and have as much endurance as possible. If it was also trained as a war horse that would be ideal, but it is not essential, so long as it does not easily spook."

Braen nodded knowingly and said, "I have a somewhat spirited gelding that might be just the thing."

"A gelding?" asked Caradog, clearly disappointed.

"Well, yes young prince. If you are going to be traveling with our Prince Llew here you would not want a second stallion. That could only cause problems. Not that Gower could not deal with them, for he is clearly the prince of all horses. Still, the gelding has plenty of spirit. He actually started with entirely too much spirit, which is why he is now a gelding."

"Actually," Llew interrupted, "there has been a coronation of sorts and Gower is now referred to as the king of all horses, by proclamation of both King Pendaran of Gwent and King Hafgan of the Spriggans."

The stable hands all cheered enthusiastically at that and someone yelled, "Long live King Gower!" To which all the rest replied, "Here, here!"

"We will bring the young Prince's new mount to you at the castle, your highness," Braen said. "I would reckon you are eager to speak with Slow Tomos."

It dawned on Llew why he was not seeing his old slow-witted friend among the stable hands. He had not really expected to, but some part of him had been looking, all the same.

"You still call him Slow Tomos now, even though he is my steward and it is openly known that he is not truly slow at all?" Llew asked in surprise.

Braen shrugged, "We always knew he was not slow but we called him that to maintain his disguise. Old habits die hard or not at all. He does not mind it."

Llew wondered if he was the only one who had never

known, nor even suspected, anything of the sort where Slow Tomos was concerned. He tried to find some way to pardon himself and could only come up with the excuse that he had been very young and considerably distracted. Why would he have thought to look more closely at his dim-witted friend in the stables and realize that he was secretly the master of the village, maintaining an outward facade such that Queen Moriganna would detect no threat to her primacy over her small dominion?

Llew recognized this as internal rationalization and had already reproached himself for it several times already over the past winter. He had also resolved that, henceforth, no one and no thing would be below his notice. Still, he knew that, while this could help, it would be no guarantee. Certainly he had been caught off guard by Gower's own capabilities and no one knew Gower better than Llew.

Leaving eight of the horses with Braen and the stable hands, Llew rode side by side with Caradog on the short ride to the castle.

"It is very unsettling, Caradog. I have known all those men all of my life and, until last year, they have known me. I still see them; I still know them. But they no longer know me. The fellow they knew last year is dead to them, as much so as dust blown away on the wind."

As they rode higher they could see over the roofs of the village. Gesturing toward them, Llew said, "Oh, they know my name, they know where I came from, but in their minds I am no longer Llew, formerly Gwri, who worked and lived among them for so long. I am some terrible royal figure of song and legend who slays monsters, consorts with the Fae, and moves at ease through the greatest courts in the land—one who shrugs off bandit attacks as they might shrug off a swarm of biting midges. But Llew, just plain, Llew . . . he no longer exists for them."

Caradog looked thoughtful. "Does that Llew still exist for you? Or is he just someone, now passed, that just happened to leave you his memories? I think that may be the case with all of us, but few have it made as obvious to them as you have."

Llew snorted and said, "I did not really wish to be a quiet brooding sort of hero, like so many of those in the old tales are."

"Then you must choose not to be, Llew, and, as with anything else, make the effort to be more like what you would wish to be."

Llew looked at him and raised one eyebrow.

Caradog flushed, "At least that is what I think I should say. I probably read too much!"

* * *

Llew and Caradog rounded a curve and came in sight of the castle on the low hill ahead. Llew had known quite a bit less of castles the last time he had seen it. Now he saw it with new eyes.

It was not Caerleon, nor was it even close. But it was well built, with very high walls surrounded by a waterless moat. It would never win any prizes for beauty but it would, Llew realized, be a very tough nut to crack if it were reasonably well manned.

More surprising was the formation of two dozen guardsmen in full kit, standing before the moat bridge and open gate. Only with some difficulty was Llew able to resist checking his weapons and continue approaching at an unvarying speed. As he and Caradog came within twenty paces of them, their leader called for attention. Shields came up and long spears snapped vertical. On a second command, every one of them took a step backwards, then pivoted, half toward the right and half toward the left. Each man took four paces, stopped, completed a rear facing movement, grounded their spears, and leaned them forward. This created a partial tunnel leading up to the bridge.

Llew continued up to them, noting as he did that their leader was Mercher, his old weapons trainer before Afaggdu had taken over that duty. The Prince of Gwent gave the master of arms for Caer Mallcoedwig a sharp nod of approval as he passed by and into the tunnel of spears. Mercher never blinked, but Llew knew he saw everything with his peripheral vision.

Continuing into the courtyard, the castle's entire population, from the least servant up, were all waiting. Llew found it all quite eerie. People in other places behaved like this for his father, but not here and not for him, yet they were. He had grown up here and knew every one of these people.

Servants stepped up to take their horses' bridles and Gower gave his appointed handler no grief. He, too, knew this place and he knew these people.

Llew dismounted and turned to face the large man standing front and center. He knew this man well and yet did not know him at all. It was Slow Tomos and Llew was finding this incredibly awkward.

"Well, Tomos, it appears we have both risen far in a year."

Slow Tomos nodded his agreement. "Indeed we have, Prince Llew. When you moved up a position it appears everyone else got to move up a position as well."

"I think I may have moved up more than one position; it would seem you did as well."

"Welcome back to Caer Mallcoedwig, your highness," Slow Tomos said, and gave a near perfect courtly bow.

To Llew, the former stable hand, whom he had always thought a mere simpleton, now sounded quite different. His sentences were longer, his tone more deferential, yet he was also far more self-confident. There was even a trace of command presence in his voice. Llew looked desperately for some sign this man was still, in some way, the stable hand he had once known. A man who had always seemed especially slow of thought and who had often needed a boy's help to make sense of things.

Slow Tomos looked towards Gower, then back at Llew again, before saying, "I see you have been taking good care of that puppy you found. It is very good to see you both."

That was enough. Llew stepped forward and embraced his old friend.

After they parted, Slow Tomos said, "My lord, I should warn you, we have guests. They arrived last night and were not certain you would come here. Now that you have, I am not certain they are pleased they have found you."

Llew looked up at this and the crowd seemed to part of its own volition, leaving three figures standing alone. The first was Cymri, with her hands on her hips and glowering at him. She was flanked by a stern looking Helgar and, on the other side, by a somewhat pained looking Addfwyn.

"Whoops," said Llew.

Chapter VIII

A Council of War

It was clear that Cymri had many things to say, but first it was necessary for Llew to say a few words to all assembled. He thanked them for their efforts and assured them that Caer Mallcoedwig was dear to him and would always be in his thoughts, regardless of how far his other duties took him. These were words that made them happy and, for his part, he meant them. It did not take terribly long and King Pendaran had convinced Llew of the necessity of such things. The fact that Moriganna had never done anything remotely like it was enough to convince Llew that it should be done.

It also gave him time to devise a plan for how he would handle things once they could speak privately.

Eventually, Llew, Caradog, Cymri, and Helgar were able to retreat inside and found themselves at the high table in the great hall. Slow Tomos saw them seated and made to leave until Llew reached out and caught him by the sleeve. "Oh no, you do not escape that easily! My faithful steward has certainly earned an honored placed at my table and, coincidentally, that is precisely where I need you to be. Please join us, and send a runner to invite Master Oswalt ap Hire of the royal kennels to come enjoy this midday repast with us as well."

Addfwyn, after a few words whispered to him from Llew, saw that the table was adequately prepared and then took over its service, keeping all other servants and guards at a distance so the mighty could speak in relative privacy.

Cymri was angrier with Llew than he had ever seen her. She had managed to contain herself in the courtyard but it seemed to have cost her some of her normal equanimity to do so.

"Bird brained idiocy! Taking off after bandits with only your sword and your horse and not even a word to anyone else! There could have been a hundred more of them just beyond the palace and you would have ridden right into them. Bad enough for the heir of Gwent to put himself in such peril, but did you have to take the heir of Gwynedd as well?"

Cymri was not nearly done. "Queen Enid is quite beside herself. It is amazing this has not killed her outright. Her niece and ward, her grandson and heir to the kingdom, and the visiting son of the most powerful king in Tethera, all vanished from the face of the earth in less than an hour's time. Did you even stop for a moment to consider what you were doing?"

Llew marveled at her. It had been a long time. Was there anyone else who would still dare to talk to him in such a manner? Afaggdu, possibly, but that was not really his way. It was refreshing and he was glad she was there.

She slowed down for a moment and Llew was able to get a word in edgewise. "I am happy to see you again, too, Cymri. But there are other things to discuss and," he held up the palm of his hand as she drew in a breath to say more, "Also, it pains me that you have some of your facts quite wrong and are willing to believe the worst of me despite that. It actually reminds me a bit of Moriganna."

The expression that came over her face told him he had probably gone too far. In an attempt to evade what he had wrought, Llew turned to Helgar and said, "Well? I believe it is your turn."

Helgar furrowed his brows. "Llew, you are my drott, and it saddened me you left without me. Suppose you had caught them? Then there would have been some real action, and what of me? Missed it completely I would have."

"Thank you, Helgar. Addfwyn? Do you have anything you wish to add?"

His man servant looked up from the goblets he was filling, startled at this. "Oh no, my lord, such would not be my place!"

"Right," said Llew, "your mouth says that but your eyes say differently."

Addfwyn hurriedly made his way back toward the kitchens.

Llew let his gaze travel up and down both sides of the table. "I was there. I was armed and armored. Gower was already saddled and ready to go. I would stake a wager that neither of you was able to be on the road in less than half an hour after I had already left and any other horse would have required Gower to slow down so it could keep up. By all rights I should have laid her kidnappers low and had the princess back that same afternoon. I would have, too, if they had not been willing to ride their horses to ruin. Even that would have only delayed things had they not had remounts waiting."

Addfwyn began delivering the first course, the first dish of which looked to be a pottage of oats and some sort of fish, possibly trout.

"We are serving ourselves as Addfwyn is the only servant we want within earshot of this table and he will be quite busy as it is, even without serving our plates as well," Llew announced. "As for kidnapping young Caradog, I would have him explain what actually happened himself."

Caradog was happy to do this. He began his tale of his horse theft, showing not a trace of remorse, while Addfwyn topped off their wine goblets.

While Caradog spoke, Llew took advantage of this time to eat his pottage, then speared and devoured a baked apple coated with spiced fig sauce. The figs could only be grown far to the south and with enormous difficulty. They were terribly expensive. This suggested to Llew that the horse and hound trade must be doing quite well. He then took a taste, just a taste, of the lamb fritters. He really did not much care for them but the rules of hospitality were unbending, what was offered must be eaten. Although, he mused, since he was not precisely a visitor here, perhaps they should not actually apply to him.

Caradog proceeded with the tale all the way to when Cai rode away with Bloddeuwedd. Oswalt ap Hire arrived during its telling but did not interrupt.

"Cai," muttered Cymri, "I knew I should have killed him when I had the chance."

"I believe you were a bird on every occasion the two of you have met," Llew pointed out.

"Do not underestimate me, Llew. Besides which, I also could have gotten Cilgwri to help if necessary."

Hearing his name spoken by Cymri, Cilgwri cawed and fluttered over to her. She gently stroked his feathers with a finger and, in general, seemed much more patient and affectionate with him than she ever had as a bird herself.

Meanwhile, Addfwyn set down a large serving dish ringed by small baked birds that were really too small to be partridges. Each was carefully positioned and staged around a bowl of peeled boiled eggs. Caradog glanced at Cilgwri, "No one you knew, I hope?" Despite his effort at wit, Cilgwri ignored him.

Addfwyn began clearing the table in preparation for the second course.

"Llew," Cymri said, "I apologize for my temper earlier. These last few days have been . . . difficult. You still have not said why you did not send Prince Caradog back to his guardsmen, and thence his palace, where he would be safe."

"It is not safe," he replied. "Those three little bandits were from Addfwyn's farm. One was their leader, Meilyr, and the other two were the ones we let flee with him. They may not seem terribly dangerous until I tell you that I think it was Meilyr I saw—at the same time he spotted us—when we rode through the town of Aber. I thought he looked familiar at the time, but I did not get a close enough look."

Addfwyn set a large pie next to Caradog. "This looks good, what is it?" Caradog asked, grasping a knife and serving spoon.

"It is carp pie, your highness, do please try some. I think you will like it," Slow Tomos said.

Caradog made a face and said, "Um, what is in it—besides carp, I mean?"

"Grated bread, sweet herbs, hard-boiled egg yolks, bacon, and tiny fish are stitched into the carp. It is then baked in the pastry shell with freshwater shrimp, capers, and more egg yolks," recited Slow Tomos.

Caradog froze until Cymri nudged him and said, "Rules of hospitality, young prince. Take your portion, a small one if you prefer, and pass it on."

Llew glanced back and forth between Cymri and Helgar. "You were both there in Aber when I spotted Meilyr. Later that same day I saw what was left of his band entering into the kitchens of the palace. I only got a look at one of them and, again, could not place him at the time but I knew he looked familiar. I pursued them but was not able to catch them after they left the kitchen and went further into the palace. What does this tell you?"

Helgar quickly stuffed his mouth full of bread. Probably, thought Llew, to avoid being called upon to answer. For her part, Cymri scowled at the tabletop, then looked up at Llew. "I understand what you are telling us. They have help on the inside. It would seem as though it must be someone reasonably well placed, too. There is no security for Caradog in that palace."

Llew nodded and pointed to the younger prince. "That is why I am keeping the prince with me. Being with me is a far cry from being in a safe place, but it is the safest place I know of from what threatens him. It has also given us an unexpected reward. Tell them the story of King Gronw, please, Caradog."

As Caradog did this, Llew found time to try the beef collops. Wrapped in bacon, and sandwiching a thick layer of venison and herbs, they were quite good. The venison normally became rather dry when cooked by itself; it really benefited, he decided, by being hidden in the protected center where it stayed moist and delicate. He would have taken a second helping, but realized filling up too quickly would be a bad idea.

Caradog finished what he had to say about King Gronw and this time it was Helgar that seemed more aghast that Cymri. "The man is a king but runs around selling his sword to the highest bidder?" he expostulated. "Llew, this is unforgivable!"

"It certainly is. This is also how we know that he does not intend to release Princess Bloddeuwedd, yet we dare not denounce him just yet. It is a secret worth his throne if exposed and there is no telling how he would react if he knew that his secret was out."

It was clearly all Caradog could do to hide his revulsion when Addfwyn brought out small bowls of green pudding topped with crushed walnuts and a sweet wine sauce. Nonetheless, he bravely took a small spoonful without flinching. Then his eyes widened and he quickly finished the entire bowl.

"Either way, there is no point in getting this torc he wants then," Helgar said. "Giving it to him will achieve nothing."

Clasping his hands together and interlacing his fingers before his face, Slow Tomos spoke for the first time since they had taken their seats. "I am not so certain of this, Jarl Helgar. It sounds almost as though the torc may not be something this King Gronw seeks for himself, but might be something desired by Lord Arawen. For what purpose I do not know. His possessing it would probably either bolster his own power with its own, or deny that power to his enemies—or possibly both. At any rate, Lord Arawen might want that torc more than he cares about protecting King Gronw's secret. In that case, having the torc when you go to bargain could make the difference between her release and her death."

"Have you any idea where we might seek it out?" Llew asked. "It has been lost a long time. If the last time anyone saw it was on High King Pwyl then I have little confidence in our ability to find it at all, let alone in the time we have."

Slow Tomos set down the piece of rabbit covered in spiced acorn paste that he had been nibbling on, then pursed his lips as his eyes took on a distant look. "Let me think on it for a little while, please. Llew, do you want to enter into discourse with

Master Oswalt, now? He is ever welcome at this table but I am certain you had a specific reason for calling him hither."

Llew shook his head at this. It was amazing him how much Slow Tomos was still Slow Tomos even though he was no longer pretending to be slow.

Addlfwyn placed a platter of roasted beef, covered in caramelized onions and garlic, next to Llew and headed back for another dish.

Master Oswalt had listened attentively, but seemed perplexed as to why he was there. "My lord, I am glad to see you come again. I know full well that, like our previous ruler, you have a true appreciation for the fine hounds we breed. Whatever you wish to ask, know that I am your most faithful servant in all matters."

Llew helped himself to a large chunk of the meat, with plenty of the onion and garlic, before saying, "Good sirrah, please know that I thoroughly appreciate both your skills and your service. As to my question today, you doubtless recall we spoke of Caer Mallcoedwig hounds when you let me tour your kennels. You also spoke somewhat of their ancestry. As I recall you said they were something Moriganna created during the century or so when she dwelt with Lord Arawen in Annwyn. That she somehow bred them from a mix of normal hounds and the hounds of Annwyn?"

Oswalt shook his head. "Not precisely, my lord. I said I believe she started with what the simple folk call hell hounds but, since normal men would not be able to control such, she interbred them with both wolves and wolfhounds. Wolfhounds were bred from some breed of dog taken from lands over the sea, long ages ago. I also believe the Pwacca are involved but I am not at all certain how, just that she developed both the Pwacca and the hounds of Caer Mallcoedwig while she dwelt in Annwyn. She had only a few of the hounds when she escaped, just enough for breeding stock really, and we have been improving the breed ever since."

"Pwacca?" Caradog inquired.

The kennel-master took in Caradog's questioning eyes and elaborated, "The Pwacca are a race of beings that are natural shape changers and rather mysterious because of it. Most people call them shape-shifters, some of the people in the remote western villages of Dyfed name them as pookas."

Remote to what? Llew wondered. *What could be more remote that Caer Mallcoedwig?*

Helgar having waited until everyone had taken what beef they wanted, dumped the still half full platter onto a fresh trench of wheat bread.

"You also," Llew remarked carefully, "said that some are born with white patches or other traits of the hounds of Annwyn and that those are destroyed."

"Indeed I did, my prince. We hate doing it but it is necessary or we might eventually wind up with something resembling a hell hound more than a dog."

The second course finished with medlar tarts. The medlars had been bletted so perfectly that no one wanted to speak while they were savoring them.

Llew waited until all were done and Addfwyn began clearing the table for the next course before turning his attention back to Oswalt. He took a breath in preparation for what he was about to ask. "When I came across Gower as a puppy he was clearly of the Caer Mallcoedwig breed. He also had a large white patch on his chest. As a horse it is much smaller, but it is still present. When Moriganna transformed him he was covered in mud. Had that not been the case—had she been able to see the white patch—would she have culled him herself, right then and there?"

Master Oswalt gave a short nod and seemed to consider his next words carefully. "I imagine she would have because, if he was a product of our kennels then it is certain he has a strong streak of hell hound in him. It is fortunate indeed that this seems to have been mitigated by his being so strongly bound to you. It could have gone much worse. There is no accounting for the vagaries of breeding sometimes. We play the dice as we roll against what seem like promising odds, but we only win in the long run by discarding those rolls we do not desire. Have you witnessed any behavior that would be accounted for solely by his hell hound heritage?"

Bringing his hands down to rest on the table, Llew said, "I think so. We were attacked by a very large hell hound not far from here. Before I was able to intercede, Gower attacked it and it rolled over onto its back and remained so, its legs in the air, until Gower nudged it and it ran away."

Cymri audibly gasped at this.

The kennel master nodded again at this. "Yes, that would fit. Gower established he was the dominant pack member. In such contests between canines it is instinctive for the loser to so submit. Were it not so then the death toll among them would be too high to maintain their numbers. So certainly Gower behaved as a hell hound would in such a situation and, not only that, was sufficiently convincing that the full-blooded hell hound did not question his right to do so. Was there anything else?"

Llew looked up and down the table and thought hard on what he was going to say next. "Yes, but I must entrust all of you to absolute secrecy on this. I will not ask that any of you so swear, for I know that my request is enough to ensure your lips are sealed on this matter."

Apparently unable to wait any longer, Addfwyn and one of the stockier servants brought out the main course before Llew could say what he intended. This consisted of a full roasted boar, complete with the traditional apple in its mouth. While Addfwyn prepared to carve it for them, the other man served up bowls of leek soup, then placed a large serving dish full of thinly sliced and grilled turnips and parsnips covered in an herb flavored pork gravy. Oatmeal cakes were quickly added to the table. The helper retreated to the kitchen while Addfwyn served up the meat, still hot off the bone.

Llew glanced about to make sure there were no more servants or guards within earshot of what he had to say next. "When Gower was fighting with the hell hound—it really was not much of a fight—I saw his mouth while it was open. It was filled with fangs and sharp teeth, just as a wolf's might be. Yet before and since I have seen only flat horse's teeth in that mouth."

Master Oswalt was completely still. "He has proved Pwacca blood then; by definition he is a Pwacca."

At the table, the silence that followed made Llew question if he had suddenly grown deaf until he noticed he could still hear many other things from further away. Then Cymri spoke, "Llew, we all love Gower but . . . we cannot risk a shape-shifter in our midst."

"No." Llew's expression was unhappy but adamant. "I am not sending him away. Not under any circumstances."

"But Llew—" Helgar began.

Llew cut him off. "No, Helgar, just no. If you recall, you would have cautioned me against letting a Spriggan travel with us and we know how that turned out. Come to that, I have never told you this but, when you first came out of the wicker man, and I realized you were a Northman, I considered, just for a moment, cutting you down on the spot. There is not a day that goes by that I do not rejoice that I did not."

Helgar looked shocked, then sheepish. "Ah, yes, I am a cook pan calling another cook pan burnt, am I not? You are quite right, my drott. Gower has earned his place with us and guard his back I always will, just as I do yours, or Cymri's, or Llewellyn's, or, gods help me, even that short piece of Spriggan smugness called Hafgan. Gower may never be able to name me friend, but I name him so."

Cymri gulped audibly, then nodded agreement with what Helgar had said, the bard apparently not trusting her own voice.

Llew looked uncomfortable. "About that—not being able to name you friend, that is—that might not be correct either." Then he told them what he thought Gower had done while they made serious inroads into the roast boar and leek soup.

Again, all was quiet around the table until Cymri asked, in a somewhat strained voice, "Llew, are you certain you heard those words?"

He was spared from answering when Master Oswalt spoke up. "It is not entirely unexpected. So far as we know, Pwacca can speak as well as a man. Although, if we accept Gower is a Pwacca we must recognize that, by Pwacca standards at least, he is different. He does not change shape very much or very often. Perhaps he is simply not as adept at this as his brethren. Likewise, he may not be as capable in speech or thought as they are. Indeed, this might be why Prince Llew found him in a bag in the stream. It is not the way we cull our hounds but it might be a way in which the Pwacca cull their own kind."

"A cruel race then," said Slow Tomos.

"No more so than men," replied Cymri. "Those Picts who, due to permanent injury or old age, cannot keep up with their tribe, have no future. Though civilized life allows us to be somewhat more compassionate, I am certain we had ancestors who were less so."

Llew tried the turnips and parsnips but found he still had no appetite for turnips, regardless of how they were served. Fortunately, the oatmeal cakes were delicious.

"Be that as it may," Helgar said, "it is good that there are so few of these Pwacca left."

This seemed to startle Master Oswalt. "Why do you say that? Is it just because there are no longer a couple of dozen living in this castle?"

"What are you getting at?" Llew asked.

Master Oswalt looked somewhat reluctant to continue but, after a moment, continued to speak. "Queen Moriganna dwelt for a century in Annwyn and took many things when she left. At least some of what she took included breeding stock for our hounds. Consider that she left despite the fact that Lord Arawen, also called the Lord of Death, had turned against her and she was in the very center of his land, surrounded by armies of barrow warriors and other, even more terrifying servants. Have you not wondered how this was possible?"

"I confess I had not given it any thought," Llew admitted. "If I had considered it I would have assumed that, since she is well-known as the Queen of Deceit, some deception or subterfuge made it possible."

The kennel master shook his head in the negative. "Not this time. Her recounts, and those of certain others, are quite clear. She fought her way free, using a large army to do so."

"A large army of what?" asked Cymri, as she accepted a tankard of dark ale from the tray Addfwyn offered.

"Pwacca, of course," Master Oswalt announced solemnly. "Granted that many, if not most of them, might have been slain in the effort, she still must have had many hundreds remaining to her. This was well over a century ago. The number existing today cannot be estimated but could be . . . immense."

This had a chilling effect on the conversation and silence prevailed for nearly a full minute.

Slow Tomos sipped at his wine a bit before speaking. "We know that there are still a great many roaming the areas around Caer Mallcoedwig. They still suppress all other threats and keep us safe from the Fae and things out of the Wild Growth, things that might not be turned aside from the misdirection spells laid upon our hidden cantref. The Pwacca do not come in to Caer Mallcoedwig but, if they did, we are not a match for them. We are also fortunate in that they do not attack or otherwise hinder our trade caravans from passing freely back and forth."

The steward turned his head slowly from right to left and regarded all the visitors at the table. "They also permitted all of you to come here without incident."

"Not entirely without incident," Caradog said.

All eyes turned to him.

"The hell hound that Gower defeated was merely one of a pack. They chased us through a forest on the way here. They were close on our heels and then we heard what sounded like the most terrible dog fight of all time. The only beast that came upon us was the one Gower subsequently ran off. It was already wounded where something had chewed at one ear."

Now all the eyes moved to Llew. He shrugged. "It is true

enough. Something quite fierce attacked them and likely killed most, if not all of them, eventually. Certainly whatever it was let us pass freely and did not pursue us."

Caradog spoke up again. "I would say perhaps it is possible a pack of predatory Pwacca were prowling in the pines. Try saying that five times fast!"

Llew quirked his mouth to one side, then said, "The question being, why would they protect us? One already tried to kill me at Caer Einionault and, if we are correct, they tried to dispose of Gower almost as soon as he opened his eyes."

Slow Tomos shrugged. "As well ask why they seem to be protecting Caer Mallcoedwig. If they are still loyal to Queen Moriganna—and that seems to be bred into their very bones—then, by extension, it is her will that they do so. Either that or she gave them standing orders sometime before she fled and has not yet had the opportunity to change them.

"I do not like this Sword of Damocles hanging over all that are here," Llew said darkly.

Slow Tomos took another sip of his wine. "We can only change what we can and accept the rest. I have taken certain precautions. They cannot get at us completely by surprise and we might very well take a good number of them with us. It is the best I can think to do at the present time.

"Come, let us speak of more productive things. You wanted to find the Torc of Tethera. I do not know where it is but your great, great grandfather, King Bran, was the one who toppled Pwyl after his year of madness and laid him in his barrow—before it was looted by Lord Arawen. If Lord Arawen did not gain the torc for himself when he breached the barrow then it stands to reason it had already been removed, or was never there. King Bran would be the logical next step; it is possible it is still around his neck."

"Would you know where to find his barrow?" Llew asked curiously.

"Alas, he went abroad to retaliate against a place called Ayreland, which had been raiding our west coast, and never returned. If he was bearing the torc that would explain why it never returned."

Cymri smacked her hand on the table. "What good does that do us? Even could we find where this Ayreland is, and where he fell, we still cannot reach it, for the sea is always death once beyond sight of land."

In a measured tone, Slow Tomos replied, "As for that, there are two things to consider, Princess Cymri. Although King Bran did not return, his man-servant did, bringing many wondrous tales of his travels. Perhaps he also brought the torc back or left some word of where King Bran lies. The other thing is that I believe I heard Prince Llew say that this King Gronw made a mention of Dylan granting safe passage for the ships of Tethera until the ransom is due. If it can be believed, he even promised to provide perfect winds for those ships that may fly the royal banner of Gwent. The idea of using this against our enemies does rather tickle me."

"Where would we find word on this survivor of King Bran's expedition," Llew asked.

"His name was Neb ap Tew, when he returned it was to Clwyd where he lived in the king's court for nearly a year, entertaining them with his many tales of exotic lands and the strange things he had found. That is as much as I know but it may be possible to pick up his trail there." Slow Tomos held his hands before him, palms up with fingers splayed, and said, "I realize that is not much to go on, and it is a very cold trail, but it is the best I can offer."

Cymri thrummed her fingers on the table as she considered it. "I remember learning of this Neb ap Tew. In addition to many other wonders, he was supposed to have a troupe of small furry homunculi that could dance, play music, and all manner of other entertainments. Some foolish people actually thought they posed a threat to bards. In bard training it is cited in a story where the moral has to do with people worrying overmuch about the wrong sorts of concerns. As it turned out, they were just exotic animals called monkeys that he had found and trained during his travel over the seas. They were not truly homunculi, and there was nothing unnatural about them. I did not know he was close to King Bran."

"So," said Llew, "I have decided to go to Clwyd. Caradog, you do not get a choice. Until we have resolved this, I want you with me at all times. Will the rest of you come? Other than Tomos or Master Oswalt, of course, whom I need here. Tomos, can you get a messenger to Queen Enid for us? Though I am convinced it will do no good, I want her to send word to Caerleon for word of this torc—" He trailed off when he noticed the look Cymri was giving him. "—ah, and to let her know Caradog is still safe, or was, at least, when we dispatched a messenger."

Slow Tomos nodded, "We will send a merchant on the morn, what else can we do for you, Llew?"

"Actually," Llew said, looking at Master Oswalt ap Hire, "aside from travel supplies, I wanted to see a man about a dog. However, before I forget my manners, Tomos, let me say that was a magnificent meal. It is very nice indeed to see standards have not slipped a bit, despite Moriganna's sudden departure."

"Oh pshaw," Slow Tomos said modestly, "you caught us quite unprepared, Llew. We both know that was not up to her standards, but just wait until supper. There will most certainly be twice as many courses, along with some real delicacies, as well as some of the more unusual dishes the kitchen has to offer. The servants are very eager to serve you again."

Addfwyn poured spiced wine for them and then brought out a good sized service cart covered with various pastries, many featuring caraway seed, as well as various elaborate confections featuring honey or fruit, some of which were even miniature models of Caer Mallcoedwig. "My lords and ladies? I do hope you all saved room for some sweets?"

Helgar grinned, ample evidence that he, at least, most certainly had.

Chapter IX

The Ride to Clwyd

They crept out of Caer Mallcoedwig the following morning. A dense mist lay over the village and the lake and even the faint noises of their horses seemed jarring in the eerie silence of the coming dawn. Each tree they approached first appeared as a looming dark giant with great twisted arms reaching for them while it almost seemed to be moving towards them, rather than the reverse.

The travelers, Llew, Caradog, Cymri, Helgar, and Addfwyn, in addition to their mounts, were accompanied by a packhorse while Caradog had, not one, but two, young Caer Mallcoedwig hounds assigned to him. Caradog had wanted a puppy, but relented when Master Oswalt assured the young prince one would be sent to Caer Pyn y Mwd within a fortnight.

Crug and Glo, as they were named, were less pets and more like mercenary guards for the young prince which was precisely why Llew had wanted them. He was confident the two beasts together would be a match for most men, mounted or not.

They had received extensive training since being weaned, and Master Oswalt had personally spent several hours on the previous day showing Caradog how to command them, as well as ensuring they were at least somewhat bonded to him as their handler. It helped a bit that Caradog did have a number of hunting hounds already but, as they were none of them war dogs, it also meant he had to unlearn a few things.

For himself, Llew had spent the previous afternoon making the rounds of the castle and the village. He did not hold court; there simply was not time and Slow Tomos seemed to have domestic matters well in hand. Instead, he merely made himself available.

Isolated as Caer Mallcoedwig was, it was remarkable how word of his deeds, and those of his comrades, had arrived so quickly. With little else to occupy them, the residents had spent most of the past year telling and retelling those stories amongst themselves and they were anxious to see him on that account, and not merely because he was now their prince. Llew had experienced this phenomenon at Caerleon as well yet, in his experience, there really was no other parallel. In their eyes he seemed to be some high ideal made manifest, glorious and bright against their everyday lives, and all who came into his presence might somehow share in, for at least a few precious moments, what he represented to them.

Caer Mallcoedwig was not a huge place. Having grown up there he knew virtually everyone by sight, even if he could not quite put a name to all of them. They remembered him, too, first as just a virtually nameless spratling who was kept about the stables, then later as one high in the favor of their dread ruler, Queen Moriganna, someone to be treated with some modicum of respect and, as much as possible, avoided. There had been none of that avoidance this visit. They had all dropped whatever they were doing and came crowding to see him wherever he went, bringing out their children, even holding the smallest ones up so they could better see him.

A little attention from him, a kind word and a clasped hand, or a pat on the head for a child, and entirely families stood dazed and pleased, as he moved on his way to meet the next. It was heady stuff, but also quite tiring. Dinner had been everything Slow Tomos had promised and quite exhausting in its own right. The travelers, with the exception of Helgar, had practiced moderation and gone to bed early, although not until after Cymri had favored the great hall with a few of her tunes.

The way Tetherans treated Helgar continued to be a source of marvel to Llew. If a great bear approached them in the forest they would be frightened and flee. Later, they might organize to destroy it or drive if off. But if a great bear was a pet of their liege-lord and could dance and sing and drink ale? Why then, in that case, they were more than willing to celebrate with it.

The other thing that struck him especially oddly was Caer Mallcoedwig itself. Llew had always thought it a small and benighted place, somewhere far off from the living pulse of the lands of Tethera. Now, by virtue of having seen a great deal of the world outside, he saw it differently. The homes were well made, dry, and secure. The people wore reasonably clean clothing that, while simple, served their needs. None of it was overly patched or threadbare. The people themselves seemed well fed and healthy. In fact, he saw no signs of serious injury or disease. Even the streets, though made of packed dirt with occasional gravel, were not rutted and it was apparent that chamber pots were dumped elsewhere. There was not even any animal dung on them, or at least not for long. There were people that took care of that sort of thing.

Part of this, he knew, was that Moriganna had actually

used her magic and knowledge to create various unguents and other medicines. The injured and ill were cared for and cured. Llew had always assumed this only made sense as it would be natural for their ruler to wish them back at work as quickly as possible. Yet he had seen this was not the case in other places. As for the rest? The people of Caer Mallcoedwig had all the land they could employ and were largely self-sufficient. Even so, the little cantref sold the finest horses and hounds in the land. Although their buyers were never told where the animals had originated from, their quality was obvious and they sold dearly. Trade caravans returned with things the village did not make for itself, or did not make enough of. These items were costly but Moriganna had not simply taxed her people, she paid for services and goods received.

There was another price. Except for those in her trade caravans, no one was ever allowed to leave, not that many would have ever wished to. Also, the people, one and all, were required to live within the boundaries of the village. This included even the farmers, who were forbidden from placing their homes within their fields. Every evening they slogged home and every morning they went back out. Ostensibly, this was to protect them from dangerous things that roamed the night, but their livestock stayed on the farms overnight and seldom seemed any the worse for it.

Llew shook his head to clear it of these thoughts. Already they had left the village and were coming to the very edge of the pastures and tilled lands that surrounded the town on three sides; the fourth side being taken up by the lake. It was a very large lake with a dock that the people built and maintained, but it never saw a boat. Nor did anyone ever attempt to fish in the lake; for all Llew knew, there were not even any fish in it. This was especially odd in that he recalled eating fresh fish reasonably often, even when he had been eating at the stables, rather than Queen Moriganna's table.

He was doing it again! It was time to look forward, not backward. In less than a week they could be in Clwyd. It dawned on Llew that he had completely forgotten where the capital was.

"Cymri, could you tell us something of Clwyd? I confess it always seemed a rather boring and unimportant place when I was younger and I seem to have forgotten much."

"Very well, Llew, but do pay attention. I will be conducting a quiz after the lesson."

Llew affected a snort while secretly hoping she was not actually serious.

"No one knows why it is called Clwyd. There is a legend that a Druid sent his mind out into the unknowable and, when it returned and he could again speak, insisted that was its name. Of course, no one has seen a Druid in hundreds of years so who can say as to the truth of that? Its capital is called Wyddgrug. In an older dialect that means 'barrow' and 'mound' so you may consider it as 'Barrowmound.' That probably means there are some major burial sites there. Not surprising as men have dwelt there almost since before there were men in this land," Cymri explained.

"King Delwyn rules, he is an older man, with no surviving children. Since the fall of Powys, the kingdom of Clwyd, by virtue of being right above Powys and adjacent to Annwyn has received far too much attention from the Lord of Death and, if nothing is done, will probably follow Powys into the grave long before you have time to become a grandfather. People have been fleeing the area for over a decade so it is already a kingdom short on subjects. It also has a ruler with one foot in the grave and no clear successor. He, too, is probably not long for this world."

Caradog wrinkled his nose. "This does not sound like a happy place. In truth, the whole kingdom has always sounded fairly gloomy and dispiriting."

"Please try not to share that with the folk that are still there," Llew said dryly. When we ask for his help, I want nothing so much as a catty remark, or even a lifted eyebrow. It cannot serve our purposes to remind this King Delwyn that he need not help us, especially as I suspect his hands are already full with other issues."

"Llew," Cymri said, "the four of us traveling alone are not enough to be safe and your guards would help in establishing you as someone to take seriously. Half of them are at Aber but the other half are with a like number of Queen Enid's men and were following you. It might be possible to link up with them."

"Nay. It is not certain we could find them at this point and we five can move far faster than five and forty. This will have to be sufficient. 'The stakes require the risk' is the lesson both your father and my own kept attempting to drive into me this past winter."

"This is not quite what they were referring to, but you have my support, as always, my prince."

"Thank you, Princess Cymri," Llew said without thinking.

"What?" she replied with some heat. "Why name me princess now?"

"My apologies, Cymri, you were getting a bit formal and I replied in kind. Obviously you are a princess since Taliesin has held all rights to the crown of Ceredigion for centuries. I never mention it but I am certainly aware of it and it simply slipped out."

"Let me get this straight in my head," said Caradog. "You, Llew, are the heir to the kingdom of Gwent, I am heir to the kingdom of Gwynedd, Helgar is the rightful Jarl of Lindenjal,

Cymri is heir to the kingdom of Ceredigion, and Gower is the king of all horses? We are five royals with no entourage of any sort?"

"We had a similar discussion last year; we are what you might call 'working royals' and, since we have no servants, we are obviously doing something incorrectly," Llew said.

From where he was traveling just behind them, Addfwyn made a light cough.

"Ah, I meant to say that the rest of you are obviously doing something incorrect," Llew amended. "Addfwyn, it is almost frightening how easily you can disappear in a group, even when there are just five of us."

"That is precisely how it should be, my prince," Addfwyn replied mildly.

"All the same, there are few enough of us. If you see something we are overlooking or should consider, do not let your natural reticence prevent you from sharing."

"Indeed," Addfwyn replied, "I should consider myself remiss in my duties if I did otherwise, your highness."

"Is that right?" Llew asked. "Then, speaking of duties, I hope the accommodations you have arranged for each night on this journey involve pleasant establishments with warm hearths, good food, and vermin free bedding."

"Alas, my lord, apparently I have been somewhat remiss in those duties, but I will endeavor to make up for my failings and henceforth ensure that we have only the finest of trees to sleep under," Addfwyn offered, by way of an apology.

* * *

They traveled all of that day and most of the next before a light, cold rain began to fall. Cymri had been drawing out Helgar's supply of Northman folk tales, but at this she interrupted his latest tale, something about a badly behaved god trying to cheat a giant, and glared at the falling droplets. "Oh, this just will not do. Sitting around in the dark, wet and cold, is not something I am ready to do again."

A keen sense of survival told Llew not to respond with assurances that they would take shelter at the next inn they passed. Instead, he said nothing and it was Helgar, a mile or two further on, who said, "Do my eyes fool me or is that not a light up ahead?"

That got everyone's attention and, in only a few minutes more, Llew could see it was a crofter's cottage. Nor was it empty. Well maintained, with a good sized croft to one side, the smoke rising from the chimney just made it look that much more inviting. The cottage was larger than most and appeared to boast a second floor on one side. This was a rather strange design for a country cottage. Who would add a second floor when it was so much easier to just make the first floor larger?

The light they had seen was escaping from a high window with the shutters partially ajar. It would have been inviting even if the weather was better than it was as this was the first dwelling they had seen since leaving Caer Mallcoedwig.

Llew had learned to be wary of crofter's cottages in remote areas, but a chance to get out of the rain was too good to pass up. They all dismounted and, leaving the animals with Addfwyn, he and the others advanced to within ten paces of the door. "Hullo, the house," Llew called.

The door rattled and opened and Llew instinctively took a step back. An elderly woman's head peered around it. "Who is it that calls on old Nan on such a foul night?" she asked.

"Ah," she said, with a welcoming smile, "company has come." Then she furrowed her brow and scrutinized them. "High born, too, if old Nan is any judge. Well, never let it be said that her hospitality was lacking. There is an animal shed to the other side. It is no great stable but it will get your mounts and your fierce dogs out of the cold and the wet. Have your men take care of your horses while the rest of you come in, please. There is a fine stew that is ready and plentiful and it may even be that old Nan has a cask of mead put aside just for some travelers such as yourselves, for she does not partake of it herself."

She threw the door open and said, "Children, set places for four, no, five." To Llew: "Your man is welcome to join us once he has taken care of your mounts. Most assuredly, old Nan does not stand on formality here, but she does know well the laws of hospitality and she is delighted you are here in time for supper."

Seeing her fully, as she stood in the lit doorway, Llew marveled that she could stand at all. He had never seen a larger woman. Though a bit shorter than himself, she had to be at least thrice his own weight. The thought came to him, mean and unbidden, that the cloth for her clothing alone must have deprived some caravan of one of their tents.

Trying to make up in some way for this unvoiced discourtesy, he turned to Addfwyn and asked, "May I give you some assistance?"

Predictably, Addfwyn declined. "Oh no, my lord, more important that you should get in there but you could reserve me some of that stew and mead, if you are willing."

Cymri leaned over and spoke close to Llew's ear. "There is much about this I mislike. We could start with why she is even here on a seldom traveled road so far from any other dwelling."

"Bah," exclaimed Helgar, "you were the one that wanted

most to get out of the cold and the wet and look at her. She clearly has no shortage of food; look how healthy she is! There is most likely a village nearby that we have not yet come to."

Old Nan waved them in and so they entered. The warmth and comfort of the place was almost a shock after the miserable weather outside. For all that it was larger than most, it was a simple cottage. Above them was not a second floor but merely two lofts, reachable by ladders. Below was a single great room, with what appeared to be an interior door opposite the entrance. There was a large fireplace that might have been suitable for cooking an entire ox. A large cauldron of something that smelled delicious was occupying one side. A trapdoor on the opposite side of the room hinted at a cellar. The furniture was rough-cut but well-made, and there was ample seating around a very large table.

The reason for the scale of things was also the cause of the most conspicuous feature of the place and that was the presence of so many children. They were everywhere, girls and boys of all different shapes and sizes, although, Llew noticed, they all appeared to be somewhere between five to ten years of age. His first reaction was to count them but they were all in motion, setting the tables, stirring the stew, cutting bread, pouring mead, and dozens of other things, all at once.

Caradog immediately asked what they were all wondering, "Why do you have so many children?"

Old Nan placed her hand upon on his arm before saying, "Oh dear, that is a story—and not a happy one. There was a village in the old glade east of here and it is there no longer. Things out of the Wild Growth came and—" she flapped her apron as if to fan herself. "Something bad happened and, as the children were all hidden, it only happened to the adults, and the older ones, and, of course, the babes still in their mother's arms, bless them. It certainly has kept old Nan busy since then, the poor dears are much too young to be on their own, why they are practically helpless."

They did not look helpless to Llew. They appeared more like a finely tuned military unit that had done so many things together that they no longer needed any command or coordination to be about whatever needed doing.

"You are a good woman," rumbled Helgar. "It looks like you are taking good care of them."

"Oh, how lovely were that true, dearie," old Nan said, "So many children. Sometimes old Nan just does not know what to do."

As she moved forward through the cottage the children darted around her, never colliding, like a school of fish around a large sea-going ship. "Come," she called to her guests, "be seated, please, the children all know what to do when it is time to eat, you could only get in their way."

Helgar was ready. He took two steps forward and found a place on a bench. "It smells good," he declared. "So much better than what we thought we would have!" Two of the children carried a large tankard and set it down on the table beside him. Helgar regarded it with interest and asked, "Did you say this was mead?"

Old Nan beamed and said, "Indeed it is." Some other travelers left it with us but we have little use for it ourselves. It is good to see it does not go to waste. As you might imagine, nothing here is ever allowed to go to waste. In the fullness of time, there is a good use for everything."

With that, they all found seats and fell upon the simple fare offered as though it were a great feast. Indeed, there was plenty of it, and it was exceedingly well prepared. Llew was not overly worried about the quantity they were consuming. He intended to press a substantial payment upon old Nan—if her pride would allow her to take it. Then he noticed Cymri had not yet consumed a thing. He leaned in close and, without looking at her, said quietly, "Cymri, refusing hospitality is one of the greatest social breaches possible. You taught me that yourself. Why are you not eating?"

It had turned out that Cymri could talk without moving her lips. This had not been a terribly useful talent during the years when she had been enchanted into a bird but, as a bard, it was sometimes useful for amusing people when she was performing. She used it now, and so quietly that none there but Llew, with his own exceptional hearing, could have hoped to hear her.

"I am not eating because I do not trust this old Nan, Llew. There are too many unanswered questions about her, starting with this huge boot-shaped cottage in the middle of nowhere, kept by just one old woman and hordes of children. Also, Addfwyn is taking too long to join us, and I am concerned on that score as well."

"She said she would give us the whole story," objected Llew, "we can judge then whether or not to believe it."

"'After we eat' is what she said. After we eat may be too late."

"How so? She offered us hospitality."

"Llew, you are so very clever sometimes but at other times I worry for you. Despite your upbringing, you trust too easily and it may yet be the death of you. Firstly, there are those who would promise hospitality and not honor it, dangerous as that might seem, but worse, she did not offer hospitality. All she said is that she knows the laws of hospitality."

Llew felt as if a great knot had suddenly appeared in his gut. "Cymri! I have already partaken! So have Helgar and Caradog!"

"Calmly, I doubt it is anything terribly toxic or fast acting. That would risk tipping her game before the rest of us could succumb. Just stay alert and be ready. I will find an excuse to play a harmless tune for the children but it is actually one that enables those hearing it to pierce certain types of illusion or misdirection and see the truth."

Taking her harp in her hands, she stood up and said, "Old Nan, your hospitality is without peer, and all the more so given the burden of this remarkable number of children you have undertaken to raise. It is poor payment for such a repast, but we bards are well used to singing for our suppers, and I would like to play the following for you and the children."

Llew looked about to see how the offer was being received and was disconcerted by what he saw. Old Nan still sat at the head of the table with her gentle smile but all around them were the children—so very many children! They filled the floor from the table to the walls and stood on other furniture wherever they could. Glancing up he could see legions more of them gazing down from the two lofts. They were neither whispering nor elbowing each other, nor were they smiling or frowning or . . . anything. It came to Llew that they were all completely motionless with not a one of them showing any emotion whatsoever. At that moment, Llew became a believer. He put his hand to the pommel of his sheathed sword.

Cymri swept her fingers across the harp and began to play a slow, regretful tune. As she played she sang:

One for sorrow,
Two for need;
Three for a parting,
Four for greed;

Five for hiding,
Six for bright,
Seven is for seeing,
With endless sight;

Eight for a death,
Nine for old;
Ten is for a secret,
That must now be told.

As she sang the word "told" it was as if a curtain was lifted from Llew's eyes. In a blink, the warm crowded cottage faded away and he and his friends were sitting on a wide expanse of decaying soil in a poorly lit cave. The only light came from some small torches set where, a moment before, there had been the massive fireplace. The stench of death simultaneously assaulted his senses.

At the center of the hummus stood a massive toadstool, easily twice the height of a man with a stalk almost too large to encompass with his arms, were he inclined to try. It stood about where old Nan had been seated. The real horror was what they had previously taken for children.

All around them were pressed rank upon rank of wizened gray beings, each about three to four feet high. No two were exactly the same; they all had arms and legs of a crude sort but for heads they had mushroom caps. There was no sign of eyes or mouths, yet, as with the great worm, Llew was immediately confident they perceived him quite well, nonetheless. The cave roof was high above them, with many ledges around the edges. The ledges teemed with more of the strange mushroom like people.

There was a single, silent, motionless moment. On the part of Llew and his friends it was shock. For the fungus creatures it might have been something similar for the result was the same. "Oh my," came old Nan's voice from the direction of the giant toadstool. "That was quite the song you sang for old Nan. You have ended your dinners early, but no matter, it is now my children's turn to feed."

Llew had been at least partly prepared for something. That was all that saved them in the first moment as the grey fungus men seethed towards them. He had his sword out in an instant and was spinning and clearing a swath. Cymri was only an instant behind him in pushing her harp back over her shoulder and drawing her own blade. Llew saw her do this with his peripheral vision, but did not expect too much from her. Since changing back to human form, she had always carried a sword, but he had never seen her draw it —not even in practice. He continued to swing in wide arcs and found he was scything down his opponents. They had neither teeth nor claws, all they could do was clutch at him while their unwholesome looking flesh cut easily. There were not even any bones in them. Nothing prevented him from chopping through several in a single swing.

Yet it was not enough. There were just far too many of them. Several had seized on his legs and he had no time to spare to cut them away or his arms would have been seized as well. He had tried to keep them off of Helgar and Caradog long enough for them to draw their weapons but a cloud of the creatures enveloped them. Helgar swore furiously and fought like a madman, he ripped several apart with his bare hands and crushed a few as well, as he flailed and thrashed with total abandon while they attempted to completely immobilize him. Caradog was loud in vocalizing his displeasure as well, but his limbs were soon immobilized by the swarm of attackers.

Llew looked for a way out but realized there was no way to find one in this confusion, let alone hope to reach it, even if that did not also mean abandoning his companions. Then Cymri slammed in to him from the side, her sword spun and half a dozen of the fungus people fell away from him in pieces. She completed the sweep and cut several of the ones gripping his legs into smaller chunks. In turn, he was able to take two steps and dispatch several that were piled upon Helgar. Perhaps, he thought to himself, we might just survive this.

It was then that the ones on the ledges above began leaping down on them. There was just no way to keep from being piled under by this fresh assault. A desperate idea came to him. Was he close enough? Yes! Llew gripped his sword with both hands as he rolled over and lunged sideways bringing the blade around with all of his strength against the stalk of the giant toadstool in the center. It was almost a waste of effort; the stalk cut very easily. The massive toadstool quivered for a moment, then toppled over onto several gray men, pinning them to the dirt floor before they exploded into clouds of black dust.

The remaining gray people stopped their struggling at once and froze in place. Llew kicked one free of his leg and it gently poofed into a cloud of black dust while Helgar and Caradog rapidly divested themselves of the many that were holding them. Any strong hit or movement and these former assailants also burst into black dust.

Still numb with disbelief, Caradog looked around with wild eyes and asked, "What just happened? I mean all of it. Not just their falling over like that when Llew cut down the queen of all mushrooms. All of it."

No one had a ready explanation.

"Cymri," Llew asked, "do you know of any tales of extremely dangerous old women living in oddly shaped cottages with lots of strange children?"

Even Cymri seemed a bit shaken from her normal calm confidence. "Nay, yet I think it may be time to create one. I very much doubt anyone before us has survived to tell of it. Perhaps too, this is not a threat from our own world but part of the Wild Growth. I cannot say, either way. As to why her cottage was shaped as it was, look about, it was merely meant to explain the interior shape of this cave."

Helgar nudged a human skull near his feet. "Thinking also, I am, that not many travelers have survived stopping here."

Indeed, the rotting humus they stood upon still smelled very foul indeed, even though they were probably becoming more used to it. The large number of bones, human and otherwise, spread throughout it were ample evidence of why.

"She wanted to kill us because she wanted our bodies to enrich her soil in this cave," said Caradog, in awe of the gruesome implications.

"What of the food?" Helgar asked anxiously. "Llew, what were we eating and drinking. Was that even real?"

Cymri examined the ground, not an easy thing as a great many of the gray people were still all over the place, even though many were now beginning to spontaneously poof into black dust. "There are real cups and flagons here." She glanced around and said, "Well look at that, old Nan really did have a great cask of mead. Doubtless she got it from a traveler, too, but I doubt it was freely given." She pointed to a large collection of barrels, kegs, and casks running the length of the long side of the cave. "It is not the strongest poison in the world but she got it for free and, as a sleeping draught, it never fails."

"Oho, "said Helgar, "let me have one of those flagons and I

will check the contents."

"Truly, Helgar?" asked Cymri. "You would drink even here? In this malodorous charnel house?"

Helgar had the good graces to look at least slightly abashed by this.

"Most of these are neither wine nor ale nor even mead," remarked Caradog, studying the markings on them after taking one of the lit torches. "I suppose old Nan could not read. Surely she had no use for oil, or vinegar, or brined fish, or any of a dozen other things that slosh inside a cask or a barrel."

"Perhaps not," said Llew, "but, for many of them, we do. Yet first we need to find Addfwyn and our noble steeds."

"And Crug and Glo," Caradog added worriedly.

The exit was a low tunnel under a ledge to one side. A short distance down this took them to another large chamber where all of their horses, along with the hounds and Addfwyn as well, lay upon the dirt floor. Pools of water connected by a small rivulet ran down one side of the cave.

Cymri ran to Addfwyn and checked him, then turned her head to Llew and said, "Just sleeping. I suppose old Nan wanted them all as fertilizer for her brood as well and she seemed to have a penchant for live food. The water here smells odd, perhaps it was drugged with something other than spirits? It could then have been enchanted to appear as though it were in troughs just as this place was no doubt enchanted to make them believe this was an animal shed."

Then she took something from one of her belt pouches and held it under the nostrils of each sleeper, in turn. As she did so, they awoke. It was not long before a confused Addfwyn was helping them herd the equally dazed horses and hounds out of the caves. They emerged near the road and in the precise spot where they had earlier thought the odd cottage stood.

Llew tapped Helgar and Caradog. "I need the two of you for a task." Then he led them back to the cave where old Nan had been and tipped over one of the large casks he knew to be beer. "I want all of these containing any sort of spirits, or vinegar, or salt, rolled over to old Nan's stump."

This took a quite a while and, when they were done, Llew said, "Now if you would, please, friend Helgar, take your axe and breach them, one and all."

"Llew?" asked Helgar, seemingly not sure whether to be confused or horrified at the waste.

"Mushrooms and toadstools have extensive roots," Llew explained. "When the cap grows old or is harvested, they simply grow a new one. I would rather old Nan not be able to do that. We are going to pour all of this on top of her stump. Beer and vinegar is said to kill warts. With any luck it will poison the root beneath."

Once that was done, Caradog asked, "Now what?"

"Now," replied Llew we will do the same with all of the oil save that we will spread it throughout. I am concerned this black powder the children wafted into may contain the seeds of future fungi."

No questions were asked, and the barrels were all rolled to various spots to provide the most even coverage possible when opened.

"Very well," said Llew, when they had finished, "Caradog, before we breach the first oil, could you please move the torches out to the cave where we found our horses? When he has done that, Helgar, would you do the honors again?"

Once the rotting humus was thoroughly covered in puddles of oil, they retreated to the other cave. "I hope this will be sufficient," Llew said, as he hefted one of the still flaming torches. "Please go on outside with Cymri and I will be right with you." So saying he walked back to the larger cavern and took one last look about at the noxious place where he and his companions had come so close to being fertilizer for old Nan's unwholesome brood. Then he tossed in the torch and ran for the exit as the realm of the mushroom queen became like unto a blazing kiln.

Chapter X

The Doomed Kingdom

Two more days travel took them to the point where they began seeing scattered crofts and villages barely worthy of the name. Although still cautious from their experience at old Nan's, they finally picked one of these and allowed the crofter family to put them up. So humbled and in awe was the poor man that he insisted he and his family would sleep in the cattle shed. Feeling marginally guilty, Llew saw to it that Addfwyn rewarded the man more than generously for his hospitality. The crofter, one Iddig by name, was quick to agree that they were inside the borders of Clwyd, and that two more days would likely see them riding into Wyddgrug, the capital of King Delwyn.

As they traveled on the next day, it was readily apparent that Clwyd was every bit as sad and forlorn as they had expected. Many crofts were empty, their thatched roofs collapsing and their fields overgrown and choked with many years' worth of weeds. The villages were no better, with at least one in every three dwellings showing the same signs of long disuse.

When they came to Wyddgrug it was no surprise to find it

a dismal excuse for a capital city. Not nearly as busy as Aber, most of the current activity seemed to be centered about people and families packing out such goods as they could and departing to the west and north.

There were no signs of gates or guards, so they accosted the first person they met near the western side of the town and asked directions for the king's keep. The fellow was middle-aged and had a marginally respectable look about him that Llew thought most likely indicated a successful street merchant—or an only somewhat successful shop owner—of some sort. Simultaneously upset and fearful, yet also resigned, it seemed likely he was carrying all his worldly belongings on the small pony he was leading toward the western road.

Llew managed to impede his path with Gower while not making it look overly deliberate. "Hullo there. Could you direct us to wherever it is the king holds court, good sirrah?" Llew asked politely.

The man started to ignore him and go around until he looked directly at Llew. Expensive clothing and armor, flanked by Helgar, Cymri, and Caradog, similarly attired and on steeds of the finest quality, complete with a servant, personal pack animal, and dangerous looking war dogs, all of these sent conflicting signals to his brain—much as he was in a hurry to be on his way, these were clearly not people he could afford to take lightly.

He gulped and said, "By your leave, my lord, you are on the right road, it is a pile of stone near the stream in the center of town. But the king is not there. Almost all of the warriors are gone, too. The forces of Annwyn march upon our eastern lands, destroying and despoiling all they can find, and he has taken what forces our poor kingdom can still muster and gone to see if they may yet be stopped."

"So is Wyddgrug in such jeopardy that it must be

abandoned to the enemy? Is King Delwyn's defeat so sure as that?"

"Wyddgrug? You do it much honor. It is a rotting husk of what it once was and most now just call it Mold. So far as being overrun . . . not today, no. But the Lord of Annwyn will eventually stop toying with us and that will be an end to it. I no longer care to wager my life that it will not be this season. Many have already left in years past and," he gestured toward the town, "many more will linger, unwilling to leave until it is far too obvious that they should, and far too late for them to actually do so."

Llew let him pass then and they went on. The castle was not difficult to find. Although not on a high place, it was right beside a large stream, almost a river, and a moat had been cut that allowed the water to flow through and around. The castle itself was not on the scale of Caerleon, but what was? It was larger than Caer Mallcoedwig and, indeed, was the second largest castle Llew had ever seen. It was soundly built, with solid lines, but it was also evident its maintenance had been neglected for quite some time, at least a generation or two.

They crossed under a barbican and over the moat, then followed the cobbled entrance road around to the side, with the wall on their right and the water on the left, until they came to a massive wooden gate. Older men with gray hair guarded it. It seemed the king had taken everyone younger.

Llew and Caradog's credentials went unquestioned. The steward, an old man named Trowyr came out to see them but seemed more concerned with how many warriors they had brought with them than in answering their questions.

He was quite dispirited when he found that number was effectively zero.

"None? You brought none? Is it the decision of Gwynedd and Gwent that Clwyd should simply be given up as a lost cause?

Do you not understand that, after we have fallen, the Lord of Annwyn will be at Gwynedd's door? There will be no Clwyd to help then. Instead you will face a foe grown even stronger from consuming us."

The steward's eyes grew wild and his voice quavered. "Why have you not sent help? Are you mad or just short-sighted? You have nothing to gain in not sending us whatever you can. You will lose everything if we fall. What you have left will not be enough to stem the tide. No one kingdom can hope to stand against the blight of the Kingdom of the Dead!"

"One moment there," exclaimed Caradog, "I will speak for Gwynedd. Why have you not sent emissaries or messengers to tell us of your plight? There is no reason to expect any aid if you do not tell us that you need it and to what purpose."

"Tell you?" the old man expostulated. "We have sent emissaries every moon for the past three to tell you. None have returned nor has there been so much as an acknowledgment that the request is even being entertained."

"Tell us?" Caradog echoed. "There have been no emissaries from Clwyd in at least a year. I am to be the next king of Gwynedd. I would surely know of them had they come."

"Your word?" demanded Trowyr. "You have truly seen none of them? How could none of them have reached you? I speak not of a single rider or even a handful. These were full delegations with far too many warriors to worry about bandits or other hazards of the road. The last even left by ship to follow the coast, a fairly short voyage."

"With Dylan out there I am certain it was short, but as for the rest? For all I know, something in the Wild Growth may have consumed them both but, my word as Prince of Gwynedd, I have seen nothing of them," Caradog insisted.

The steward seemed to collapse a bit at this and some of his frenzy fell away. "So no one knows . . . anything of what we face. We are assuredly lost."

"We know now," Caradog said. I will speak with my grandmother and we shall do what we yet may."

Trowyr shook his head. "Nay, it is futile if nothing is already on the way. Even if misfortune does not befall our fourth emissary, there simply is not time for him to travel there and for reinforcements to arrive here."

"It is not futile until I say it is," Llew said. "I need to speak with your king, now."

"Impossible! He is in the field, trying to stave off our fall for another day. Even if you could find him and even if you could reach him, I doubt very much that he is holding court at present."

"Just point the way, then," Llew said, "if you please."

They took the eastern road out of town. Although it had seen much traffic, and recently for that matter, there was little upon it now. Smoke was rising in the distance from numerous locations.

"Does it seem odd that there are so few upon this road?" Caradog asked. "I would have expected carts of supplies being taken to the king's army, messengers between it and his capital, and even refugees from the lands further east."

"What is odd," said Cymri, "is that we have the heirs of Gwent and Gwynedd both, and we are taking them into a war zone with no escort and none of us are trying to stop this madness."

Llew chose that as his cue. "Peace, Cymri, I believe Caradog has a point. That there is no one going to and fro may be an indication that the road is blockaded somewhere between us and the king's forces."

Tugging thoughtfully at his beard, Helgar said, "That is a very good point, Llew. The king must not yet know of it or clear it he would. He could not let it stand." He checked his axe to make sure it was easily reachable, then added, "We would be doing him a favor by taking care of it for him."

"If there is one, we would be doing ourselves a favor by avoiding it altogether and going around it," declared Cymri.

Helgar grinned, "Where would be the fun in that?"

"This is where it would be handy if you were still a bird and could scout ahead for us," Llew remarked to Cymri.

"I am rather glad I am not, all the same. Have you not trained Cilgwri to do that little chore for you?"

"Alas, I am afraid his uses are not quite that broad. The best we can hope for is that he will detect an ambush and give warning in advance."

"We will not need him to do that, Llew," Helgar said. "The blockade is just ahead at that crossroad. See where those trees have been piled across the road? Just beyond them is a fight."

"What!" exclaimed Llew. "That is it then! Cymri, please ensure Caradog remains safely out of it." Come Helgar, we have already flanked them, now it is time to attack."

"Very well, Llew," Cymri acknowledged. "Addfwyn, please remain here and ensure Prince Caradog is kept from harm."

Despite misgivings, Llew knew he could not win and so chose not to argue over this further delegation of duty. He was worried though. Although she had done well enough slashing down the minions of the mushroom queen, that had not exactly been a test of swordsmanship so much as a desperate thrashing about. With no practice, how well trained could she be for open combat? He and Helgar donned their helmets and all three of them readied weapons. With no signal given, they galloped down the road and around the makeshift roadblock.

More than a dozen men in a motley assortment of armor battled a beleaguered group of six that bore the colors of Clwyd. One of the latter was mounted although many dead horses indicated that number had recently been greater. Men from both sides were also down as well.

Electing for efficiency over gallantry, they attacked from behind with surprise fully on their side. Llew trampled one with Gower and cut down a second with a full sweep of his sword. Helgar took down two with a heavy mace, swinging forward into one, then back into another as he rode through and past. In similar fashion, Cymri managed to slash two more. Although one of those still lived, he would no longer fight.

Having passed through the contested area, each of the companions turned their mounts for a second pass. The odds had changed considerably; instead of at least twelve on six in favor of Annwyn, it was now nine on six against, with four of those nine mounted. Two of the remaining enemy attempted to run while the other four tried to fight. It was over in less than a minute.

The single rider that had been there when they appeared now turned his attention fully to the newcomers. He appeared to consider them briefly, then passed his sword to one of his men, who wiped it clean on the furs of one of their fallen enemies, then handed it back. The rider then sheathed it.

"Good day to you, my lord, and our thanks for your swift intervention. I am Subaltern Ian."

"It was a pleasure," Llew replied. "I am Prince Llew of Gwent, and it is urgent I speak with your king as quickly as possible. Could you, per chance, give me the directions I need to seek him out?"

"I can do better than that, your highness," the mounted warrior said, "I can take you directly to him as I likewise have a message for him. He must be told that, although he did not order it, we are bringing up our reserves from the south. It was the only reasonable thing to do and, with no order forthcoming, we began to suspect our lines of communication had been cut."

"Your men are unhorsed," Llew pointed out.

"No matter, your highness. They can attend to our fallen brethren and clear this blockade from the road. We need our lines north and south, as well as those to Mold, kept open."

"As you desire," said Llew.

* * *

Two hours later, Subaltern Ian led Llew and his companions into a large clearing not far from the road. There were tents here, as well as camp furniture, fire pits, and piles of firewood. Various barrels and boxes were also in evidence but there was no trace of men or horses, despite the ample evidence of their recent presence.

Ian looked perplexed and said, "This is most certainly our king's headquarters. I cannot say where or why he has gone. The camp is not overrun but neither was it struck and loaded."

"Perhaps it was about to be overrun?" suggested Helgar.

The subaltern shook his head in the negative. "In which case I should think the king's men would have burnt it themselves, rather than let it be captured. I also see no half eaten meals or other debris that would indicate an unexpected retreat. No, they saw an opportunity that involved moving quickly, but not in a panic."

"It is certainly not difficult to see which way they went," Cymri said. "Tracking an army is not a difficult task for most. At this point we can either quit this quest altogether or follow and I believe I already know your will in this matter, Llew."

They followed the trail the men of Clwyd had left, skirting around a great hill and down through a small vale, then over a ridge-line before they began to hear the sounds of battle from ahead. Llew was liking this less by the minute. For his own part, he was not averse to seeing what lay ahead, and Helgar was practically champing at the bit, but he did not want the rest of his party drawn into a full-scale battle, or even a small one for that matter.

Passing through a ruined field of barley they reached the next hill and were able to see. On a wide plain before them were the armies of Clwyd and Annwyn. Having approached each other from opposing sides, the skirmishers of both were already engaged in the center.

Llew was surprised to see that so many of the forces of Annwyn appeared to be humans of one variety or another. To be sure, there were a significant number of barrow warriors and other things as well, but they were not at all the majority of Lord Arawen's combatants.

Cymri frowned as she took in the scene. "The forces are so evenly matched it is impossible to say who is going to win. Neither side seems to be using any sort of deep strategy that could otherwise sway the outcome."

"King Delwyn appears set on defending his kingdom then," Llew said, "but it seems odd that the forces of Annwyn would risk themselves when they might simply withdraw and seek a more advantageous encounter. Either Lord Arawen values them not at all and is content to wear down Clwyd through attrition, or the second boot has yet to drop."

He continued to regard the battlefield before them, then snapped his fingers and pointed. "There! In the trees across from us. Reinforcements for Annwyn and all of them barrow warriors!"

Caradog peered out towards them and said, "I see them! They will attack when King Delwyn's main forces come to the center and collapse his right flank. Llew, he will be destroyed!"

Llew continued to regard the tableau before them. This was so much like one of Afaggdu's map games that he was having a hard time getting his mind around the fact that men—a lot of men—were fighting and dying out there even as he considered the situation. "No," he finally said, "they will not be destroyed. King Delwyn has a goodly number of mounted warriors. They can screen his other forces while they make an orderly withdrawal. Yet," he paused while he considered further, then said, "whoever commands the forces of Annwyn must see this as well."

Caradog began to say something but Cymri held up her hand, palm towards him, and he desisted.

"Of course," Llew continued, "the enemy will not know that King Delwyn's reserves are already on the way but he must assume that, sooner or later, King Delwyn will succeed in summoning them and it will be back to two large forces squared off against each other."

He drummed his fingers on Gower's saddle while he further considered the situation, as the skirmishers below continued to kill one another. "I do not believe this is just for purposes of attrition, it is too complex for that. If a military victory is intended it will not happen while—"

Llew turned his attention to Subaltern Ian. "Where is King Delwyn? He is not at the forefront of his troops I hope?"

"Oh no, my lord," the subaltern reassured him. "While he might like to be, his majesty is getting on in years. That would be his observation post and command center on that hill to the south of us. You can plainly make out his house banners."

Llew looked, then looked again. "How much of a guard does he have with him?"

"I would guess it would be around seventy warriors, although most of them will not be his best. There is little need for more in this case as the enemy would have to punch through nearly the entire army in order to reach him."

"But," Llew persisted, "if he falls, and his command center with him, then the forces of Clwyd will be bereft of the leadership they need for a smooth withdrawal from the ambush. Many Clwyd warriors would be lost. Together, with the loss of their monarch, they might very well be completely routed."

"If that happened then few would ever leave this place and those that did would be a broken force," Subaltern Ian agreed. "The rest of Clwyd would fall almost as fast as the forces of Annwyn could march."

Llew gave a heavy sigh, then said, "The king did not choose this location. He moved to take advantage of it, and he did so quickly—too quickly. Notice the brush and stones at the backside of the hill your king is on? A hundred or more men could easily be hidden there."

Clearly Ian did for, as he glanced at the area Llew had indicated, he froze. "You are quite right! We must warn him instantly!"

"Agreed," Llew said. "Cymri, you and Addfwyn take care

of Prince Caradog, please, and remain here as long as it seems safe. If the battle is lost, get to Aber and persuade Queen Enid to summon every warrior she can. Messengers must be sent to my father and to Dyfed and Ergyng. We are nowhere near ready for a final showdown with Annwyn but, with Clwyd gone the way of Powys, it would be now or never."

"I am your shield-bearer. My place is at your side!" pleaded Caradog.

"I am sorry, not this time, Caradog. The message you must carry, and what you must do should we fail, are far too important. It is so important that even Cymri will remain behind this time for it will be all the two of you can do to raise the alarm and salvage what is left."

Llew looked sharply to Cymri. "Any disagreement? Tell me now, please."

She shook her head. "Nay, Llew, I spent years of my life trying to prepare you. If it was not to save kingdoms then it was for naught." She reached out and seized his armored forearm. "Just do not die. You still have far too much to do."

"A happy thought," replied Llew.

Speed was the order of the day. Together with Helgar and the subaltern, he charged down the southwest side of their hill and made a direct line for the hill on which King Delwyn stood. They ascended it from the west side, both so as to remain unnoticed by the forces they assumed were in hiding at the foot of the eastern slope, and to show the king's guardians they were approaching head on and clearly not trying to go unseen.

Chapter XI

A Skirmish for Clwyd

As they approached the top, Llew let Subaltern Ian lead. A messenger from their own army would surely be the best guaranty of their good intentions.

And so it was. Helgar drew some sharp looks from the royal bodyguard but, as he was accompanied by their own man and another that their man identified as royalty, no one made any attempt to take the young Northman's weapons from him.

They were quickly led into the presence of King Delwyn. In truth, despite his armor and cape, he did not look much like a king to Llew. He was somewhat short in height, with stooped shoulders and a small pot belly that even his armor could not hide. He was also bald on top with just a wispy white fringe around the sides of his head. Without the armor he could have been anyone's uncle who sold fruit from a cart at the market— were it not for the face. That face! It was one that had seen sorrow and disappointment, then looked too long into the mouth of despair. Dark circles under the eyes gave every sign of permanence, while the rest was a study in sagging, worry-lined, flesh.

Ian started to speak but Llew quickly held up his hand for silence. "My pardon, your majesty, I know you are terribly busy but I believe your person is about to be attacked by forces of Annwyn already positioned in hiding at the foot of this very hill," Llew managed to get it out in one breath, then gasped for another.

King Delwyn looked at him as though he had just risen out of the earth at his feet. Then he bit his lower lip and looked to either side before looking back to Llew. "Who are you?" he asked.

"My lord, I am Prince Llew of Gwent, firstborn son of King Pendaran and heir to the throne. You may know of me. Please, I believe the threat to be quite real and imminent. This hill is a trap; this entire engagement is a trap. They mean to kill you before anything else. That this will effectively decapitate your forces and doom them to complete destruction is only a bonus of sorts. There is a second force in the tree line across from here that is preparing to attack your right flank when it reaches the center."

The King sighed and said, "I know about that. It disturbs me primarily because it is a bit too obvious, as if they meant for it to be found. As for the rest? I am of Clwyd, show me."

Llew led them to the eastern side of the hilltop and waved an arm at the thickets below. "I believe they are hidden down there, your highness."

"You believe?"

Llew gestured to the black bird sitting on his left shoulder. "Sire, this is Cilgwri. He is a very clever bird. Among other things, he is trained to fly high over potential enemies and caw one time for each enemy he spots."

King Delwyn regarded the bird. "Once again, I am of Clwyd, show me."

Llew pointed to the area below and then shrugged his left shoulder, saying, "Cilgwri! Go!"

The bird took off in a flurry. In seconds he was orbiting high over the questionable terrain. Abruptly, he broke off his flight pattern and came flapping back for Llew as fast as his wings would carry him. "Caw, caw, caw, caw, caw . . . ." It went on without end. He landed on Llew's shoulder still cawing for all he was worth."

King Delwyn watched this, quirked his mouth, and waited for Llew to quiet his feathered friend. Then he said, "I am not certain I have been shown anything, but that was very interesting."

"Your majesty, before I came across Prince Llew, I was coming to tell you that the reserves are in motion and will be approaching from the south," Subaltern Ian interjected.

King Delwyn, reached out and gripped Subaltern Ian on the upper arm. "So my message got through? Good man, I hope to use them to redefine the situation here."

"Sire, there was no message. The enemy had blockaded the crossroads. I might not have gotten through myself but for the fortuitous arrival of Prince Llew and his people coming from the capital. We were sorely outnumbered until they turned the tide."

King Delwyn cast a thoughtful glance at Llew, then said, "Captain Gwallawg, have your men form up here and prepare to resist a charge. Baddon, signal our commanders on the field to withdraw—however much they must do so—in order to refuse engagement. Yet I do not want them in full retreat, just enough to lure the enemy onward."

He turned his attention back to the base of the hill before anyone could move and said, "And then there is that. Baddon, while you are signaling, get another couple of squads up here if you can do it quickly, but it may not be quickly enough."

'That' was barrow warriors now rising from the thickets at the base of the hill. Apparently, whatever commanded them realized they had been revealed by Cilgwri's noisy overflight. The revenants began forming up to attack, even as more continued to emerge.

It was worse than Llew had imagined. They were outnumbered by at least four to one. Even with the advantage of being uphill from their attackers, this did not look good.

"Your majesty," Llew said, "Surely most of your men here have mounts, can we not simply remove ourselves from this location?"

King Delwyn shook his head in the negative. "Most of the horses are hobbled and unsaddled. Many more were taken to where they could find better grass. We wanted them as fresh as possible for later."

"At least take yourself to a place where you can continue to command the army, regardless of what happens here," Llew persisted.

"And leave all these men to die? The men on this hill were chosen to serve as my field command for a reason. They are my very best at what they do. Their loss would cripple Clwyd more surely than my own death. Further, I could not stand myself if I did so and how could I command thereafter if I could not even live with myself? And who of my remaining subjects would respect me? Besides which, it is not I that is needed to command the army. Baddon, does that better than I ever could, he was born for that role. No, I stay, but I will understand if you wish to withdraw. Should Clwyd fall, all hope will fall to Gwent and whatever alliances it can cobble together. I would not wish to impede that."

Nearly every man on the hill was now forming up on the king to resist the coming attack. King Delwyn called to the one he had called Baddon, "Take yourself down to the forces and command from there in my stead. You know my intentions and of the reserves on their way. Whether we stand or fall here, I do not want the field officers losing their heads and doing foolish things while we on this hill are engaged."

Helgar glared at the massing barrow warriors below and said, "Llew, the king is right. Hie yourself from here. I will give a good account for you. No worry should you have on that!"

"There is no chance of that, Helgar. This is what we are given to do today and we shall do it. If I mount Gower at all during this, it will be to slay more of our enemies, not to escape."

"You are indeed my drott, Llew."

The men of Clwyd had only just formed a line when the first barrow warriors arrived. To their credit, they did not blanch or cringe from the horrors that assaulted them. They were, all of them, veterans of endless skirmishes with the forces of Annwyn. They had met barrow warriors before and come away alive, even if in doing so they had sometimes been the exception and not the rule.

Llew had met Lord Arawen's barrow warriors before—he had even vanquished one—but had he not been given a significant bit of help, the encounter could have gone much differently. Now he had no militant sister to seize his foe by the ankle, yet even though beyond death, they were not all powerful. The Lord of Annwyn would have marched forth long ago and conquered all the world were that true.

Over the previous winter in Caerleon, Afaggdu had taught

him several things about fighting these fearsome foes. That knowledge now buoyed his confidence. Helgar, not known for keen attentiveness in most educational settings, had also paid close attention. It was time to see how well those lessons would serve them.

As the first barrow warrior reached him, Llew took a half step backward, letting his opponent advance just that much further, then he blocked his opponent's blade with his own and used the weight of his entire body to slam his shield into his foe. The smell that erupted from the impact was almost overwhelming, but the barrow warrior was knocked to the ground by the impact. It was true! For all their strength and energy, the walking wights did not have nearly the mass of a living man and this stood against them when it came time to hold their ground.

As it tried to rise, Llew and the warrior next to him used their swords to shatter its bones and chop it apart. More crowded in behind it and Llew ceased to notice the smell, his other senses far too busy just keeping him alive.

The same tactic worked repeatedly and Llew lost count of his individual victories after defeating half a dozen. The dead did not learn from each other's mistakes. Confidence soaring, he was tireless and unstoppable. It took a while before he understood part of this was the intense relief he felt at finally having foes that he could address with weapons, while clad in armor, precisely as he had trained all his life to do. Moreover, it came to him that there was another component to it as well. That was because—unlike with men—he could feel no guilt over destroying them, nor even guilt for not feeling guilt.

In time, he had to give more attention to protecting his left side when the warriors of Clwyd, weakened with exhaustion as their initial energies faded, could not keep pace with him. Llew lost all track of time although he remained aware of Helgar, still at his right side, giving as good or better as Llew was himself. Then, so unexpectedly that he nearly stumbled, the way down the hill before him was clear. They had punched a hole completely through the enemy's center!

Llew spun about and tried to take in the current situation, almost casually destroying a stray barrow warrior that came at him from the left. Incredibly, the line still held and, although the barrow warriors were still pressed against it, many warriors deep in the center, their numbers overall seemed greatly reduced. They also seemed all unmindful that a pair of warriors had come out behind them. All of their thrust and all of their attention was still for the direct center. This was marked, Llew realized grimly, by King Delwyn's banner. Even as he saw it, the banner fluttered and started to fall as the original bearer went down and another warrior seized it in his stead. It was clear they were in trouble there, the men's stamina fading in the long fight while the foe kept coming, unmindful of such mortal concerns.

Llew's own initial rush of energy failed him then and he sucked in a deep breath while trying not to collapse on the welcoming ground. He turned to Helgar, who was swinging about with a wild look, froth foaming from his mouth, and called his name. The Northman turned to him, eyes wide open and great axe raised for another swing. Not liking what he saw, Llew dug deep and found what he needed to surge forward, stepping inside the weapon's effective range, his face just inches from his friend's.

"Helgar! I am your drott! Duty calls and honor compels, you must answer!"

Helgar's eyes rolled in their sockets then snapped to Llew. "Ll—Llew?" he asked dazedly.

"There is no time, Helgar! The king is in mortal peril and it falls to us to turn the tide, follow me!"

The Northman seemed to seize hold of himself then, "Yes, my drott. Your man I am!"

The two of them then fell upon the barrow warriors at their thickest point, directly opposite King Delwyn's banner, and began hewing a path back for all they were worth. It was considerably faster going than it had been earlier as the barrow warriors were entirely focused in the other direction and, while those they attacked might begin to turn around, it was only those so attacked that attempted it. Very few of them got the time to complete that turn.

A dozen, then two dozen, of the fearsome warriors of Annwyn went down in broken pieces. Yet, as quickly as the two could dig a hole into the line, it continuously filled in from the press of more barrow warriors from the sides. All of them were as singularly forward focused as the newly fallen they replaced. Llew attempted to redouble his efforts. Surely even the barrow warrior's numbers were not without end; this could not continue forever.

At last Llew was so exhausted he could barely see. A blackness was closing in on his vision from all sides. He felt he was looking at the world from the bottom of a deep well, one that kept him at some remove from reality. It was a remove that kept him from being overly terrified at what would happen when that tunnel closed completely. Despite this, when a sword began to descend toward him, it jolted an instinctive reaction. He knocked it off course with his own blade, then grabbed the arm that held it with his shield hand. It was the armored arm of a living man and his remaining strength served to pull the man's face close to his own.

Who was this man? He looked familiar. Surely he was not someone Llew knew especially well? "Your highness!" Llew gasped. And then, "Enough, cease! It is over and we have won."

King Delwyn let his arm go slack then, ending its resistance to Llew's iron grip. Llew let it fall as he staggered back a couple of steps, nearly tripping on the many broken enemies that covered the ground. It was true! Up and down the line, exhausted men were putting the finish to the last thrashing barrow warriors. Some warriors were already sagging to their knees or collapsing to the ground in exhaustion. Of the men who had stood their ground that day, nearly half, Llew noted in his daze, would likely never rise again. Yet no one had run. If it had come to it, he was suddenly sure, they would have died in place to the last man.

Cymri arrived then, followed closely by Prince Caradog and Addfwyn. Shortly after, a hundred fresh warriors came, sent by the cantref king named Baddon.

After seeing that the injured and the dead were being attended to by the newcomers, Llew found a large rock that Helgar was resting on and sat down upon it on the opposite side, their backs helping to hold each other up.

From there they had a fine view of the opposing factions in the valley below. As battles went, it was not really much of one. The forces of Clwyd attacked and the forces of Annwyn retreated. Yet it was a very calm and methodical retreat. The retreating force was not in a panic and clearly meant to leave as they had come. The attacks were met and defended against even while they continued to withdraw.

"It is a shame they did not run without fighting, is it not, Helgar?"

"Aye, Llew. I guess not so scary fellows we be today, eh? We get more exercise this way though. Perhaps the next we meet will have better judgment because of this."

"Scary?" came another voice. "I would say you were both positively terrifying today. Between the two of you there is little doubt you accounted for over a third of the enemy's force sent against my person. And had you not borne us warning of them then they would likely have accounted for all of us, in any case."

Llew looked up to see King Delwyn standing before them. Llew started to muster the strength to stand but the king held out his hand to prevent it. "Nay, do not rise on my account. You have this day preserved my kingdom—for a time."

"How goes the battle, sire?" asked Llew.

"It goes as well as can be expected. The reserve has arrived. Thank the stars they did not stupidly wait for a messenger to arrive—the advantage of having good people working for you. Occasionally, there is a danger they will take too much initiative, but the ones who take too little are the ones that will break you. You will learn this when you are king, if not before, or even already.

"Baddon commands the field and has destroyed goodly numbers of the foe. Yet they retreat in good order and will gain the safety of Annwyn, their numbers still mainly intact."

"That still sounds like a victory," Llew observed.

The king sighed heavily. "It would, save that this battle has taken all of our strength to repel and it was not even an invasion, just a raid to test our strength. Taking me off the board would have been a bonus. They have learned how weak we are and will now prepare for final conquest. I fear we do not have a full year, perhaps not even this season, remaining to us."

Unbidden, Prince Caradog had approached. He now asked, "Is it so certain as that? How could it have gotten this bad?"

King Delwyn lifted an eyebrow at the intrusion.

"King Delwyn," Llew said hastily, "I bid you greet Prince

Caradog, future king of Gwynedd. Prince Caradog, I give you King Delwyn of Clwyd."

"What is this? And the two of you just trotted in without any more escort than that single amazing Northman you have?" King Delwyn asked. "Never mind, it was a rhetorical question. It got this bad," he continued, "because Powys faced a threat greater than any single kingdom and, receiving no aid—no, not even from Clwyd, to our shame—it fell. Which left Clwyd facing an enemy grown even stronger. With no assistance, we, too, will fall. And then an even stronger Annwyn will expand its borders and pick off another Tetheran kingdom, ripe for the plucking. When there are only two left, will they at least assist each other, even though it will be far too late to triumph? Alas, I have become a cynic and inclined to believe the worst."

"You believe two kingdoms together, could not stop the Lord of Death?" Caradog asked.

"Caradog," Llew said, "For myself, I am not certain even all the remaining kingdoms together could stop Annwyn, yet it must be attempted."

"Ah, wisdom at last," said King Delwyn. "If it is not merely a ruse to support your father's desire to name himself high king."

"It is not a ruse!" Caradog said hotly. "On my cousin's coronation, or," he gulped, "on my own if she is lost, Gwynedd will swear allegiance to the next high king!"

"Lost? How is it that she may be lost? Is she not your future bride?" King Delwyn asked Llew.

"She has been taken by someone who thinks he is smarter than he really is," Llew said. "He has demanded a ransom we are not sure we can find, but the trail, tenuous as it is, leads here, and it is to seek information pertinent to our search that we came to you this day."

"That you shall certainly have if it is knowledge I can command," the king pledged.

"Thank you, your highness. On your previous point, however, rebuilding the great kingdom and creating a new high king is the only way all of the kingdoms will ever come together on anything," said Llew, while trying not to take insult at King Delwyn's earlier insinuations. "It is hard news indeed that Clwyd is already in such deep straits. We cannot let it fall, yet we may not have time to prevent that. Still and all, the effort must be made."

King Delwyn eyed him speculatively. "I will go this far, young prince, if you can prevent our fall until the end of this year, and however much longer it takes before you are crowned, I will come to Caerleon and swear true allegiance to you at your coronation."

Llew was taken aback. "It is a generous offer, your highness. I will take you up on that and only hope that we can keep Clwyd safe."

The king held up his hands and said, "There are but two caveats I will not swerve upon. The first being that I will have King Baddon as my heir and none will seek to prevent that. There can be no finer steward for Clwyd."

"Done," said Llew, "and the second?"

"I will only swear allegiance to you and your heirs, not to your father, Pendaran. I mean no offense, but I will not do that. That is why I specified it would be upon your coronation."

"I cannot sway you on that condition?" Llew asked. "It is a bit awkward."

"And I am sorry, particularly given how much you have already done for me and how much I am asking for you to do for my kingdom, but no, on that I will not bend."

"If that is the best we can hope for then, for myself, I accept. I will convey that to my father."

Llew found he had recovered somewhat. "Please excuse me for a time, your highness, I would like to visit the wounded; it may be I can be of some help there. We can discuss the information I need this evening, after things are better situated, for we will need to start out first thing in the morning if we can."

* * *

Llew made his way to where the wounded men were laid out in a crude field hospital. Together with Cymri and Addfwyn, several warriors with varying degrees of skill in healing were doing what they could.

Cymri looked up at his arrival. "Did you have a good talk with King Delwyn?" she asked.

"Unexpectedly good," Llew answered. "I will tell you about it later but first I thought I might come here and recite the healing chant you taught me. Will an hour be enough?"

"An hour? Healing chant? What—" She suddenly looked nervous. "You cannot do a healing chant here. There are too many who would hear. It would be difficult to explain."

"What do you mean?" Llew asked.

"We were alone in the wilderness, even Llewellyn was not able to fully notice it. These men, these warriors of Clwyd, they would notice it—know it was enchantment. It would raise questions about you."

Llew was perplexed. "And so?"

"Llew, not everyone can do it." As he opened his mouth, she raised her hand to prevent his interruption. "It is not just because they have not been trained, it is because they are not able to do it, even if they knew the enchantment."

"What?" he asked. "I can do it. I have to assume you can do it. Why can they not?"

She hesitated, then said, "It has to do with your ancestry. Only those with at least a little bit of Fae blood can perform enchantments. Most men have none and so cannot. Because of this they distrust those who can, despite the fact there are quite a few who can and even more who could, but never know it."

"Ah, yes," Llew said thoughtfully, "it would follow that you would have Fae blood as well. I have seen Taliesin employ his harp to create enchantments."

"He possesses an enchanted harp, Llew. For myself, I have studied the lore of the Druids somewhat."

"The Druids could create enchantments without having Fae blood?"

"Of a sort, yes, for while not all Druids were capable of it, the priest class developed certain arcane abilities. Their powers for enchantment had a different source; they instead learned to channel divine magic through years of intense training. With the aid of their goddess, they attuned themselves to the world about them and all the living things within it. You can forget about them for now. Their order died out centuries ago."

With a tug on his ear, Llew said, "Not to get too far off topic here, but you just said 'for now.' Why did you phrase it that way?"

Cymri made a wry face. "Among other things, they could supposedly travel across the waves of time itself. If that is true then the possibility will always exist that one or more did so and will appear at some time yet to come."

Llew considered that, then shook his head from side to side to clear those thoughts. "I am sorry I asked. So far as Fae blood goes, I already know I have a bit of it. Hafgan told me." A thought occurred to him. "If I can do this then Llewellyn could as well, if she were taught the chant."

"That does not necessarily follow, Llew. The ancestry may be necessary but there may be more to it as well. Just as a blue eyed brother might have a brown eyed sister; their ancestry might be identical but that portion which they were each bequeathed was different."

"All the same, Cymri, why should anyone distrust a little Fae blood? I doubt the common knowledge that I had a bit would invalidate my claim on the throne. Half the people of Tethera claim some kinship somewhere with the Fae, if given the chance."

"Claiming it and providing proof that you have it are two different things, Llew. It could be detrimental to your coming reign if it were too well advertised."

Llew gestured to the wounded men about them. "As much of a detriment as dying would be to those who need not necessarily do so? I am of a mind to proceed, regardless."

"Wait. Very well, Llew, let us try this instead. I will play a tune and you will accompany it. It will have much the same result as the two of us chanting away, but the difference will be that none will suspect us of enchantment or possessing Fae blood."

"You expect me to sing?" Llew asked, aghast at the idea.

Cymri smiled then and replied, "What? Is the healing of

these men not worth so much as a song to you?"

Chapter XII

The Traveler's Barrow

"Neb ap Tew," said King Delwyn, stroking his chin thoughtfully. "Certainly the House of Neb is known to me. My grandfather granted their founder his title and lands. They have been valued subjects of our realm ever since. We are nearly on the border of their lands as we sit here."

'Here' was the seemingly abandoned camp they had found earlier that day. It was anything but abandoned now. Indeed, it was a veritable hive of activity as the army trickled back from the field to other encampments ringing this one. Everywhere men were cooking, eating, erecting additional shelters, or just looking for a place to lay their heads. And not just men, Llew could hear many horses being tended to all about them at the other camps. Those with smithing or leather-working skills were in full swing repairing weapons and armor. All knew that, while the enemy had retreated, he could and would return, in time.

"Neb ap Tew's descendants may have evacuated to the capital," continued the king, "but I rather doubt it. The family has a lot of pluck and is ill-disposed to give up what they feel is theirs. This is even more understandable in that my grandsire was quite generous with Neb; he must have greatly endeared himself to the old fellow. Moreover, the family has done well since that time. I expect, however, that they have been hit as hard as anyone by the ongoing downturn in Clwyd's prospects."

"No doubt you are correct," Llew agreed. "Nevertheless, their progenitor was the last known companion of King Bran and we hope to find some clues as to where he might have left a certain item that he may or may not have had. It seems a thin reed indeed, but it is the only one we have."

"It seems so thin that perhaps it would be better if you devoted your time to gaining the support we need to save Clwyd. From what you told me earlier of what must have happened to our own emissaries, it is not going to be easy getting word to your kingdoms."

Llew was having some serious doubts himself. It did seem very little to act on, yet with two weeks to go and no other leads it was all he could do besides wait. "It will not be a problem this time, your highness. Send your next emissary by ship and it can carry on to Gwent after Gwynedd. It need merely fly the royal banner of Gwent and it will even receive favorable winds—but only for the next two weeks, so it must be done quickly."

King Delwyn smiled grimly. "I will summon my scribe forthwith. We may all dictate letters to him now. By tomorrow night my emissary will depart for Abergwyngregyn from our port at Hull. You are certain about the banner granting free passage?"

"The enemy wanted us to be able to travel quickly so we could more quickly gather his prize. I do not believe he realized that this might be made to work against his interests. I am curious though, that is a far ride for one day."

"We can do it," King Delwyn said confidently. "We have been on a war footing for a considerable time. Despite the cost, I have purchased the finest horses we could obtain. They come from a single merchant who does not reveal their origin—and I have stationed at least one at each of various strategic points within Clwyd. When a rider comes in it is possible to change either horse, or horse and rider, on a moment's notice. In theory, even with the Wild Growth and the terrible state of some of our roads, we could send a messenger from any place in the kingdom to any other in less than twelve hours."

"Amazing," replied Llew, meaning it. The king was obviously referring to Caer Mallcoedwig horses. Using them for their speed and endurance to tighten his communications, rather than for mounting a few of his warriors, was a fair way to leverage their value and justify their cost against the limited coffers of a failing kingdom.

"If, come the morning, young prince, it looks as it does now—that the enemy will have completely withdrawn beyond our borders—I will lend you a guide to take you to Caer Neb."

* * *

"This is the place," Subaltern Ian announced. "Behold, Caer Neb."

"Well, it would seem they are at home," Llew remarked, observing the smoke curling from what was probably the kitchen chimney.

Caer Neb had obviously begun as a sort of fortified manor house. And then, Llew thought, the neighboring area became a much rougher place. Annwyn had grown closer, Powys had fallen, but, rather than move on, the folk here had built high walls of stone, with anchoring towers and an entrance protected by both barbican and a removable bridge over an earthen moat. Caer Neb was not precisely a mighty fortress, yet Llew had never seen anything like it in the hands of anyone less than a cantref king. The descendants of Neb were serious about keeping what they had.

Llew was deliberating on their best approach when it became obvious they had already been observed. Armored men appeared atop the gate house. Llew started to hail them when the subaltern cleared his throat. "I am not unknown here, my lord, allow me to introduce you."

And so it was that ten minutes time saw them ensconced at the lord's table, while an old woman brought them mulled wine and pastries. The steward assured them Lady Vanora would greet them shortly once she was finished with some pressing duties. The steward also seemed to know Subaltern Ian rather well. They at once began taking turns asking and delivering updates on various people they knew in common.

"So," Caradog said brightly, "maybe we should consider what precisely we are looking for. It seems too much to hope that old Neb came back with the torc himself and it sits to this day in the lady's jewelry box."

Helgar snorted. "No no, lad, that is not how it works with our Llew here. She will probably just have some strange markings on an old hide and it will fall on us to figure out it is the name of a great fire breathing drake whose lair might include the torc."

As she shook her head in disagreement, Cymri said, "Oh, no. It will not be in the lair, the drake itself will reveal the cave that is the location of the torc, but only after it is defeated in battle, along with its two bigger brothers—"

Llew laughed despite himself. "—and the cave itself will be at the bottom of the sea guarded by an army of Fomorii and trained sharks. No, seriously I only hope for anything that might give us some hope this is not a wild goose chase. It may be that Neb left some word with someone about where Bran lies buried. In which case, maybe we could find him and see if the torc is about his neck."

"Ooh, Llew," Helgar exclaimed, "violating his barrow, maybe? Hafgan would not like that at all."

"In a good enough cause I believe he could be reasoned with. Certainly saving Tethera from piecemeal destruction at the hands of Lord Arawen would seem to qualify." Llew glanced around the table at the modest dining hall. It was well appointed, tastefully decorated with a collection of the usual hunting trophies and weapons, but also some very handsome tapestries and an odd variety of things that Llew knew must have family significance. A matching pair of pewter mugs, one dented and both mounted on a plaque. The wheel off of an old spinning wheel. A small leather saddle. A single tiny slipper, bedecked with ornamental glass beads. Such things and others would not be here if they were not significant to someone and, even though they were not significant to him, their presence was comforting, reassuring him that real people lived here with real lives and that, even this close to the very gates of Annwyn, their lives were not completely dominated by dark enchantment and prophecy.

"I like this place," he said to his companions. "Something in it speaks to something in me."

"And to me as well, my lord," said the old woman who had served them their refreshments. She took a seat at the head of the table. "Now that I have completed my initial duties of hospitality, what else may I assist you with?" Then, as if in afterthought, she said, "Lady Vanora of Caer Neb, at your service. Oh, and thank you young Ian, for not giving me away too soon."

Everyone stared at her, open-mouthed, for a moment, then Helgar pounded the table with one huge fist, laughed, and pointed at Llew. "Ha, my drott, I think she took you in completely."

Caradog looked about, confused, then said to Helgar, "I think she got us all, you as well."

Helgar folded his arms triumphantly. "Yes, but that is not so unusual. With this one," he said, pointing at Llew again, "you have to laugh because, unless enchantments are at work, it is not so very often that it happens."

Llew shook his head and began explaining the reason for their visit.

After a time, Lady Vanora interrupted him. "I think I have the meat of the thing, dear. My great grandfather was the last to see this ancestor of yours, and he may have been the last to see this torc that you are looking for?"

"That is it in a nutshell, my lady. Are there any tales that have come down to you that might pertain? Or, perhaps there is something amongst whatever of his things you still have?" Llew asked. "I know he brought many amazing things from his travels, yet what we are looking for may not be so terribly amazing, just terribly important."

Lady Vanora furrowed her brow in concentration. "I am trying to recall but I think the story goes that, after King Bran was poisoned, his entire body was seized by paralysis and he lost the use of his legs, then his arms, and the poison's work continued to climb before they found a way—or perhaps it was a place—where they could prevent the poison climbing any higher. Once there, however, he could not leave or the poison would recommence its dreadful work. My great grandfather did not abandon him, however. I know he did not. It seems to me King Bran wanted him to return to Tethera to bring word of all that had happened. It was very important to him. Perhaps because it also concerned this torc you have spoken of?"

"It is possible," Llew replied eagerly. "Perhaps he even brought back the torc himself so that it could be passed to his heirs. May I see the things you have that you know he brought back?"

Lady Vanora shook her head regretfully. "I know all the things we have of his. Truly, some are quite amazing and it was these that helped him gain favor with the then king of Clwyd such that he was granted these, our lands. There is no torc amongst them, nor anything else that might secretly contain such a treasure."

"Ah," said Cymri, "that is too bad. Are these all of the things he brought back then? Have none been lost or given away in the time since?"

"Oh, no, of course not. There were quite a few amazing animals he brought back with him that also amazed and entertained all that saw them. There was a creature that ate nothing but ants with a long sticky tongue, and another that looked like a spotted cat but was the size of a wolf. It supposedly followed him about as devotedly and well-behaved as any dog ever whelped. There were also a pair of wingless birds, each taller and heavier than any man. If the stories are true, they laid eggs the size of a man's head. Another bird, a much smaller one, could talk and tell jokes.

"Most astounding of all was an entire tribe of homunculi. In appearance they were little men about knee high and covered in fur. He trained them to do all manner of things and their antics were said to be endlessly entertaining. Alas, none of his menagerie fared well in our climes and all eventually passed on, each leaving a hole in his heart, tis said. My grandfather says that all of them were interred in his own barrow such that when his time came, he merely joined them there."

She snapped her fingers then. "It comes to me now! Many of his items were so intricate or contrived such that only he could make them work as they were meant to. All of these were interred with him as well as a small fortune in riches. Some of these were things that he had acquired on his journeys. Your torc could easily be amongst them or even around his neck. Then, too, even if the torc is not there, something else might be, perhaps a lodestone that points to King Bran's refuge, or even a simple star chart."

"These things are resting with him in his barrow?" Helgar asked, looking a bit uncomfortable.

"Aye, young man, they are," Lady Vanora replied. "Is that a problem? I can grant you permission for I know your cause is right. I also know you cannot simply be afraid of the dark."

"I am certain he is not," Llew said. "Caradog, we will not be plundering this barrow but, all the same, I think it is not something I should wish to have you involved with. You can remain here with Addfwyn until the three of us return."

"What three is that?" Cymri asked in a sweet voice. "I certainly would expect that the two of you are fully capable of doing this without my help."

"Bah, you just do not care for getting a bit of dirt on you," Llew accused. "Subaltern Ian? Would you care to join Helgar and me in a short excursion?"

"Alas, much as I would actually wish to, I must return to the army forthwith. It was only with the insistence of King Delwyn, over the repeated protestations of my father, that I was permitted to come even this far with you."

"Your father is in a position that he is permitted multiple protestations to his liege before carrying them out?" Cymri asked with sudden interest.

"Well, yes," the subaltern replied. "He is the lord commander of Clwyd's royal army, King Baddon."

"And yet you named yourself a subaltern and not a prince?" Llew asked, his curiosity evident.

The young officer flushed, "It is my father's idea. I will no doubt be promoted swiftly, but to his way of thinking I should not completely escape the process of working my way up to command. He believes it will make me a better leader of warriors."

I will need to keep an eye out for Prince Ian, Llew thought to himself. If the young man was his father's heir then he would likely be king of Clwyd someday and, if not, then it might be possible to recruit him away from Clwyd, whether it stood or fell.

Young man? It suddenly occurred to Llew to wonder why he was thinking of the other that way. Subaltern Ian was at least five years his senior, and not even that terribly far removed from him in social standing. When had this condescending—and it was condescending, he realized—attitude towards others crept up on him?

"I wish you good fortune in that," Llew said, clasping wrists with him. "I also expect I will see you in Caerleon one of these days and I look forward to it."

"The barrow you seek is not far," Lady Vanora said. I can have one of the current watch standers take you there to ensure you do not get the wrong one. The two of you should be enough to open it if you take a long pry bar. Just please do close it up again afterward."

* * *

"This is it, my lord," said the watch stander. Regardless of his title, he was merely a guardsman going by another name, Llew decided. It dawned on him the difference in designation might be due to the fact that Lady Vanora was maintaining a significantly larger military force than the laws of the land allowed to one of her station; she was at least one or even two steps removed from the level of a cantref queen. Naming her warriors as hired men gave her—and probably her cantref ruler—a public way around this that they could both wink at in private.

Cymri had told him many times that desperate times called for desperate measures. Afaggdu had simply told him that he liked being in wars because people threw away all their silly rules as they needed to and just concentrated on getting the job done. Afaggdu was not one for dealing with rules when he felt they were in the way of what needed doing.

The barrow the man had led them to was one of a group of five that stood out in an area almost devoid of trees of any sort. Grass had grown over all of them and it was, Llew imagined, the kind of place children might have liked to play tag in and even hide-and-seek. In the tall grasses, with the mounds to mask their movement, it might have been ideal. Barrows had a bad reputation, however. No children would come here to play.

"Please pardon me, my lord," said the watch stander, "but I would liefer not remain while you unseal the old lord's barrow. Over there, by the road we came in on," he gestured to a point about a quarter of a mile away, "looks to be a much better place to let the horses graze while I wait for you."

Llew chose not to comment on the abundant variety of grasses around the barrow itself. "Very well, please watch for our egress. We may need assistance with whatever we bring out."

"Aye, my lord, as long as it is not chasing you."

"What?" Llew asked sharply.

The watch stander realized his mistake at once. "My lord, if you come out fighting I will come to your assistance at once and—oh by Mab's many mates!" He licked his lips and started over. "My mouth runs away from me and I mean no disrespect. I will come forthwith regardless of what you do or do not emerge with, my lord, and I mean that."

Llew allowed himself a wry smile. "Thank you, I will not ask you to check in on us if we are gone overlong."

Sweat was evident on the watch stander's brow as he replied, "And I thank you for that, my lord."

Using a pair of ash wood shovels, and the information Lady Vanora had given them on where to find it, the two of them rapidly shoveled and scraped away all the dirt over the capstone.

Looking at its size, Helgar exclaimed, "Look at this hulking rock! There is never a Spriggan about when you need one. Hafgan or his lads would make short work of rolling this away, but I am not certain we have brought a large enough pry bar."

"Count your blessings, my friend," Llew counseled. "Do we really want a Spriggan about just as we prepare to loot a barrow? I recall that is one of the things they are rather sensitive about."

Helgar shuddered. "On second thought, I think we are two strapping fellows who can certainly manage this little task. At any rate, Spriggans probably cannot summon the strength for this until after dark and after dark is not when I would ever do this thing."

With quite a bit more digging, and considerable effort, they forced the keystone to roll to one side. This revealed an earthen tunnel braced with old rotting logs. Nothing about their condition inspired confidence.

Helgar whistled thoughtfully as he regarded them. "Llew,

we had best move very lightly here. How strong these supports are is probably not how strong we would like them to be."

"This is a very unusual barrow," Llew remarked after they had lit torches and were gingerly following the tunnel downwards.

Helgar grunted. "How so?"

"My understanding is these things are built by excavating a hole, then they build a room and fill it with bodies and grave goods. Finally they close it up and cover it with dirt until it is a mound. They do not build a tunnel down to the chamber. There is never a need for one. They would not want one as it would make it easier to do precisely what we are doing."

"And yet we are in one," Helgar observed. "Llew, I am confused. It is as you say; why would they want such a thing?"

"In truth, other than that he planned to rise from the dead and wander out, I can only surmise that someone planned for the addition of something—or else the removal of something—at some point after Neb's interment. Whether it was Neb himself, or someone else I cannot say."

"Llew," Helgar said excitedly, "perhaps he had the tunnel made for us! He meant for us to come here one day and recover the torc."

"I confess the thought had occurred to me but, even if the torc is here, it may not be easy to find; yet it gives me reason for hope. And here is another reason for hope."

"What reason is that, Llew?"

"This large stone slab blocking our further progress. I now have a reason to hope we can get through it with that pry bar we brought."

In short order, they did manage to roll it aside, the primary difficulty being the narrowness of the passage they had to work in. Darkness loomed behind it and they brought their torches forward to see what could be seen.

The slab-lined chamber was perhaps fifteen feet wide and eight feet high. Stone columns down the center held up the slabs that formed the roof. The far end was in darkness their torchlight did not extend to. From the entrance, Llew could make out a raised stone slab lying in the center between two pillars. On top of it, on each side of the pillar on the nearer end, he could see the bottom of a heavy boot, toe pointed at the ceiling.

"This is very odd," whispered Llew. "A barrow this size should have dozens of bodies in it. I have never heard of one with but a single occupant unless, perhaps, he was a great chieftain or king."

"Are we whispering because he might be a barrow warrior and hear us?" Helgar asked quietly.

Feeling somewhat sheepish, Llew adjusted his voice to a normal level and said, "No, we are whispering because I am silly. If proximity to the fell dweomer of nearby Annwyn has not yet animated this man's body then I do not expect my voice will. If he were already a barrow warrior he would be up and prowling about, seeking a way to reach his master, the Lord of Annwyn."

"Then I hope he does not awaken as one while we are here."

"We destroyed dozens of barrow warriors yesterday," Llew reminded him. "One more should not be a problem."

"Somehow it seems different outside in the sunlight, Llew."

Not contradicting him, Llew moved into the chamber, casting the light from his torch where he could. "There appear to be boxes piled at the far end. I believe I would prefer to check them before we see if it is on his person."

"Oh, I do agree, Llew. But I am wondering what these are?" Helgar pointed to a double row of rectangular stone blocks running the length of the chamber on one side. Each was about two feet long and half as wide and tall.

"How odd. It looks almost as though they were planning to build something with them and never got around to it, but that cannot be right because they are far too orderly placed to be merely leftover building materials."

Helgar regarded them and said, "Ya, they almost look like little versions—" Something came bounding at incredible speed out of the darkness at the back of the chamber and attached itself to Helgar's left shoulder and upper arm. The Northman bellowed and dropped his torch to grab at it with both hands.

Four more came streaking from the back and leaped onto him. "Argh!" yelled Helgar. "They are biting! Get them off!"

Llew gaped for a moment, not sure what to make of it. Then he was rocked by multiple impacts, staggering several feet to the side as at least six hit him at once and were clinging to his hair, cape, arms, belt, seemingly anything where they could get good purchase and yes, they did bite—and claw!

Panicked, Llew almost dropped his torch before he realized that could only make it worse—alone in the dark with things that dwelt there. As more clambered onto him he somehow managed to struggle closer to the central stone table and drop his torch there so that it was more or less held upright as it leaned against the ancient corpse of Neb ap Tew. Then he seized the one trying to claw at his face and ripped it away.

If something small and furry and resembling a man

175

attempted to become something like a barrow warrior, then that was surely what he held. Even in the flickering torchlight, broken dried bones were clearly visible through a torn covering of dried skin and fur. It writhed and twisted in its attempts to claw him with nearly as much energy as a shape-shifter might display in similar circumstances. In a sudden fury, Llew closed the hand that held it into a fist, crushing most of its body.

They were fragile then! Llew threw himself backwards against the wall behind him. Any number of the little monsters were crushed between his armor and the wall. Using his forearms to protect his face, he threw himself forward on to the floor and crushed still more. He rolled as he could to catch a few more, then rolled again to facilitate regaining his feet.

As he came erect, still more of the things hit him, driving him a few steps backward until he felt the slab under Neb ap Tew against his back. Attempting to grip a particularly troublesome one on his left arm, he succeeded only in waving it about until it brushed the flames of the torch he had half dropped there. It caught flame as though it were little more than crumpled parchment.

For a moment, Llew exulted. He had found a major weakness of his tiny adversaries. Then he realized that, despite the fact it was now burning like a torch itself, the hateful thing had not relinquished its grip or its attacks. It simply did not have the level of self-preservation a living animal would have had. If barrow warriors were stupid, these things were less clever than insects! Worse, the heat of its burning was causing him more hurt than the simple creature itself.

It was fortunate indeed, Llew realized, that they were so little capable of any sort of thought or they would all have gone for his unarmored head. By contrast, most were busy ripping at armor they had no chance of penetrating, even were it not enchanted.

Llew took care of the burning one by the simple expedient of smashing that arm repeatedly against one of the columns until it fragmented and its flaming remnants had all fallen away.

He continued in this manner, pulling them off himself, one by one, and crushing them into broken bits. It was working, he could tell, but only because no more were joining. The supply was apparently finite, thankfully. Llew pulled off his last attacker and whirled about, looking for Helgar.

Helgar had one in each hand and flung them down on the earthen floor before him, then leaped high in the air and came down on them with both boots and a ferocious yell. He looked about, panting, eyes wild, until he saw Llew, then he slowly relaxed.

The Northman was a sight, dripping with sweat, covered in scratches and cuts where his flesh had been exposed. Even his clothing where his armor did not extend, was sliced and rent. Llew knew he himself could look no better.

"I guess we were not so scary to them, my friend," Llew said.

"Better for them that they had been scared," grumbled Helgar, as he picked up his dropped torch and re-lit it from Llew's.

Llew counted the stone blocks, there were fully two dozen. It now seemed obvious that the little animals had once been laid to rest upon them as their owner had been on the larger central slab. Unlike Neb ap Tew, they had eventually gotten back up. Llew tried to assess the damages. He and Helgar would require a lot of cleaning and bathing to get the stench of the small ones off of them. Then he considered the situation and realized his earlier qualms about long dead corpses were currently in abeyance. He stalked over to the corpse of Neb ap Tew and searched it. He was disappointed, but hardly surprised, to find there was no torc on it.

"What do you think?" he asked Helgar. "May as well search the grave goods while we are here is my thought."

Helgar grunted, "This we had best do, for I will not come down to this terrible place a second time."

"I do not think they can be turned into little barrow warriors a second time, Helgar."

"Why were they turned at all? I have never heard of anything other than men becoming barrow warriors. And why did they become—whatever it was they were—before their master became one?"

About to open the first trunk, Llew hesitated to consider these questions. They were good ones. "Perhaps," he ventured, "they changed because, although they are not men, they are closer to men than most animals, and that was close enough for them to be affected by Annwyn's growing power. As for why they changed before their master? I can only surmise that it takes more something—power, maybe—to convert a man. If nothing prevents the power and influence of Annwyn from coming closer then I expect even our friend Neb will be affected."

Helgar nodded slowly. "I sense you have the right of it, my drott. One moment, please." He then walked back to the dead man on the slab, drawing his axe on the way. Llew focused on searching the first box until Helgar returned.

There were six trunks in all and they contained a myriad number of strange and potentially interesting things, but none of them appeared to be of any help and they were not there as looters. Llew closed the last trunk, hugely frustrated, and rested his hands on it as he leaned forward upon it, using it to partially support his weight.

"I am open to any suggestions. Helgar, have we missed anything?"

"I think we may have, my drott."

Llew looked over his shoulder at Helgar and saw that he was holding his torch and looking up. Turning back he followed Helgar's gaze and saw it himself. Painted on the wall over the trunks was what could only be a map. It showed a vast body of water bordered by coastline along the bottom and right sides.

"I know it," Llew said. "The southern coastline is the northern borders of Gwynedd and Clwyd. That would make the eastern coastline that of Annwyn."

"I think you are right, Llew, but I do not see anything showing where the torc would be."

Llew pointed to a small island far out in the blue of the sea. Symbols identified it by name and it was the only thing on the map that was labeled. The island was also adorned with a carefully drawn crown. He frowned before saying, "I am really going to have to learn to read, and soon."

"All that is written there is the name in Old Pictish, Llew. I think you would say it as 'Avilion,' or maybe 'Avalon.' Have you heard of it?"

"Aye, and I have. It is not supposed to be a real place. We will speak to Cymri of it but it appears we may have to find out for ourselves."

A thought occurred to Llew. He had just heard something that did not sit right. A moment's consideration and he realized what it was. "Helgar, you say this is written in Old Pictish? Are you saying that even Picts can read and write?"

"Well, no Llew, not the wild ones here in the south."

"There are others?"

"Oh, ya, they have several kingdoms to the north of Annwyn." Discerning the look of general disbelief that Llew was now evidencing, Helgar continued. "Do not think they are at all like their wild cousins down here. The northern Picts live in castles, wear armor, ride horses, plant crofts. All in all, they are much like Tetherans but perhaps a bit better at most things."

Llew simply stared at his Northman friend. "Such as?" he asked, in a clipped voice.

"They are more given to scrolls and such and they make better jewelry and steel. It would make them a good choice for raiding, but they are very jealous of their land and are themselves so very fierce that the effort and risk exceed the value of any likely plunder. Instead, it is much more profitable to simply trade with them."

"And they have a written language that you know how to read?" Llew was not certain which part of that statement was less believable.

"Oh, aye, Llew. They have two. They are fairly similar except that the newer one is written with the same letters as used in Latin."

"Latin being the language of the Roman Empire?"

Helgar nodded agreement. "Yes, that is right."

"Helgar, tell me, what languages can you read?"

"Ah, Pictish of course, a little Old Pictish, although not so much. Also a little Latin, but mostly best I am with runes written in Futhark, the writing used by most of my kin. I suppose I shall have to learn to read the way Tetherans write, but I am not so fond of learning such things and have put it off. Perhaps we can learn together?"

The prince of Gwent started to say something but instead took his tongue between his teeth and held silent.

"Llew," Helgar said at last, "our torches are growing old and will soon gutter out. Can this be something we talk about once we are out of this tomb?"

* * *

Emerging into the sunlight felt good beyond words. The watch stander, good to his word, was there with their mounts within two minutes. If he thought anything amiss about their bloody, shredded, and begrimed appearance, he wisely said nothing.

Cymri, still in the company of Lady Vanora and Caradog when they came in, had rather a bit more to say. "Phew, that smell is dreadful. Please do not sit anywhere until you are cleaned up a bit."

Though he did not sit down, Llew strode right up to her. "Neb's monkeys—more than twenty of them—had risen under Annwyn's influence. You suspected something like this might happen and you deliberately missed all the fun," he accused.

"Fun?" She said the word as though she had never considered its use before. "Is that what you call it? Helgar, is this true? Did the two of you have fun?"

Sarcasm was not a common practice for Helgar, but neither was it unknown to him. "Oh, aye, my lady. What could possibly be more fun than a barrow full of monkeys?"

Chapter XIII

On a Stranger Ride

"There is, of course, a problem in reaching Avalon," were Cymri's first words after hearing of their discovery.

By this time, Llew and Helgar had bathed and had their wounds seen to. While none of these were serious, there had been another consideration; given the rotted nature of those that had inflicted them, the risk of sickness festering in even such shallow cuts could not be disregarded. Likewise, their armor was being cleaned, and new clothing had been found for those items beyond restoration.

"Normally there would be, certainly," Llew replied. "But now it is as we told King Delwyn, we simply need a ship with a royal banner and we are free to travel where we will."

"I agree. I was not referring to that as a problem because, for now at least, it is not. No, the real problem is that Avalon is an otherworld."

"The otherworld?" Caradog asked. "Is that not where the dead go? The place where the gods and the Fae dwell?"

"No," Helgar corrected, "she said, 'an' otherworld'. I was taught that there are nine otherworlds, eight if you do not count our own."

Cymri compressed her lips together, then said, "Perhaps things work differently in the Northlands. Here we have worlds and otherworlds. In defining otherworlds, I must first explain what worlds are so that you may have some sense of the differences.

"Tethera exists as part of this world. Are there worlds besides this one? Yes, of this much we are certain, but those worlds are not what we refer to as otherworlds. How do we know this? It is because of the Druids. They were said to be able to see through time itself, and perhaps even travel across it as easily as you or I would move up and down a river. Doing so would probably also create additional worlds, akin to ours, but in some way different, or perhaps those worlds already existed and the Druid's art was merely in being able to travel between them. There are no Druids left to tell us, even assuming they knew themselves."

"What happened to the Druids?" Helgar asked.

"We do not know. Perhaps they merely died out. Perhaps Lord Arawen or the Fae saw them as a threat and had them destroyed. Or perhaps they saw something so frightening that they all fled somewhere. I like to think they found a world so much better than ours that they all just left ours behind and went to it."

"At any rate, we suspect Tethera was once in a different world and was only brought here later. Because it was not an especially good fit, we still see adjustments taking place, the principle of those being what most people call the 'Wild Growth.' This is most likely a process where Tethera is being forced to settle into its new world and that process stretches at the very fabric of whatever Tethera is. Worse, that fabric sometimes becomes torn and when this happens, rather than see open space, we see only that part of the world that was there before Tethera was placed over it."

"That is terrifying," Caradog whispered. "Who knows what elder evils may live on in that other world and could thus become part of ours? Why, in cases like the great worm that Llew slew, and the queen of the mushrooms, that may be exactly what is happening!"

"It may be worse even than that," Cymri replied. "It is also possible that, in the process of settling itself in this new world, the weight of Tethera may rip the fabric of that world as well. When this happens in a place where our own fabric is also torn, it could allow things in to our world that were never meant to be in *any* world. Things that, save for the meddling that caused the Wild Growth, never would have come into existence at all except, possibly, as some dark unrealized potential between the worlds."

Helgar held out his bare forearm to show the others. "Look at the way my hairs are all standing straight up. Feels very strange it does!"

"Very well," Llew said to Cymri, "you have succeeded in making all of us very uncomfortable with your discussion of worlds. Do you have anything else to say on the subject before getting around to otherworlds, which is more properly where our current interests lie?"

"Just this, Llew, I have told you before that the Wild Growth began when Annwyn started to take form in our world. The coincidence is too great; the conclusion too obvious. If anything could, this fact alone should lend greater impetus to our drive to resist Lord Arawen in all things and at all costs. Annwyn is an otherworld, yet it is drawing itself forth into our world, an inch at a time. It does not belong here. It should not even be possible for it come here, but this may be the entire reason why Tethera was brought into this world—because here it is possible."

"Meaning," Llew said, "that the Wild Growth may be an unintentional, perhaps even an unexpected, side effect of his plan to turn all of Tethera into a land of the dead, with himself as the self-proclaimed, and all powerful, Lord of Death. In his hubris it may not even have occurred to him that he could open doors to things potentially worse than death itself."

"Be that as it may," Cymri continued, "the point being that, Annwyn aside, otherworlds are not like unto worlds themselves, except perhaps in miniature. In simplest form, they are simply other places, not nearly as big as a real world where different rules of nature and enchantment prevail. Some are horrible places, some are wonderful, others are neither. Some are home to Fae, some to the dead, some to . . . other things, and some are even empty. Some are well known and some are not."

"Avalon is a somewhat famous one. It is said to be like unto paradise itself. A place where great heroes are sometimes taken to rest after their labors—there to abide until such time as they are most desperately needed. It would have been a reasonable place to take King Bran."

Llew smacked his right fist into the palm of his left hand. "Then we should be on our way at once, or as soon as our repairs to our equipment are complete. It is barely noon and Lady Vanora set five seamstresses and two leather workers to it before our baths were even drawn. We can be at the port of Rhyl early on the day after next if we leave now."

"And that," replied Cymri, "goes back to where I said there is a problem with simply traveling there."

Llew sighed, then asked, "And that would be?"

"Avalon is as much an otherworld as it is an island. Further, it moves about the sea, and by no discernible pattern. The only way one can travel to it is after standing on a Fae stone. Only when you do so can you learn how to get there and, if you turn aside on the way for any reason, you will no longer be able to find it without first going back and standing on the Fae stone again."

"Easily done then," boomed Helgar, "we will simply stop at the nearest Fae stone along the way and then proceed to yon island."

Cymri shook her head. "To do that you would first have to know where to find a Fae stone and the only way to find one is to ask someone who knows where one would be."

"So who would that be?" Helgar asked.

"Oh no," Llew exclaimed, as he realized the likely answer.

"To find a Fae stone?" Cymri tsked and shook her head resignedly. "Why one of the Fae, of course."

* * *

"I have never seen a tumulus before." Helgar scratched his head and continued to regard the grass covered earthen mound before them. "I must confess it looks a great deal like a barrow mound. How do we know that is not what it is?"

Cymri slid off her horse and passed the reins to Addfwyn. "The differences are subtle, but they are there. As we have approached it today, I noticed the early morning dew hung more heavily on the spider webs than is its wont. Likewise, toadstools have been appearing in the form of little fairy rings and, last night, we heard tinkling bells in the darkness beneath the trees. It is a tumulus, a faery mound, and the Fae know that we are coming. More than that, they have permitted it."

"If you say so," Helgar replied dubiously. "I will fashion a shovel and we will soon see."

"Ah, no," Cymri said quickly, "that would probably not be the best way to go about it."

"Then how shall we go about it?" Caradog asked.

Cymri smiled enigmatically. "It is just as you say, we shall go about it."

"Huh?"

"We shall go about it, all of us, three times. If they mean for us to enter they will make it evident. If they do not, why then, we are done here."

"Why would they wish to meet with us at all?" Llew asked.

"The Fae are nothing if not capricious. They may decide to do it just 'because.' Or they may see some place for us in their machinations. Or they might just be bored; it is a frequent complaint of those who are immortal. Mind you, despite whatever they say, never believe them to be your friends. They are capable of lies but scorn to use them. Despite that, there is no limit to their ability to mislead mortals and, this is important, you are neither to eat any food nor drink any liquid while we are inside, save for what we have brought ourselves."

"Wonderful," said Caradog, "are we at least allowed to breathe?"

"Yes," she replied, "but do not sleep. The main danger of their food and drink is that it will make you very sleepy."

"What happens if we sleep?" Caradog asked, now quite

attentive.

"Then belike when you awaken you will discover a century or more has passed in the world of men. For now, however, remove all items of iron and steel; we will leave them with Addfwyn and he will await our return, along with Crug and Glo. Hounds do not always do well in otherworlds and the realm of the Tylwyth Teg is, potentially at least, more confusing for them than most."

"You would have us enter this dangerous place unarmed and unarmored?" Llew asked, aghast at the prospect.

"Unless the armor is of leather or bronze, then yes," Cymri replied. "We may each keep one weapon apiece for appearance's sake but do not draw it unless you mean to kill, and do not kill unless there is no other alternative. Even the touch of cold iron is painful to the Fae and prolonged exposure will kill them. They will not admit us—they will not even speak with us—if we do not first make this gesture."

The forest bordered the tumulus closely but there was room there for them to ride single file around it, once, twice, thrice. As they came around the third time they found a great portal, with doors of stone flung open wide, on the side of the tumulus. Oil-fed cressets, burning brightly, lined a wide tunnel of worked stone leading into the hill. A figure stood in the opening, wearing clothes of green that were more finely made than any Llew had ever seen. It also bore a long bow and quiver across its back, one visible over each shoulder.

Llew sensed that timidity would not work in his favor here and nudged Gower to approach. *So this*, he thought to himself, *is a Fae.* The creature did not move at all, frozen, with an almost too welcoming smile upon its face. Its face? Llew looked again. The being wore neither beard nor moustache. The golden hair was worn long but that meant little. The features were very fine, both delicate and beautiful, while the clothing gave nothing away. Was this member of the Fae a male or not? There was simply no way to tell and so Llew tried to push the question aside.

The figure abruptly came to life as he ventured closer and exclaimed, "Welcome, Prince Lleu, to the realm of the Fae. I am Aite and it is both my duty and my honor to bid you and your companions welcome in the name of our august majesties, King Auberon and Queen Mab, and to escort you all to them. They even now await your arrival."

The voice was, there was no other word for it, beautiful. Mellifluous and strong, without being overly loud, the words came to them precisely at the level they needed to be to cross the distance between, and no more.

Caradog then displayed a gracelessness that Llew was certain had to be feigned. "Greetings, Aite. I am Prince Caradog of Gwynedd. Pardon me for asking but I have never encountered the Fae before. Are you male or female?"

The Fae seemed to be at a loss for words. After a moment, it asked, "Do I understand that you are questioning me as to my gender, Prince Caradog?"

Caradog, rather than taking the verbal retreat he had been offered, instead smiled agreeably and replied, "Yes."

There was an awkward pause. Then Aite laughed and said, "Surely I must stop receiving visitors in my hunting clothes if it confuses the issue this much. I am a Fae maiden, of course, but," and she waggled a finger playfully at him, "do not get any ideas. I am much too old for you!"

Score the first round to us, Llew thought to himself. He was fairly certain that Aite's androgyny was only one of many attempts that would be made by the Fae to keep him and his party off balance. 'To what purpose?' remained the question. Was it in service of harmless pranking or something else?

"Come," Aite invited, "and please bring your mounts. You are entering by one of our least used gates and from here to the courts is still a fair distance."

Cymri raised a finger. "Pardon me, Aite, we would be most pleased to visit with your royals, yet we are sorely pressed by time. Is it possible you could simply tell us what we need to know and we could be on our way? We would certainly be willing to return after the present situation is concluded."

Aite dipped her head apologetically and said, "Nay, and I do apologize, Lady—"

"Cymri," Llew supplied.

"—Lady Cymri, but our majesties were quite specific. Whatever it is you wish, you will need to speak with them directly."

"I see, thank you."

"Ware, Llew," Cymri said without moving her lips, and in a voice so low only Llew could hear it. "There is mischief at work here and we have little choice but to play along with it for the moment. Keep her talking so that she, at least, might be distracted."

Llew gave no indication he had heard her; she would know he had.

Aite made a gesture and a large white stag trotted up behind her. She mounted and with a grand sweep of her arm indicated they should follow. With her leading the way, they rode down a short passage of worked stone blocks and then under a translucent portcullis and out from what appeared, on this side, as a gatehouse of intricately worked glass. The whole thing looked about as sturdy as a large crystal goblet. Before them was plain of rich green grass, covered with a thick mist that hid anything more than a hundred paces away. The sky, if there was one, was similarly obscured. There was no visible trail or road, yet they continued out onto the plain without stopping. The crystalline gatehouse was soon swallowed by the mist behind them.

Llew glanced behind to see how his companions were taking this. Helgar and Caradog were looking about confusedly. At no point since entering the tumulus had their path ever angled down. By rights, they should now have been emerging from the far side of the mound. Cymri seemed to be taking this completely in stride and Llew decided to emulate her example. She had told them in advance that otherworlds did not lie within the world of mortal men and he, of all people, knew not to be surprised when she was right.

"Aite," Llew ventured, "you called me Prince Lleu at the gate. Although it sounds very similar, I am actually Prince Llew—unless, of course, you know something I do not?"

She regarded him with an enigmatic gaze. "Perhaps," she ventured, "I do know something you do not?"

"What?" exclaimed Llew, startled.

She laughed at that, a delicate sound that conveyed commingled amusement and delight. "Listen to you! How could I possibly? It is an easy enough mistake to make; you would have been better served had I said 'Prince Llew'."

"Ah, so tell me, Aite," Llew responded, "that is a magnificent creature you are riding. Is it by any chance the Stag of Rhedynfre?"

"Nay, do not be saying such! You will only turn his head

and make him vain. His name is Hyddod and he suits me better than any other steed. Do I look like one who would care to muck out stables and lug food and water to any beast? Hyddod is wonderfully self-sufficient. I have merely to set him free and he takes care of all that he needs, as any wild beast might, then returns to me when I require his services."

"Aite," Cymri interjected, "I have a dreadful suspicion that you intend to show us some of the great wonders of the land of the Tylwyth Teg, yet as I have said, our time is quite short. I assure you no one could regret that more keenly that ourselves, but I must ask you to take us to your liege lords by the most expeditious route that you know."

For a moment, Aite dropped her chin and appeared to sulk. Then she lifted it again and smiled. "Very well then. Quick it shall be; follow if you can!"

With that, Hyddod gave a great bound and was off. Gower needed no urging, he gave chase immediately and Llew found himself holding on for dear life. Had Gower ever run this fast before? Even so, little by little, the white stag was pulling away. This was a new experience for Gower and Llew could tell that his steed did not like it. Llew also did not have to look behind to know that he and Gower were far outdistancing his friends. Was it better to keep the party together and lose their guide, or keep the guide in view by at least one of the party? Without knowing more about this place—and about Aite's purpose in doing this, if there even was one—this was not a question he could answer.

Aite and Hyddod had gradually faded into the mist ahead of them when, a short distance later, the mist relented somewhat and Llew saw he had entered a vale. Great boulders and smaller stones were set amidst a backdrop of ferns and incredible flowering plants that were quite unlike any Llew had ever seen. Great trees, of a species Llew had never seen before, so big that it have taken ten men, linked hand-to-hand, to wrap their arms about their trunks, shaded almost everything, yet the ground cover seemed to flourish in such faint light as there was. Flowing through it all was a large stream, periodically forming large pools, each different, each beautiful, before tinkling waterfalls descended to the next level.

It was so spectacular, Llew forgot to breathe for a moment. A thought came to him that, if men had lived here, someone would surely have built a mill to take advantage of the water and its elevations, creating a mill pond at the expense of all these pools.

Hyddod, now riderless, was grazing near the edge of one such pool. Of Aite, there was no sign. Llew slowed Gower to a cautious walk and ventured between the stones down toward the stag.

His caution did him little good as Aite dropped onto Gower behind him and put her hands over his eyes. "Guess who it is!" she queried playfully.

Llew had his hands full as the equally surprised Gower snorted and reared, forelegs flailing at nothing. Gower calmed almost immediately but Llew had only barely kept his seat.

"Aite, you are trying to get me killed," he accused.

The hands came off his eyes immediately as both of her arms snaked around over his chest holding him tightly while she brought her mouth close to his ear. "Silly," she husked, "of course I am not. Were that the case I would have used my bow." Then she licked his ear and he nearly fell off of Gower again.

"You know I was only jesting when I told your little friend he was too old for me, right?" Still holding him fast, her hands began to slide down his chest. "After the first few centuries it really does not make any difference. You, certainly, are not too young for me."

Llew manage to say something, but it was not comprehensible, even to himself.

She giggled again. "Oh, do not worry about them, they will catch up to us, but not before I want them to. Come, let us wait for them on the soft moss by the largest pool. I assure you it is quite a unique sensation and one you should not miss."

"Uh . . ." Llew said brightly, not certain what words went after that. He had the feeling he should be attempting to picture Bloddeuwedd in his head and focusing on that image, yet it just seemed exceptionally difficult to do so at the moment.

There was flurry of hoof beats as the rest of the party rode in at a gallop.

"What!" Aite exclaimed, as they came to a stop. "However did you—"

"Let us just say that I have had a little experience with a misdirection spell in the past," Cymri said dryly. She then looked first to Helgar and then to Caradog. "We all have, for that matter. "Caradog, turn around, look away. Llew, do not move a muscle. I will tell you both when you can do otherwise.

"Now," she said, apparently speaking to Aite again, "if you would be so good as to find the rest of your clothing, we will go directly to present ourselves at court."

There was very little said for some time after they rode out of the vale. Helgar waited until the riders were sufficiently strung out that it would be necessary to raise one's voice to be heard by another. He then let his horse catch up with Gower so he could ride beside Llew."

"Psst, Llew," the Northman said in a muted voice.

"Yes, Helgar?"

"Cymri never told me not to look, Llew. You do know what the forest lady was trying to do, do you not?"

"Yes, Helgar, it took me a bit but I figured it out."

"Ah, good then. This was very serious, Llew. You are betrothed and this could have caused big problems, dangerous problems."

"I would expect it could have," Llew replied, wondering where Helgar was going with this.

"My drott, it is my duty to help protect you from danger. Bear that in mind. The next time some woman tries to do something like this you must tell her it is my duty to stand in your stead."

Llew sighed. "Thank you Helgar, I appreciate your bravery and devotion to duty. It is good to know you are always ready to keep me safe, regardless of the personal sacrifice involved."

Helgar nodded once in acknowledgment and smiled. "I could do no less, Llew."

Chapter XIV

The Court of Auberon

After a bit they came to a crystalline ramp. The sides were filigreed and multicolored and the entire construct spiraled up into the sky until it was lost in the mist. There was no central newel, suggesting the entire thing just held itself up. That would never be possible outside this otherworld, Llew realized.

Aite gestured towards the ramp. "Your animals may remain here. They will be quite safe and they may consume the grass without any undue effect. It will, in fact, make them stronger and increase their stamina to graze from the fields of Tir-Na-Nog."

"Tir-Na-Nog?" asked Caradog. "That is not a Tetheran name."

Aite shook her head from side to side before regarding him with an air of forced tolerance and saying, "Silly mortal, did you think the Fae are Tetheran?"

Llew was hesitant to leave anything here, but he leaned forward and spoke quietly into Gower's ear for a few moments, then slid off and patted the great horse on the neck before heading to the ramp. The others dismounted and followed.

The Fae-woman regarded him curiously. "Forgive me for asking, Prince Llew, but what was it you said to your mount?"

"I told him to keep the other horses here and, if anyone attempts to harm them or take them away, to kill them."

Aite seemed amused. "Your horse speaks?"

"Only a little," Llew replied, "but I expect he listens very well."

She hesitated, then laughed, apparently convinced he was trying to be funny.

As they ascended, the ground eventually disappeared, hidden in mist. Given that the ramp was largely transparent, this was a blessing, despite the fact none of them had an inordinate fear of heights. A short time later, the fog seemed to be lifting when, without warning, they emerged above the mist. Llew heard Helgar and Caradog gasp. It looked as though the sky were turned upside down. Clouds extended to the horizon in all directions, forming white, soft hills and mountains with deep fluffy gorges and valleys, but these clouds were all below them. It was an eerie and awesome sight.

Aite waited silently for them to take it in. Llew marveled that the mist below had just been the result of clouds lying across the ground itself. Perhaps that was all that fog really was? Up here the sun beat down as on any bright summer day, despite the mist and fog on the ground. Except that it was sunlit only to one side of them. The other half lay dark under . . . stars. Llew blinked, surely any kingdom of the Fae must be strange but this was beyond strange. It had not been half day and half night on the ground below.

His thoughts on this were brutally interrupted as his gaze continued to rise to the sky directly above them. It was a castle, but only by the widest possible interpretation of that word. The thing was vast, larger than even Caerleon. Yet Caerleon was not made of fantastically shaped multi-colored crystal, spun into elaborate representations of towers and turrets, flying buttresses, and curved translucent walls sporting fantastically shaped crenellations, and all of it extending both up and down with nothing resembling a ground level, either below or above.

It is floating in the sky, Llew told himself. *Of course its towers and walls extend both up and down. Why would they not?* Yet this meant it could never come down. No matter how carefully and slowly it was set upon the earth, such an action must surely destroy at least half of the structure were it ever attempted. Then it occurred to him wonder how it could ever have been built in the first place and never mind what arcane enchantments now held it there.

Above and beyond them, the spiral ramp grew into larger spirals, finally meeting the eldritch fortification precisely in its vertical center, passing through a circular entry with a gold and silver portcullis raised above it. In further service of the strangeness, half of the floating castle lay in what seemed to be permanent night and shone with the light of a thousand stars reflecting from its myriad surfaces, with many more ghostly glows of endless hues emanating from within. The other half lay in the noon-day sun and reflected sunlight in all directions, most especially from the silver and gold conic peaks of the highest and lowest towers. These so dazzled any eyes attempting to assay them that they were soon forced to flinch away from that task.

Aite spread her arms and said, "Behold Cae Wydyr, also

called the glass fortress, bastion of the rulers of the Fae, the all-powerful King Auberon, Lord of the Seelie Court, and the incomparable Queen Mab, Lady of the Unseelie Court. Here their combined will and power is both manifest and absolute. Let us move on, our time is now nearly in step with their own . . . and it is not good to keep them waiting."

In time, they entered under the portcullis and proceeded into a hall of terrible splendor. Incredibly well wrought suits of transparent crystal armor plates lined the hall. They all held weapons of similar construction. Helgar slowed and asked in wonder, "Is this where the valkries bring the slain heroes of the battlefield?"

Aite laughed and replied, "As if we would want a grand collection of dead mortals here, of all places."

She led them on through armories and antechambers, up grand staircases and through narrow halls they could barely slide through sideways. They passed a grand high ceilinged chamber where hundreds of Fae danced with each other to a haunting melody. Finally she led them through enormous double doors into a feasting hall when many dozens of Fae were at feast, sitting at a crystal table in crystal chairs, drinking from crystal flagons, and eating foods Llew had never seen before—off of crystal plates with crystal implements.

They angled to the left and went around the table. None of the revelers took any notice of them. At the far end of the room the floor was a step above the rest. Here they came to the high table, perpendicular to the larger one and with seating for only six, although just two sat there now.

Llew looked to Aite for introductions and discovered she was no longer with them. The sounds of the feasting abruptly faded away, and they all looked behind to see that a translucent green wall had appeared between them and the lower table. The feasters could only now be dimly seen as faint blurry shapes beyond it. He turned back to the seated figures.

King Auberon, for it could only be him, cast an appraising look over them as they approached. In appearance he was much as the other male Fae they had seen in the castle. His skin was perfect and showed no trace of wrinkles or other imperfections. Likewise, although the hair streaming out from under the silver coronet he wore was also silver, it was in no way the gray of age but most likely the color he was born with. Even so, something in his eyes betrayed one who had lived and seen more than any mortal ever would.

"Ah, and here we are, blessed with a surfeit of mortal royalty." He held up his hands before Llew could speak. "Nay, do not bother yourselves, we know who you all are and you certainly know who we are, so what point introductions, eh? To Mab he said, "Look, my dear, the prodigal son has returned."

The Queen of the Fae was already looking them over. Unlike her mate's, her long braided hair was dark—darker than night. It could really only be seen as a silhouette for it seemed to absorb all light that struck it, giving nothing back. Her face was sharp with very high cheek bones and piercing eyes, eyes with black pupils and white irises that seemed to pierce right through him. For all of that, she was so striking to look upon that it required an effort to pay attention to what she was saying. "And so he has," replied Mab. "The terms were specific. I do get to keep him this time, do I not? It is only fair, an eye for an eye, a son for a son."

Llew felt, more than saw, Cymri stiffen next to him.

Auberon held up a finger to Llew, in the kind of signal people make when they wish someone to bide a moment while they say something to someone else. "Now, dear lady, there is nothing I would wish more myself than to place him as captain of my personal guard. He would be splendid in our livery and truly set the tone for such an important position. Then, too, I would be delighted to be able to keep him so close, but it cannot be. I was not being cruel before. A bit sneaky, perhaps, but I was not being cruel."

"My child is dead because of him and there he stands, very nearly the precise image of my own precious babe as he would be today. I want him for my own, I deserve it."

"What is she saying?" Llew demanded. "Have I been here before? Am I then as Hafgan hinted, no true-born prince of Gwent but merely a changeling? A temporary thing purchased for Moriganna's foul schemes?"

"A changeling is no temporary thing!" Mab declared, rising from her seat. "Never that!"

"Come now," said Auberon. "I am certain the boy did not mean to insult, he simply has not had the benefit of a proper education. Patience, while we get a few things out of the way.

"Llew, hopefully Pendaran has already had that little talk with you that mortals like to give their sons. If so, it should come as little surprise to you that sometimes babes are born with one parent Fae and one human. It really happens rather more often than one might think for we have very few pure Fae children, despite our efforts to the contrary, and we do love our children. Even if the other parent is human we bring them here and raise them as our own for they are dear to us.

"However, I am certain you have heard much of the proclivities of some of our number. Alas, there is at least a little truth in them. There is also the fact that any Fae may change their form to that of any other creature, and they may do this once each day. There is a goodly number of offspring born where one parent is Fae and the other is something else."

"What is this 'something else' you are speaking of?" Caradog asked.

Auberon pursed his lips and regarded the younger prince. "I think we must put down that question to the fact you are very young and have not had that talk with a parental figure yet. You ask 'what else' and I must say, 'almost anything else.' Use your imagination! The Fae certainly do.

"Now these progeny are more problematical. Certainly we do not want children running about that are half troll, or half Firbolg, or whatever else. Goodness no, it is difficult enough to keep a floating crystal palace clean without some half-giant putting his great grubby fingerprints everywhere." Auberon affected a mock shudder.

"It is further complicated by the fact that we Fae are an extremely practical lot and it goes against the grain to just throw something away that might be valuable. So what is frequently done is the babe is taken to someplace humans live and exchanged for a human baby as we find those the least objectionable. Indeed, properly raised, humans adapt readily to living among us. The only drawback is we become inordinately fond of them and, just about the time they should start getting really interesting, they waste away and die, usually in less than one or two centuries. It is always very tragic, but that never stops us from doing it again when another changeling is available."

"You do not see the human mothers losing their own infants as being a drawback?" Helgar rumbled.

"Oh goodness, no. They never even know the swap took place because a special enchantment is laid upon the changeling so that it will always look nearly exactly as the original child would have. We are doing them a favor, really. Many of these changelings die of course, because mortals do not know how to take care of them—they need a lot of magic in their environment—but the ones that do live are the ones that keep things interesting.

King Auberon returned his attention to Llew. "I expect this concerns you most because we have just admitted this is not your first time here and you already suspect you might be a changeling. Am I right?"

"So that is it," Llew said bitterly. "Hafgan was right, I am not my father's son, just some unwanted by-blow of the Fae, left in place of his real son. This is not the knowledge I came here for."

"No, you have it quite wrong, of course. Amazing how often mortals do that. You are not half Fae, not even a quarter, although there is some. You certainly did not start out as a changeling. The changeling was left in your place and you were taken here. The problem that arose was that the changeling was then murdered."

"My son," Mab said in a low voice, those frightening eyes fixed full upon Llew. "Murdered by the one you call Arawen because he thought the child was you."

Auberon shrugged. "We had agreed to deliver a changeling and, before the principal could even acknowledge that the job was complete, it no longer was. Our own standards, and one must have standards, required that you be returned to your mother. Yet it appeared your mother was dead by then and things became rather complicated."

"He was such a beautiful child," Mab said in an unsettling voice that made Llew wonder at her sanity. "He looked so much like you."

"What was the purpose? Why would you exchange a son you valued for me?" Llew asked of Mab, yet he got no response.

"Uneasy rests the crown," Auberon replied. "No doubt someone villain saw an opportunity to pay Mab back for some imagined slight and swapped her child for the changeling that would have been sent. This is doubly unfortunate in that any other changeling would not have fooled Arawen and he would not have bothered to have it murdered."

"Murdered," Mab echoed in a low voice.

"Sooner or later," Auberon continued, "we will find out who and Mab will express her unhappiness with that person or persons responsible."

Mab only smiled tightly at this.

"You came for the location of a Fae stone you can use to find a path to the Isle of Avalon. It has been a long time since any of us have ventured there. Sailing about in ships is not really what we like best; we have not the patience for it. Nonetheless, you may find a Fae stone where the river Elwys meets the river Clwyd. The juncture is about a mile south of Caer Rhuddlan which is, itself, just about two miles south of Rhyl, so it is right on your way."

"No, Lleu is not leaving this time," Mab declared, using the same slight mispronunciation of his name that Aite had initially used. "He is so much like my poor lost son that he belongs with me and it is time and past time for him to take his place here at court." She smiled at him then, apparently sincere, and said, "Your life is so very short, but while it yet lasts we will have the grandest of times, you and I!"

"Oh dear," was Auberon's response.

Cymri's face was grave as she approached Mab and ventured to lay one hand on the queen's. "I am sorry, your majesty, but Llew is needed in the realm of men. Only a male of his blood can inherit Gwent and go on to reestablish the great kingdom of Tethera. This is all necessary if Arawen is to be stopped and punished for his crimes. You do want that, do you not?"

"You are trying to manipulate me?" Mab shrieked in a sudden rage. "Mortal woman you have gone too far! Did you enjoy life as a black bird? Now you shall spend the rest of it in the same manner!"

Cymri took several steps back as a short wand appeared in Mab's hand. Before anyone could do anything, she pointed it at Cymri and spoke a word.

As it was, nothing happened.

"You are holding my flute," remarked Cymri.

Mab's mouth opened, but not to speak; her jaw had literally dropped with surprise.

"I think this is what you were looking for," the young bard said, showing another flute-like object in her own hand. Before Mab could say anything else, Cymri said a word and Mab disappeared, leaving behind a large black bird, flapping in midair.

The bird cawed once, perhaps in disbelief, then winged its way out the nearest window.

"And that," King Auberon said to Cymri, "was absolutely priceless. You are a very precocious mortal and there may be little I admire more in mortals than that. That look on her face when you did not change is one I will always cherish. You must now beware, though. In a day's time, as with any other Fae, she will be free to resume her own form and she will not be happy with you."

"I am already not happy with her," muttered Cymri.

"I would suggest you all make haste in leaving our fair realm," Auberon suggested. "The Seelie Court is mine and none there will do anything to prevent your departure but, handicapped as she currently is, Mab may still be able to rally some part of the Unseelie Court to her aid. Llew, please do come back some time when all this unpleasantness is over, assuming you survive. You are not precisely family, but I like you."

"Wait," Llew said, finding his voice, "it was you that sent her son as a changeling for me. Why? She will be furious with you if she eventually figures it out."

Auberon shrugged, "It has happened before. She will make a few half-hearted attempts to kill me and will not speak to me for a century or even a millennium. Then we will make up and with Mab that is always its own reward."

"As for why I had to send that particular child as a changeling for you? It is because it resembled you closely enough that it would fool Arawen. He can see through a changeling's guise as readily as any Fae. For you to be safe he had to believe he had killed you."

"Why, would having Mab as its mother make the changeling so closely resemble me?" Llew asked.

"Really, Llew, to defeat Arawen and save Tethera you will need to become quicker on the uptake than this," chided King Auberon. "The resemblance had nothing to do with Mab. It was because you both had the same father, of course. Now go, hurry!"

Chapter XV

The Hunting Trip

The wall between them and the revelers disappeared with a wave of King Auberon's hand. That, thought Llew, still reeling from Auberon's last words, was a rather brief visit. They made their way out of the feasting hall and, with only a few hesitations, they were able to retrace the path they had used coming in. Fortunately, Cymri and Helgar both had some talent at this. Llew was quite certain that had he and Caradog been alone, the two of them would have wandered forever, irretrievably lost in the labyrinthine glass fortress.

They did not sneak or run. By common agreement they marched along in the same manner in which they had entered, making every effort to look as though nothing was amiss in a party of mortals taking a walk through the seat of power of the Tylwyth Teg. Many Fae saw them, but none attempted to impede their path. Despite this, no one was more surprised than Llew when they had found their way to the final exit and the top of the spiral ramp to the ground so far below.

"Llew," Caradog cried urgently.

He turned and saw what the prince of Gwynedd was seeing. Although they had previously seemed to exist solely for the purpose of ornamentation, the many suits of strange multi-colored crystal armor were now in motion, and all of them coming after the group! They held their weapons like warriors rushing into a fierce battle, fully intending to use them.

Helgar drew down his axe from across his shoulder and turned as though to meet them.

"No, Helgar, no. There are far too many and I expect they are considerably more difficult to break than so many empty wine bottles. In any case, it is not necessary. They are not as fast as we, especially as we have no armor—another reason not to engage them! They will not catch us before we reach our horses, nor afterward either."

The Northman reluctantly nodded agreement and the four of them fairly ran down the ramp. Llew did not like how very far it was to the bottom. Who could know what deviltry Mab might have waiting for them if they too long to get down?

At that moment, Caradog managed to step on the hem of his cloak and tripped, falling heavily on his back, with his head angled downslope, he landed on his cloak and his momentum from running kept him in motion. With a despairing cry he picked up speed at an astounding rate and slid down and around the ramp far faster than they could hope to catch him.

Llew goggled for a moment, then gave a short laugh. "Ha, we must not let him forget that this was simply a happy mishap due to his own clumsiness. He will likely become insufferable otherwise."

"Happy?" Cymri said. "He will die if he slides off that

ramp!"

"He will not," Llew contradicted. "The side of the ramp angles down from the outer edge, probably to help prevent that very thing and, even were it not, the outer balustrade seems purposely designed such that it will steer those that stray so far back on to the ramp." He looked back at the multitude of crystalline warriors pursuing them. "Quickly now, our cloaks! Remove them and hold them in front of you, then take a quick run and dive upon it!"

With some misgivings, Cymri and Helgar did just that. Helgar had to try a second time as someone of his weight and size apparently required quite a bit more speed to get in motion initially. Even on the second attempt it seemed as if it just was not going to work for him, then he began slowly picking up speed. The Northman gave a great whoop as he slid out of sight around the curve of the spiral, still accelerating.

Their pursuers were nearly upon him when Llew raced forward and leapt onto his own cloak. For a moment he feared he was going to have the same problem as Helgar initially had but, reassuringly, he realized that although he had slowed considerably when he landed on the cloak, he was now picking up speed. The reassuring part went away rapidly as his speed continued to increase. He let out a great bellowing yell as the balustrade to his right became a blur. At least Llew thought it was a yell, when he recalled it later. Even though it might have been on a bit of a high note, he was certain it was still a yell; screaming in fright was surely not something he ever did.

The rest of the ride down was an almost incoherent compilation of impressions. The thrill was tremendous, once he convinced himself he was not about to die in the next given moment. After that he did scream most of the way down, but in glee and exhilaration, not fear. Then he hit the grass at the bottom, was torn free of his cloak, and rolled for at least twenty paces before slowing to a stop. He picked himself up shakily, a bit dizzy from the rolling, and still overwhelmed by the ride itself. Caradog was there giving him a hand.

"I see you made it down safely," he said to his young shield-bearer.

"Llew, when this is over we must come back and do this again! Can we? Please?"

Llew glanced to Cymri who was up and looking more than a bit grass-stained and disheveled. She looked him in the eye and, in a voice colder and more brittle than ice, said, "Never . . . ever . . . again!"

Both of them looked to Helgar, who already seemed his usual self. "Me?" the Northman asked. "Agree with Caradog I certainly do."

"You would," Cymri said, in a two word condemnation. "This is what I get for traveling with three young boys and no other adult supervision."

"Quickly now," Llew advised. "They will not be forever getting down."

Their mounts were grazing nearby. As Llew went to mount he noticed that Gower's front hooves were splashed with blood. He dropped to his knees and began a careful inspection, which his steed bore phlegmatically. Llew soon realized the blood was not Gower's.

"What is it, Llew?" asked Helgar as he rode his own horse over to them.

"Nothing of consequence," Llew replied. "Just watch what you step in around here. Apparently Aite was incorrect when she said our horses would be safe here."

Helgar shook his head. "Gower was here so our horses were quite safe. It was something else that was not safe here. Assuming Gower is safe is very dangerous, but it seems to be a common mistake. Even so, few make it twice."

Llew snorted and said, "And thank goodness for that!"

As there were neither trails nor roads, nor even stars, to guide them, they might have wandered aimlessly across the plain of Tir-Na-Nog for ages, lost in the mist, were it not for some strange tune Cymri knew that allowed her to find her way to things she wished to locate.

They came to the glass gatehouse from which they had entered Tir-Na-Nog and found it closed. Llew slid out of his saddle to see if he could find a mechanism to open it. It was for that reason alone that the arrow, the one that would have skewered his head a scant part of a breath before, now passed through the empty space where his head had been.

"Gah!" he exclaimed, and turned to see Aite at the edge of the mist, bow in hand and the great stag, Hyddod, at her side. She already had another arrow notched.

Stall, thought Llew, *play for time to think of something, anything.*

"That was most impressive, Aite. I would not have anticipated that even the amazing Hyddod could have brought you here so quickly."

She grinned, keeping the next arrow fixed on him. "Hyddod is amazing that way, I always keep him close at hand to ensure I can travel swiftly. Do not be sad. You could never have escaped. Had I failed to get you myself it would still only have been a matter of time."

Then she changed into a white doe, sometimes called a hind, while her bow and other equipment fell to the turf.

"She really should not have talked so long if she intended to kill us," Cymri remarked, as she lowered Queen Mab's wand.

The doe regarded them with her wide doe eyes, then glanced to Hyddod. If anything her eyes grew even wider. Hyddod sniffed her, then shook his antlers and stamped a fore hoof. A moment later he threw back his head and roared. At that point, Aite went racing off into the mist at high speed, her trusty steed in close pursuit.

Cymri gave an evil-sounding snicker and said, "It seems she was right, Hyddod will certainly ensure she travels swiftly. Doubtless, she will most certainly change herself back tomorrow when she regains the power to do so, but I think she will be much too busy to interfere with us again before then."

While Helgar and Caradog chortled, Llew glanced to Cymri in amazement. "Cymri that was—"

"—inspired?" she asked.

"I was going to say 'mean' but now that I think about it, perhaps cruel."

"How cruel? She tried to use you as a play thing and then tried to kill you. All I did was teach her a little lesson."

"From what I have seen," said Llew, "the Fae behave according to their nature and possess no sense for right or wrong. Nor do I believe this is something they can be taught, any more than fire can be taught not to cast light. Was it not you who once taught me that to punish something that could not learn was just a form of cruelty?"

"It was not me," Cymri replied, "you must have heard that

from Moriganna before I came on the scene."

"Really?" Llew frowned. "What an odd thing for her to say—at any rate, I have quite decided that I spoke in haste. That was terribly amusing and, rightly or wrongly, after the way she attempted to work her wiles on me at that glade, it does feel like she had it coming. Does this mean I am cruel? Perhaps it does, or perhaps it just means that I am not perfect. I suspect the latter is closer to the truth."

No one said anything while Llew found the mechanism to open the silver and gold portcullis and they passed through. The stone doors at the opposite end proved equally easy to operate and everyone sighed in relief as they all passed out of Tir-Na-Nog and back into the lands of Tethera.

Addfwyn was still there. Llew spared a moment for greetings, it felt like long ages since they had left him there, while Caradog reintroduced himself to Crug and Glo. They then donned their armor. He hated to take the time to do it, but if the Fae did not like it then it seemed especially worth doing. Aite's blithe comment about how something else would have done for them, even had she failed, was troubling. She had failed. Did that mean something else, whatever it might be, was coming for them?

"We will go west and north," Llew said decisively. "That should let us intercept the Clwyd river so that we may follow it up to where it meets the Elwys and find this Fae stone that King Auberon told us of. We have only a few minutes of daylight remaining but we cannot stop until we are well away from here."

There did not appear to be any way to close the gate to Tir-Na-Nog from this side so they left it open. Surely the Fae would be along to close it in time?

As they rode, Llew realized something Cymri had said earlier was troubling him. "Cymri, you said you were the only adult traveling with three young boys. Is that truly the way you feel about us?"

"Forgive me, Llew, I was a bit testy at the time."

"No, well . . . yes," he amended, "but that is beside the point if that just caused you to give voice to a belief you already had."

Cymri grimaced and said, "Sometimes I feel old beyond my years, Llew. When we met you were nine years of age while I was sixteen. Now you are fifteen and I am twenty-two. Some would already consider me a bit of a crone, to be unmarried and without prospects at this point in my life. It sometimes colors my thinking."

Llew did some rapid calculations. "Moriganna turned you into a bird when you had been with us a year, and it was less than a year ago that I broke the enchantment. Have you examined yourself in a looking glass since then? Time apparently stopped calling on you while you were a bird. Of a surety, you are not even quite eighteen yet. The difference in age between us has narrowed to less than three years. "

Cymri looked as startled as Llew had ever seen her. "How blind have I been?" Then she smiled and examined the backs of her hands. "Perhaps you are right, Llew, thank you for that. But it is not just age of the body that constitutes true age. Consider Moriganna. She does not even look a day over forty yet we know she is centuries old. Also, do you recall what Queen Enid said to you? I can quote it verbatim, of course. 'Youth is in your mind and in your soul, not just your body."

"She also said to take whatever opportunity you have to enjoy your youth," Llew reminded her. "You seem intent on making yourself old before your time."

"Hmm," she said, "Llew, is this about me or more about how you would like to make us peers?"

He flushed at that but answered, "Cymri, I remain extraordinarily fond of you but I am betrothed now and happily so. As to in the past? When I was much younger? I freely admit I might have sold my right arm if it would have brought you closer to my own age. I suspect that it is probably fairly common for young boys to become enamored of a pretty young tutor—or it would be, if there were many boys so fortunate as to have one."

"Why, Llew, you say the sweetest things," she said, laughing gaily as she did so.

Llew, for his part, quirked one corner of his mouth and replied, "Yes, that is me, sweet through and through."

Night had fallen completely and they were lighting torches when, from behind them, a deep horn blew a long somber note that resonated through the forest.

Cymri was instantly serious again. "Llew! Mab must have found a way to summon the Wild Hunt!"

"And here I thought it might be a relief if I knew what Aite meant when she said that if she did not get us then something else would," Llew replied.

Helgar had one hand resting on the handle of his axe. "I suppose you are going to say we cannot fight them, either?" he asked plaintively.

Caradog's eyes were wide as platters. "This is the Wild Hunt, Helgar. Gwyn ap Nudd is likely leading it himself. Against him there is no victory. To have him come upon you is death!"

"You say so?" Helgar asked, with a dangerous grin. "And will he not be surprised when that death is his own?"

"You misunderstand," Caradog insisted. "We cannot fight him and his huntsmen and their dogs."

"Cymri, is there any chance we could outrun them?" Llew asked. "We have a sizable lead on them."

She shook her head slowly. "From what I have heard, Gower might be able to, but it is far from certain."

"You will be ready with Mab's wand?"

In answer, she withdrew a handful of black dust from her pocket. "Like many of their more esoteric creations, it does not hold up well when removed to our world."

Llew winced internally and said, "Then you get your wish, Helgar. We fight."

"Ya!" the Northman's axe was in his hand.

"But first," said Llew, "we prepare the battleground. Caradog, you and Addfwyn must take the horses, except for Gower, and tether them off the trail and at least two hundred paces further on. Take Crug and Glo with you and keep those horses safe! If we fall you must leave, quietly, and take word at least as far as Caer Neb. King Delwyn will need to know what has happened. And lend me your daggers, the ones with the wrapped steel wire on the hilts . . . ."

"Llew! I can fight! Crug and Glo can, too! Keep us here, please."

"Nay, you are our fallback. Think on what would happen if we do fall here and no word of it escapes? Who would ransom your cousin then? Also, Crug and Glo are not here as weapons of war but to defend you and you specifically. Practice patience; Afaggdu will give you all the fighting you can stand, and then some, when he takes over your training."

Their preparations did not take long. Llew waited in the widest spot on the trail as the baying of the hounds grew closer, and the horn sounded and sounded again, each time louder, as it, too, came nearer. Hoof beats, became audible, even to those other than Llew. Abruptly, the baying became yipping and whining that, after a moment, receded back the way the baying had come. Apparently the Fae hounds did not like stepping on the steel arrowheads that had been scattered upon the trail like so many little caltrops.

The hoof beats came again although much slower this time. The lead rider came into sight, a dark armored figure on a midnight black horse. Antlers rose from its helm. Other mounted figures were crowding the trail behind it.

Waiting astride the trail ahead of them, behind two torches set to either side of the trail, was a great black horse, even larger and more foreboding than his own. Astride it sat another dark armored figure with antlers rising from its helm.

The lead huntsman snarled. "Insolent mortal! You dare mock me? For this alone you are dead!"

"Ah," said Llew, trying very hard to keep his voice sounding deep and steady, "you were going to leave me alone otherwise? Would that be a bald-faced lie? That is rather poor form among your kind, is it not?"

With a wordless shriek of fury, the huntsman couched his lance, spurred his mount, and charged forward. The riders behind him did the same.

So badly did Gower want to leap forward to meet them that it was all Llew could do to persuade him to hold motionless.

The steel wire across the trail unhorsed the first four riders before it broke.

With the light from the torches still interfering with their night vision, they never saw the second wire either.

The second steel wire got three more before it snapped. That was the cue for Cymri, hidden off the trail to one side, to cut a rope holding one end of an extremely heavy log several feet off the ground. As it fell, it pulled up another rope that had been lying across the trail, hidden by leaves and looped over a branch before it reached the log. This rope snapped up, two feet high where it crossed the trail, and was held completely taut by the hanging log. None of the riderless horses made it past that point. They all fell and went sprawling, some breaking legs or otherwise badly injuring themselves in the process. It was complete madness. They are Fae horses, not real ones, Llew told himself, seeking to absolve the terrible guilt he felt for the animals. Curiously, he had no reservation at all about the huntsmen themselves.

There had been at least four more riders, but only two were able to draw up short of the mass of fallen riders and horses, the other two lost their seats as their horses stumbled into the chaotic mass of fallen, flailing, horses and riders. Helgar lunged out of the woods next to the two that remained seated. His axe rose and fell and one of those two still in the saddle came crashing to the ground. If anything, the second one fared even worse. After Helgar hit him, he also fell to the ground—on both sides of the horse.

Llew sat and watched the carnage. The ground was covered with thrashing Fae—and some that were not thrashing. All of them of were faintly smoking where the wire, or Helgar's axe, had hit them. One especially loud screamer had managed to get himself thoroughly entwined in one of the broken wires. There was actual smoke rising from him. The screams and cries of injured Fae horses contributed to the chaos, several would certainly have to be put down. In the meantime they were immensely dangerous, in their anguish, some even rolled over their own fallen masters. Those that could get to their legs and run away eventually did so, heedless of what further damage they inflicted to the unhorsed riders.

The lead rider struggled to stand, his face was still a mask of fury, but he was having trouble breathing and clutched at his throat with one hand. With a slight squeeze from his calves, Llew let Gower know to be prepared to charge. The big horse snorted and stamped with anticipation. All of this was far more butchery than battle, but Llew did not feel he had the luxury of mercy. He and his friends would have received none and, still outnumbered, he was unwilling to give the Fae any chance to turn things about.

An enormous voice suddenly shouted, "ENOUGH!"

Chapter XVI

The Concordance

Llew froze, he knew that voice!

A dark giant strode into their midst. His great hammer rose and fell three times, putting the most grievously injured Fae steeds out of their misery. Then he removed the entwined steel wire from the smoldering huntsman and tossed it aside. He dropped the unmoving huntsman on the ground.

"You!" the giant turned and pointed a massive finger to the leader, who was now standing, one hand on a tree for support, the other still massaging his throat. "Hunting a bit early this evening are we?"

In a rasping voice, the huntsman said, "Queen Mab wishes it, I but serve."

"Ha," said the giant, as it shrank in size until it was no larger than a dwarf. "And since when does Gwyn ap Nudd rush to do anyone else's bidding? Even his own queen's? You exist only for the love of the hunt and its simple pleasures."

"As I said, it was for Queen Mab," Gwyn ap Nudd insisted. "Really, Hafgan, you of all people should know how persuasive she can be."

"You say that as if you do not know she is raving mad these days. Very well. Yet so perspicacious a huntsman as you claim to be must surely realize these are mortals. You have license to hunt them, of course?"

Gwyn ap Nudd remained silent and looked at the ground.

"Oh my. You do not have license? That would put you in direct violation of the eighth provision of Boudicca's Covenant. The penalties are listed under paragraph twenty-three of Math's Concordance and, I must say," the dwarf leaned closer and glanced from side to side before putting one hand, palm open, to the side of his mouth and whispering loudly in a theatrical aside, "they are somewhat unpleasant."

"Please, your majesty," said the huntsman in voice that while urgent, was not panicked either, "there is no need for that. Mistakes were made, clearly."

The king of the Spriggans looked pointedly at the other members of the hunt. Most seemed to still be alive, but none had yet ventured to stand. In a laconic voice, he said, "Aye, I would say some mistakes were made. Two mortal boys just about ended a ten thousand year tradition. If I had been a moment later they would have, too, and we would have had to put a couple of centuries into training your successor."

"Boudicca's Covenant though?" Gwyn ap Nudd complained. "Seriously, Hafgan, how long has it been since that has been enforced?"

"Ack," said Hafgan, "you ask a question like that with Boudicca's heir a hair's breadth away from ending you where you stand?"

Consternation written across his face, Gwyn ap Nudd looked up to Llew, still seated astride Gower, naked sword in his hand.

"Your Royal Majesty," he said haltingly, while putting an odd inflection on the form of address, "my sincere apologies. Truly, we were misled. You must understand I would never have knowingly violated the covenant between our houses?"

Llew understood no such thing but he now had a feel for how Hafgan wanted this handled. "As that may be, there seems to be no harm done to any of us so it may be that I could. However, because of this . . . incident, I find I now possess neither arrows nor the materials to fletch more. Likewise, I had to ruin two fine daggers that did not belong to me. Will you make restitution?"

Gwyn ap Nudd actually smiled at that, "Ah, there is some of us in you. Yes, Your Majesty, I believe I can give you and your man each a full quiver of arrows that are so finely crafted that no mortal fletcher has ever seen the like. Likewise, please accept my own dirks, a matched set, of a quality beyond all mortal blades, and of a metal that will neither pit nor rust, nor ever become dull."

"And these will not be destroyed when the morning sun rises?" Llew inquired.

"They are not made out of Fae dust, Your Highness, my word on it."

As soon as these had been presented to Llew, Hafgan spoke up again. "Alright then. All friends and made up. That is what I like to see. Mortals, go stand over there a moment, I will get to you. Gwyn, I want this place cleaned up by dawn—all of it. Take all the huntsmen now. Yes, I know they are not in wonderful shape. That poor fellow there does not even have a head, does he? Still, no excuses. The ones that are still able to walk can gather the horses. Then collect all the wounded and worse, and get them home—and do not forget to find that head and take it with you as well!"

Hafgan put his hands on his hips and regarded the horses he had put down. "Your dogs are probably already home by now but, if they are not, round them up. You can send back half a dozen pet trolls, or a gwillion or two, to get the dead horses, otherwise I am certain you know where to find a few dozen boggarts that would be happy to do it for the meat. If you do not know the enchantments yourself, get a water nymph or a dryad and summon some rain here when you are done. This place needs a really good washing down before anyone stumbles upon it and draws the wrong conclusions—or the right ones. None of us should want this shining moment of Fae pride advertised. Got all that? Superb, be seeing you by-and-by."

Hafgan turned to Helgar and Llew. "As for you lads, you got that Addfwyn character parked somewhere around here?"

"He is with the rest of the horses," Llew replied.

"Good, let me walk you to your horses then. Besides, I think he owes me money."

Helgar looked up at that. "Addfwyn? Are you certain?"

Hafgan shook his head, "Not at all, I just said that in jest. Actually, I think you are the only one that does."

"What! Who owes who?" Helgar exclaimed. "We said we would split the last round and someone that was not me—well, short he was and someone much taller covered it!"

Hafgan frowned. "That sounded suspiciously like a short joke. Llew, are you teaching him bad habits?"

Maintaining a straight face, Llew replied, "Not I! You taught him enough for the both of us."

Once they were out of earshot of the hunt's survivors. Hafgan half turned to Llew and shook his index finger at him. "You see now why we Spriggans do not care to be put in the same bucket with those twisty Fae? Not a one of them is right in the head."

"What was all that about concordances and such?" Llew demanded. "Despite all that pomp and fury, the master of the Hunt behaved like a village thief caught with his hand in his lord's coin purse. And what are you doing here? And why did you save him?"

"My goodness, lad, three questions all at once, just boom, bang, slap! No hint of payment for answers either. Is that the way of it with young people these days? Just demand whatever they want and with never a thought of recompense?"

"I think we are a little past that, Hafgan. Now, do you need me to ask them again or has your memory slipped away in your dotage?"

Hafgan affected a hurt look. "Ah lad, it is like that is it? Of course I remember. Fae are the ones with odd memories; they seem to forget whatever they find inconvenient. Such as that, under their agreement with High Queen Boudicca, they are not permitted to hunt mortal men without either dispensation or legitimate cause. After a few wars, with High King Math trouncing them each time, they agreed to put some teeth in the rules on how folks that violated the covenant would be dealt with. The punishments really are quite unpleasant. All the same, these Fae still seem to forget all about them when they think they can get away with it. The master of the Hunt failed to get away with it. Funny thing about Fae, they will fight and die for a point of honor only they can understand, yet catch them lying or breaking rules they have committed to and they will rollover and show you their belly like a beaten hound. Stranger still, that one probably will not even bear you any ill will over this; he may even be happy with you for letting him off so cheaply."

"Why was he so subservient to you then? You are king of the Spriggans; are the . . . what did Cymri call them again? Tylwyth Teg? Are they sworn to you as well?"

"Gah, lad, I still had two questions to go and here you are asking another!"

"My apologies."

"Accepted, and no, of course they are not sworn to me. They are far more likely to swear at me. I have told you about Spriggans though. We do not like oath-breakers and take it upon ourselves to communicate that dislike to others—and no one wants to be on the wrong side of a bunch of Spriggans. I have also told you what we do when brute force is not working, have I not?"

"I seem to recall," Llew said, "that when that happens your tendency is to use more of it."

"Too right!" affirmed Hafgan. "As for what I am doing here, well, this is a bit delicate but we also guard barrows and someone opened up one to the south just two days ago. One of my boys followed the trail of the perpetrators and it led straight to you. It is our good luck he is a politic fellow. When he found out who you were, instead of dealing with you himself, he had word sent to me and here I am."

"I can explain, and we did not take anything!" Llew protested.

Hafgan humphed. "That is what they all say."

Llew opened his mouth to make a retort and Hafgan cut

him off, holding up his hands placatingly. "Easy, lad, I did not say you would not be the first to be correct on both counts. As for why I saved some of the huntsmen from what it looked like you were about to do to them? Do you have any idea how long it would take to train up a whole new bunch for the Wild Hunt? Decades, and that is a fact! Meantime, who is doing all the things they are supposed to be doing? Just because you ran afoul of them does not mean the world would be a better place in their absence. You just have no idea what a mess things would soon be in if they were not out there taking care of business. One of the few cases where the Fae are actually a good thing."

Hafgan pursed his lips. "Just how did you get Mab so annoyed with you, anyway?"

"Cymri turned her into a black bird with her own wand."

"Yep, that would do it," he said, nodding knowingly. "Still and all, it sounds like a pretty good trick. So that means she is with you? Where is that freckled lass?"

"If you mean me then the answer is 'here I am' and now you can tell me why you asked," announced Cymri stepping out of the trees from one side of the trail.

Hafgan pretended to be hurt. "Ah, lass. Is it not enough that I have missed you? Very well then," he continued, suddenly appearing in good spirits again. "It may be that I just wanted to make sure these lads had a bit of adult supervision."

Cymri gave Llew a meaningful look and Llew rolled his eyes.

"Although I would really have to wonder what kind of example you are setting for them if you are running about turning queens into birds."

"She started it," said Cymri, darkly.

"No doubt, no doubt," Hafgan demurred as they arrived at where the horses had been tethered. "Ah, Addfwyn, good to see you again. Nice to see you have taken on some help and no longer have to tend to this entire lot by yourself."

"Greetings to you as well, your majesty." Addfwyn said respectfully, not showing the least bit of surprise at the Spriggan king's unexpected presence. "But this is not my helper; this is Prince Caradog of Gwynedd."

"Your majesty," Caradog greeted him.

Hafgan gave a quick nod to Caradog then frowned at Addfwyn. "So they are doing it again. We have what? Four royals, well, five if we count Gower, and no one but you in their train? Can the dogs at least give you a hand gathering firewood and taking turns on the cooking?"

"I am afraid they are the wrong breed for that, your highness."

"Ah, that is a pity," replied Hafgan. He regarded the rest of the party. "So, any reason why you people are playing at being 'working royalty' again?"

There was a moment of silence, then Llew said, "It will take some time to explain and I can grant you anything but time. If you care to camp with us tonight we can give it all to you as we travel tomorrow. We are heading for the Fae stone where the Elwys river meets the Clwyd."

Hafgan thought about it a moment. "That might be entertaining enough to justify the trip. In any case, you will need me to help find the thing as that is not exactly high ground there. More to the point, that stone is probably under six feet of mud by now."

* * *

They were nearing where the rivers met, early the next afternoon, before Hafgan had heard the entire story and clarified what questions he had concerning certain points.

He closed one eye while tilting his face and squinted, as if to scrutinize Llew extra closely. Then he gave it up. "Nope, still cannot see you. I kind of thought you would be coming to grips with who you really are by now."

"Verily, King Hafgan, you cannot see Llew at all?" Caradog asked.

"Nay, lad. Spriggans see things, not as they are, nor as they appear, but as they see themselves. In most cases this makes no never mind as, in the case of a stone, for example, all three are normally the same."

Wait," objected Caradog, "a stone has a way of seeing itself? It has neither eyes nor a mind."

"Correct on both counts, lad, but everything, even a stone, has a certain sense of awareness. If you rolled it into a fire, say, and the heat caused a crack in it, would not that crack be a kind of memory? In its own way, the stone is now forever aware that it was once rolled into a very hot place. Or it could just have a bit of soot on it and, when that soot has worn away, the stone will have lost all awareness that it was ever in a fire."

"As you say," said Caradog, dubiously.

"To go on," continued Hafgan, "we Spriggans find it is usually a tremendous advantage to be able to see things as they see themselves, but we have never seen—er, not seen, as the case may be—a being less aware of who he is than our Llew. Speaking of which, you can call me Hafgan. I get little enough respect as it is and it seems silly to start now."

"You say that I am still not at all aware of who I am?

Surely that is not right," objected Llew. "King Auberon told me who and what I am. As the highest of the Fae it seems unlikely he would lie to my face and before witnesses, mortal or not. Is there anyone, anywhere, less likely to lie, even to their enemies?"

Hafgan frowned. "No, you have the right of it there. Even I have been known to let slip an occasional bit of whimsical speaking—all in jest, you understand, but one such as he would lose much dignity were he caught in such an exaggeration. Nonetheless, think back carefully on precisely what he told you. Just as he may be the least likely amongst all the Fae to tell a fib, he is the wiliest of them all. That makes him the best able to speak the truth to his own purpose and make others believe as he wishes."

"I cannot believe that leaves us mere mortals no means of seeing through the webs of such as he," Llew said flatly.

"Well," said Hafgan, "it helps to have some experience in dealing with these shifty Fae. Your best hope in discerning the truth is to create a kind of shadow image of what they have told you and what you already know. Then, instead of looking at it, you must look where it does not cover, then do what you can to cover those places as well. Their strategy is, after all, to distract you from looking at those parts at all, completely absorbed in what they have shown you."

"For example?" Llew asked.

"Take what he told you and see what it really covers; it is probably less that you would first think in some areas. Then we see if some parts of it can be used to assemble something that reveals a bit more than what he actually said."

Seeing his audience still looked blank, Hafgan continued, "Here we go then. He told you that you have Fae blood, but it is less than a quarter. Since we know you are not some strange beastie out of the Wild Growth, we know that you are a mortal man.

"He also said that, as a babe, you were taken by the Fae and a changeling left in your place. You share a father with that changeling but, unlike you, the changeling was a son of Queen Mab. Still, that means you are half-brothers. Do you notice anything missing there?"

Llew shook his head. "It seems clear enough, although I confess I am having a difficult time imagining my father having a dalliance with Queen Mab."

"Oh, as to that, do not forget she is Fae. She could have come to him in the form of your own mother and how would he have known the difference? You must not blame him."

Llew allowed himself a relieved sigh. "It is good of you to point that out. I was beginning to feel rather disillusioned. Our liege has never seemed one who would knowingly engage in adultery. If there is even the slightest prospect that he was without knowledge of this then I would have it so. In truth, I would just as lief never speak of it again."

"Ah, and there you show how Auberon shaped your thoughts with you none the wiser," Hafgan declared.

"Whatever do you mean?" Llew asked, thoroughly confused.

Hafgan looked around at the rest of the travelers. "Anyone else see it?"

"Ah," blurted Caradog, "King Auberon never said that the father of the two was King Pendaran."

Hafgan chortled. "Got it in one."

"What?" cried Llew. "What are you two saying?"

The Spriggan king held up his hand, palm out. "Do not read too much into it, lad. He did not say King Pendaran was *not* your father, yet neither did he say King Pendaran was your father. At least not in so many words. It smacks of misdirection. Let us move on. The exchange was carried out under King Auberon's orders on behalf of a mortal."

"A mortal? He did not say that it was for a mortal," Llew corrected.

"He did not say it was done at the behest of a mortal but, had it not been, then that would have been a violation of Boudicca's Covenant; he is too wily to risk being caught at that."

"Then I think we can safely assume it was Moriganna," said Llew. "Assuming anything that old that does not die still counts as mortal."

"Aye, she still counts as mortal, lad. Short of ascending to godhood, she always will."

Llew shuddered, "Now there is a thought."

Hafgan ignored that and continued. "Now he did tell you why the changeling had to be Mab's child. It had, however, nothing to do with her and everything to do with the father. Because of a shared father, and a bit of fate, the child closely resembled you. This was necessary because it was Lord Arawen plotting against you and he would not have been fooled by a changeling's illusion. Even if he is not Tylwyth Teg, he is still Fae, or something else that sees right through Fae illusions.

"So Moriganna—if it was indeed her—thought to save you and was able to persuade King Auberon to give up Mab's child to do it. Either she made Auberon an offer he could not refuse, or he is allied with her. For whatever reason, they spared you from the changeling's fate."

Llew tried to follow the threads. "It seems to fit. Yet it still begs the question of why it was so important to save me that Queen Mab's own child became expendable. Moriganna might not care who she sacrificed in order to place her own candidate, usurper or otherwise, on the throne of Gwent—but surely her desire would not have been sufficient impetus for King Auberon to save me?"

Hafgan gave him a sober look. "Have you stopped to think what things might be like for the Fae if Arawen destroys Tethera? Trapped in their own otherworlds, they would eventually be overrun themselves. They are not great ones for planning ahead but I would wager that thought has at least crossed Auberon's mind, although probably not Mab's. They need Tethera to win and that means they need you."

"If that was important to them then surely they could find another way," Llew objected.

"Do not be too sure of that, laddie; when prophecies are involved, and they surely are, then even the Fae can find their options limited. The whole thing is bothersome and the pieces do not quite seem to fit as closely as they might, once you examine them. That is a sure indication old Auberon was holding back on things we need to know.

"Odder still, Auberon is a fickle ally at best, but he has saved you three times now. Once by using Mab's child to save you from Lord Arawen. Once when he managed to sneak you out as an infant after you had been exchanged for your half-brother, and then again just this past day. Whether she was changed into a bird or not, there in his own demesne he could have prevented your escape and held you for her but, by not doing that, he let you escape."

Llew frowned. "That is right, is it not? Mab wanted to keep me when I was an infant but he found a way to smuggle me out of Tir-Na-Nog. I suspect it was as a changeling for someone else's child. That would explain why he only said I did not start as a changeling, not that I was not one. Perhaps it was for the stable master's child at Caer Mallcoedwig. While I do not remember his wife at all—I only barely remember him—yet, while he lived, I never doubted he was my father. If I was the changeling exchanged for his own son, why then, neither one of us would have known otherwise."

"This would be an interestingly backward take on things. Usually they leave changelings because they want a human babe instead of some Fae crossbreed," Hafgan said, as he scratched his head. "In your case it sounds like they would have been willing to toss the baby out with the bathwater as what they really wanted was to place a changeling."

"Of course," remarked Llew, "if that is true then I have to wonder where the real Gwri is."

Hafgan humphed. "If they took him then they are raising him as one of their own. They like to do that. Do not get any ideas about rescuing him though. They would treat him like royalty. Back here he would be an orphaned stable boy. Besides which, by now he would be more Fae than human—in mind if not in body—and he would not welcome the attempt, not even if you were to offer him a human kingdom."

Helgar raised his voice then. "Llew, have you forgotten what Garl said? Moriganna sent her own men to make the exchange for Llewellyn's brother. This they did. Then they were captured and Garl made them his. They still took you to her but they told her you were the changeling. It seems very much like luck you were not left in the forest to die as Arawen must have intended."

Llew grasped at his own head with both hands. "Enough! As Hafgan said, we are, perhaps, still missing pieces and are beginning to double and triple think ourselves."

"It is still progress, lad. Let me know when you have it figured out. Those of us with minds that like to inquire would like to know. Ah, and here we are."

As Hafgan had predicted, the Fae stone was covered in several feet of mud. Fortunately, he was able to show them precisely where it was and they soon had it relatively clear. The stone itself was unremarkable in appearance. So far as any anyone could tell, it was just a large flat slab of rock and had no runes or carving on it. The mud had to be cleared around it for a short distance as it had an unfortunate tendency to begin flowing back into the hole, given a few moments to do so but, as Caradog pointed out, they did not have to keep it uncovered longer than it took to stand upon it. The instant it was clear, Llew did precisely that.

As soon as he stepped onto it, he had the oddest feeling. It was as though, in some way he could not readily describe, part of his mind now had its attention diverted in some other direction from the rest of his thoughts. In another way it was almost like something was in his peripheral vision yet somehow stayed there, in his peripheral vision, even as he moved his attention to it. In a sense, he could see it; he just could not focus on it. It was, he decided, quite distracting.

Except for Hafgan, the others looked at him anxiously as he stood there, trying to make sense of this new strangeness. After a full minute of inactivity, Helgar had to ask, "So? Work did it? Guiding us to Avalon is now possible?"

In answer, Llew raised his arm and pointed slightly west of due north. "That is where it is now, two hundred and twenty-three miles in that direction, as the crow flies."

"Suppose it moves while we are making our way to it?" Caradog inquired.

"That will not pose a problem. It does not move fast and, regardless of that, I am now able to feel where it is. Not where it was. We must now hope to procure a ship in the port of Rhyl, just a few miles further on."

"And this is where I must leave you fine folks," Hafgan announced with obvious regret. "There are things that must be done, and soon, and there is no one else to do them."

Llew's face fell. "Ah, must it be so, Hafgan? We have only just been reunited and, much as Helgar might deny it, I am certain we were all hoping you could travel further with us than this." Helgar's eyebrows went up as Llew said this but he did not gainsay him.

With a rueful smile, Hafgan slapped Llew on the shoulder, something of a reach for him in his normal form. "Hey now, I will miss you all, too, lad, but it is just as well. I would be of no help to you. Spriggans do not do well with sea travel. In point of fact, leaving Tethera is not really something we can ever do; we are thoroughly bound to the land. This is but one of the ways in which we distinguish ourselves from those swervy Fae who still seek to count us in their number.

"I would still feel a bit guilty about skipping out on you while you have so much on your plate but, to hear your account, you have the worst of your quest done. All that seems to remain is a short voyage to Avalon and then a quick meeting with this would-be bandit lord Cai. Whether you retrieve the torc or not, I would wager you will make short work of him!"

Chapter XVII

Voyage to Avalon

Three days later they got their first sight of the fabled Isle of Avalon.

By great good luck they had found a well-appointed ship by the docks at Rhyl that was actually built for travel on open seas, as opposed to simple coastal traffic. A rarity in Tethera, it was Northman built and of a type Helgar called a knarr. Better still, Helgar had actual experience crewing knerrir. Found wrecked along the coast after a storm, it had been rescued and restored, before seeing heavy service as a coastal cargo ship. Nearly forty feet long and clinker built, its interior was completely open to the elements, with two half decks to either side of a central cargo area. Helgar admitted that, for a knar, it was a bit on the small side.

He laughed before commenting, "I think maybe its father was a knarr but its mother, she was a karve." After Helgar said this, the rest of them looked at each other blankly. Was this Northman humor or sea-faring humor? None could say.

With a single mast and a square sail, the little ship was designed to be operated primarily by sail. This was especially fortunate as it was currently without crew or master, and there was simply no way they could have hoped to get by had it depended on oars.

From his days of assisting Braen at the stables in Caer Mallcoedwig, Llew was no stranger to bargaining. He purchased the ship for a good price, despite taking pity on the local shipwright who owned it. He deliberately avoided pressing as hard on the price as he thought he could have. Despite the economy involved in moving by water, many people had become very chary of venturing onto ocean waters, even when they were staying within sight of the coast, and this was probably why the ship was currently not in use. Further, Llew was offering coin and, due to their difficulties, the people of Clwyd valued cold hard coin far more than in other kingdoms. For all of that, when they attempted to hire a few deckhands, offering high pay for a few days service, there were none available at any price, not once the sailors learned their intended course would take them out of sight of land.

"Good such a small one she is," Helgar remarked to Llew, upon hearing this. "Normally, a ship like this, she would be a fair bit longer, and need at least ten men as crew. Since we have but five it will be difficult enough as it is, especially to hoist sail."

Cymri and Caradog, meanwhile, had arranged with a local sail-maker, all but unemployed in his primary capacity these days, to have a reasonable facsimile of the royal banner of Gwent available first thing the next morning.

Addfwyn arranged for the horses to be pastured until they returned, leaving strict instructions not to approach or hinder the big stallion in any way whatsoever. Llew had never been separated from Gower before and found himself at a loss as to how he felt about that, but he took some solace from the fact that there probably was not another horse anywhere that would be better at seeing to its own safety.

Their remaining daylight hours were spent purchasing and loading such supplies as they might need for an early morning departure. Usually prone to be rather casual about most matters, Helgar suddenly became very particular on where things were stowed, and how they were secured, after Llew named him captain.

As promised, with the banner flying from the mast, the weather favored them and it was a good thing it did. For all of his experience, Helgar was not a sea captain by trade and, of the rest of them, only Addfwyn had any experience at all on sailing vessels. Llew wondered briefly where he had come by it, then forbore to ask.

Despite knowing precisely where they were going and having favorable winds, their own inexperience, and the strange way the ship often had to run at an angle in order to move closer to its objective—Helgar called it tacking—two nights passed at sea before what they sought appeared off the port bow. Llew privately called it the left forward side but was willing to indulge Helgar's nomenclature.

Avalon itself was impressive enough. Although not a large island, the front presented high cliffs that were surmounted by a rough and wild looking plateau. This sloped gradually upwards until it reached bordering mountains on the opposite side.

Helgar chewed on his lip as he surveyed it. "Llew, I am seeing no place to go ashore. There is no quay visible anywhere, not even a beach where we might at least ground her."

"Nor will you find any as there are none," Cymri announced. "There should, however, be a narrow break in the cliff just to the left of the island's center, if we enter it carefully we should be able to find a second break to the right that will eventually take us into a hidden cove, almost a cave with the overhanging rock, but high enough that, if we are careful, we should not even have to unstep the mast."

"That is a good thing," Helgar declared, "because there is not likely to be any of the facilities we would need here for taking down the mast—even less, I think, for putting it back up again. What is in this cove?"

"A stone jetty, I am led to believe. From there, we should be able to gain access to the rest of the island."

Llew whistled, "That certainly sounds as though it would be a better alternative to swimming up and attempting to climb those cliffs."

Caradog laughed at that. "I think most anything would."

The first break in the cliff was anything but easy to find. Even from a few ship lengths away it was difficult to see. After that, it was just as Cymri had described. Within an hour they found the quay. It was built of aged stone and covered in many layers of barnacles where the tidewater reached. There was no indication that it had been used in decades, or even centuries. The end that met the cliff wall was so sheltered as to be something of a cave. It was there that a tunnel, cut through living rock, was floored with wide stairs leading upward. Deep indentations in the stone steps indicated that at one time they had seen heavy traffic. Caradog set the dogs to guard the ship while Addfwyn passed out lit torches. Then they made their way up the stairs in the tunnel.

They traipsed upwards for a considerable time, taking only occasional breaks to rest. During one of these, Llew motioned everyone to be silent. Then he bent his ear to what might be heard. It took a moment, then from a far distance above he heard it. "Music!" he told the others. "I hear music, quite well played. It is not what you might expect here—if you were to expect music at all. It has a peaceful and decidedly glad note to it."

"That is a good thing, is it not?" Caradog asked. "If people still dwell here they might know something of King Bran."

"If they are people," remarked Cymri.

"Ya, if they are even alive," was Helgar's contribution.

"My, we are an optimistic crew, are we not?" complained Caradog.

The stairs ended as they emerged into a marble pavilion. The stonework was utterly without flaw, looking as though it had just been quarried and polished on the previous day. Light furniture was present, as were long gauzy curtains in bright shades of red and green. On a low table, a sampling of food had been laid out that included grapes, both white and red, and a variety of cheeses, sliced into small thin shapes and garnished with fresh herbs. Wine cups were also present, along with uncorked, yet quite full, bottles of wine.

"Well," exclaimed Helgar, "it looks as though they know how to greet guests," and made for the table. Cymri held up one hand and shook her head in the negative, indicating they should leave it alone.

"Until we know more, we should not chance the local food. It will not do us physical harm but we do not know what other effects it might have."

Llew pushed aside a curtain and looked out on carefully manicured gardens and lawns that stretched off into the distance. A variety of flowers were in bloom, although no gardeners were in sight. Marbled paths ran through the flowers and between the carefully planted and pruned shrubs. Here and there he could see artfully placed pools of water, as well as fountains throwing water into the air in diverse and complicated patterns. He signaled the party for silence then set himself to listen. Specifically, he wanted to find out where the music was coming from. After a moment he turned to the others, amazement writ large on his face. "This music, it comes from nowhere and everywhere. It has no specific source."

Cymri laughed. "Are we really surprised to find magic at work on an enchanted island that floats about the sea?"

"Magical or not," Llew said, "I cannot even perceive how that is possible, for it seems to contravene all logic."

No one else said anything until Helgar came and looked out with him. He gaped a bit, then said, "Llew, we saw this from down below, it was just wildness and rocks."

"Can we go out? There seems little point in stealth. All indications are that we have been anticipated," Caradog pointed out.

Llew had to concur. As a group they moved out of the pavilion and down the few steps to a nearby path. "There is a large central structure," he pointed out, "It looks something like what a castle might look like if it were made all of marble and with no concern at all for defense, only aesthetics. If we are to learn anything then that is surely where we should start."

The others assented and they moved towards it. At one point, while passing over an elevated area of terraces above a large square pool of water, they had an especially good view of the sea. Caradog shaded his eyes with one hand and scanned the water below. "I wonder," he ventured, "had we left our ship anchored offshore, do you suppose we would actually see it from here? I mean, we could, normally, but I think the top of this island is not in the same place as the bottom."

"Aye," agreed Helgar, "it is an otherworld, like where the Fae lived. Could it be the same one?"

Llew shook his head in the negative. "No, I do not think so, it feels different. Just being here seems to invigorate me and make me feel . . . pleased, this despite the fact I was, just recently, worried about how little time remains before we meet Cai, even if it must be empty-handed."

Cymri gestured to a line of apple trees, heavily laden with fruit, extending down one side of the garden before the pool. "That is fitting. This is Avalon. It is a place for healing and rest and it was enchanted even before the Fae cast their first spell. If the old stories I have heard hold true, we could neither fight nor do any harm here, even were that our intent. No force may be used against others here, nor can they be harmed in any way."

Helgar snorted. "Small wonder Hafgan found himself unable to accompany us. He would not know what to do in such a place where brute force could not prevail." Upon his saying this, everyone turned and looked at him.

"What?" the Northman asked. "What did I say?"

They reached the central structure, a blend of pavilion and palace. As they made their way in, so gradual was the change between plantings, trees, lattices, and vines that it became impossible to truly tell when they ceased to be outside and were, instead, inside. Of the construction and the furnishings, it was difficult to believe that all the craftsmen in Tethera, working together, could have accomplished such a wonder in less than a century or two. Further adding to the inexplicable nature of this place was that, while seemingly bereft of any inhabitants, it all looked as though it had only been completed mere hours before they had entered.

The music continued everywhere they went, never overly

loud but present, nonetheless. It distracted the senses, and it was for this reason that Llew had no warning when, upon entering a great hall towards the center of the palace, they came upon the others.

A dozen men stood around a great table, laden with a feast, making a toast. On a raised dais at one end sat a throne wrought of countless gold wires of varying widths to somehow convey a representation of an apple tree. A giant of a man wearing a crown of gold sat atop the throne. Although he had not risen with the others, he laughed with them as one of them inadvertently slopped his wine in the process of clinking it against the others.

"Have a care, Barris, you must realize wine does not grow on trees," he admonished.

The men at the table thought this comment terrifically funny and burst into renewed laughter.

The men were all finely dressed and, although not in armor, wore swords in addition to their very fine clothing; they also looked as though they might be no strangers to using them. Still and all, Llew did not feel threatened—then mentally clubbed himself for forgetting what Cymri had said about conflict on the island being impossible. He entered the hall and strode forward. The men at the table looked up at him and seemed to see him and the others following, but none sought to rise. Instead, one called out, "Please, take seats and join us, there is assuredly plenty for all."

Llew frowned slightly at this. "But there are no more—" He had meant to point out there were no more chairs, for the table only sat twelve and twelve were already there yet, looking down to the table again, it was clear he had been in error. The table now held seats and settings for five more, yet he was certain that, just a moment before, the table had been shorter and had held no empty place settings.

Rules of hospitality applied and he should have sat and eaten with them but this was just too strange. The men at the table had gone back to making small talk with each other and were giving the intruders no further attention. Llew looked to the enormous man on the throne. By contrast, the laconic king had his eyes fixed upon them.

"Your majesty," Llew called to him, "I am Prince Llew and heir to the kingdom of Gwent. I know it may seem rude, and such is the farthest from my intention, but we have traveled far and time is quite short. May I approach and speak with you directly?"

"Aye," agreed the seated man, "that would be best, I believe. Your compatriots may sit and partake. The food is quite nourishing and safe. There are no side effects, either; this is not the land of the Fae. I suggest this because you and I do need to speak and I would as lief it was just the two of us for the moment."

Llew looked to his fellows and nodded once, then approached the figure on the throne.

"Greetings, young prince," said the throne's occupant, "I would rise to meet you but, as you may not yet have realized, I have only the use of my head. My arms and legs are as lead and no effort on my part may move them, indeed, I cannot even feel them."

"That is a great tragedy, and I am most unhappy to hear of it," replied Llew. Privately he was horrified, to be so trapped in his own body! He could scarcely imagine a worse fate. "Was this the result of some injury in battle then? You have the look of a fighting man."

"Ah," the king replied, "of a sort. We fought in a place

called Ayreland and their ways are not as ours. My opponents used a cruel poison on their arrows. I was struck in the leg and, as the poison worked its way up, it left each part of me paralyzed and useless. It would have reached my head in time, and I would surely have passed on, but one of my men knew of this place and brought me here. No sooner had they carried me up from the quay did the poison cease its cursed spread. Sadly, it has done nothing to restore what was lost and so I have remained for many years. But you . . . you say you are Prince Llew of Gwent?"

"So everyone tells me, your highness."

"That is remarkable—truly remarkable—you see, until you told me this, I supposed I was still king of Gwent. I presume people must think me dead and so have crowned my son in my place. That would make you my grandson, would it not?"

Chapter XVIII

An Exile on Avalon

"It is odd, though. You are a strapping lad but had not yet been born when I left. I would not have imagined I had been gone so long."

"Who are you?" breathed Llew. Although the room was at quite a pleasant temperature, he could feel gooseflesh rising on his arms.

"Oh, and where are my manners? Perhaps I have been gone a rather long time. I am King Bran of Gwent, although some simply refer to me as 'The Usurper' for overthrowing my liege lord, King Pwyl. It had to be done. He had gone quite mad and was intent on destroying everything he could, which includes rather a lot when one is high king. Indulge me; has my reputation eased with the passage of time?"

"King Bran?" asked Llew. "Truly?"

"Yes, it is most certainly I."

"You overthrew the mad king, Pwyl, and took the throne of Gwent yourself?" Llew heard himself inquiring.

"Yes, that is me. As I told you, it had to be done. I hated having to do it. Pwyl had once been my best friend before he changed so."

Llew slowly shook his head. "We came seeking only your barrow. We never imagined finding you alive. The events you speak of occurred almost precisely one full century before I was born."

King Bran sighed heavily. "Has it been that long then? It is impossible to keep track of time in such a place as this. One perfect day fades into another, and then another. I realize now I have feared something of the sort might occur. What purpose to live on and survive my doom if only to be forgotten in an enchanted paradise?"

Llew was not sure he could answer that and did not make the attempt.

The king looked up at Llew again. He stared hard, as if to take in every detail that Llew's person presented. "Perhaps you are aware that I was something of an enchanter. Although my powers were never enormous—there are far too many intrusions on a king's study time for that level of proficiency—I was still quite capable. Yet using no power save only my wit, I can already see two truths about you that you are not aware of."

"And what would those be?" Llew inquired, respectfully.

"The first is that you are not in my line of descent or, if you are it is only an incidental relationship—someone married a close cousin or some such thing."

"So," said Llew slowly, "there was some changeling nonsense going on around my birth. If what you say is true, then I am not the rightful heir of Gwent." After all this time, Llew did not know quite how to feel at this news. There was a sense of relief, coupled with a certain sadness, too.

"I did not say that," Bran retorted.

"Did not say what?"

"I only said that you were not of my line. The second thing I notice is that you are undeniably Boudicca's heir and I do not doubt you have every right to take the throne of Gwent and name yourself high king as well."

"How can that be true if I am not even my father's son?" Llew demanded.

"For now I will only assure you that what I have said is completely correct. If you want more I will employ the power of my third eye to see what more I may tell you. Before that, however, I would have you tell me why you came seeking me. I am certain there must be many more pressing things in your life."

As he had for Hafgan, Llew gave King Bran a summary of where things stood in the kingdoms and then another on Bloddeuwedd's kidnapping. When he was done, the ancient king pursed his lips and considered matters before speaking.

"So, young prince, you came this way on the odd chance that you might find my bony corpse and, around its neck, Math's Torc? I hate to disappoint you but I do not have it. I never did, and, if I did, I could not wear it. I am an usurper; do you not recall? I am not of the line of Boudicca and so could not have worn it; although you would have no such trouble. Ah, Cai did not tell you about that requirement, did he?"

"No, he most certainly did not," Llew said bitterly. "It certainly would have saved a lot of time if he had."

"You think coming to find me a total waste of your efforts then?"

"I did not say that," Llew protested, "although I must admit it has not proved to be an effective course towards rescuing Bloddeuwedd."

"Do not be so sure," said Bran. "As I said, I always had a bit of the second sight and it has become much stronger during my time in this place. I have also reviewed things with my third eye as you told your story and I believe we can do quite a bit for each other."

"And what would that be?"

"I tire of life in this place, of life like this, and would fain help you. I know you will take good care of my descendants that you spoke of, this Pendaran and Llewellyn. How I wish I could meet them, but that will never be for you must take me from here when you go. I will then tell you all you need know about the location of the torc and, also, how to buy time for poor beleaguered Clwyd."

Llew was aghast. "But you will die! You have said that it is only the powers of this place that prevent the poisons from passing up into your neck and then your head. Just tell me these things now. There is no need for you to leave. If fate is kind, Pendaran and Llewellyn may someday visit you here."

"Nay, Prince Llew, I wish it were so and I am glad you would have it thus, but it cannot be. My condition must stand, take me with you and I will aid you considerably, in life and in death."

"What of your men?"

Bran sighed. "Best to leave them here. They are good men and loyal, it is true, but, sadly, they refused to leave without me.

Only Neb ap Tew ever did, and it took all my eloquence to convince him to finally do so. I am glad to hear that he survived and did well. Although he is now long dead, I believe he fared far better than he would have here. A century of long life and total leisure without purpose has not been especially good for these men. They are no longer what they were; they have become more like poor copies of themselves, running through day after day and year after year, with the same amusements, the same feasts, and even the same conversations and japes. I do not believe they could function in the world of men any better than I could in my present state. They have no curiosity or drive and seem unable to even recognize or long recall that which is new in their experience. Their bodies cannot die or atrophy here, but I wonder if the same holds true for their minds?"

Llew shuddered. It came to him he would rather die than live on in such a state but, for them at least, it was not his call to make.

"Come," said Bran, "your companions have finished their meals. While I tell my men farewell, I would suggest you take some things to go, it is all quite good and safe, and then we should be on our way. You did indicate that speed was of the essence, did you not?"

Bran was a true giant. In his day he must have stood nearly eight feet tall and was built to scale. Surely he must have been a singularly dreadful opponent in battle, most likely being able to handle most opponents as though they were no stronger than children. Now, however, he was a very great burden to carry. Fortunately, his ancient companions still had their full strength, if not their mental acuity, and were well used to carrying him from one venue to another. With their help, King Bran was carried down to the quay and on to the ship. Cymri then shooed the confused men back up the steps to their eternal gardens.

After they descended the steps, it became increasingly clear that Bran could not last long, His color had become suffused with an awful gray pallor and his breathing grew more labored almost by the minute. Their little ship had barely cleared the reefs around the island before he called for Llew to attend him.

His face was now a thoroughly unhealthy shade of pale blue, and his speaking somewhat slurred, when Llew reached his side. "As you can see, Prince Llew, my time grows short indeed. Please listen well. You have in me the power to frustrate Annwyn and its dread lord, at least for a time. All you need do is take my body to Clwyd—the top of that hill where you defended their king seems a likely spot—and build a simple throne, loose stones will do. Seat my remains upon it so that I am looking towards the otherworld of Annwyn. Then cover me over with a great cairn of stones, but use no earth. Do this, and neither Lord Arawen, nor any of his creatures or enchantments, will be able to approach from that direction for a long time. That protection will last at least one year for every year that I lived beyond my time on yon island."

"Truly?" Llew asked. "Would the Lord of Death not then simply come at them from another direction? It will take much less than a century to do so."

"He assuredly will," Bran wheezed, "but it buys you time. He certainly will not be able to do it this year, and possibly not even the next. I must assume you will not waste this time."

"No," said Llew, "I certainly will not, but what of the torc? You said you knew something of its location?"

Bran smiled weakly. "I said I would tell you all about the location that you need know. Specifically, the torc was never found after I laid King Pwyl to rest. It has a way of disappearing when it is not in use. No one quite knows why. Perhaps it has gained a certain awareness of things itself, over time. In any case, when it is needed then that is where it will be. You see? You do not need to find it. If you truly need it and are meant to have it, why, then, it will come to you."

"I fear it will not," Llew replied. "We need it for Princess Bloddeuwedd's ransom. What chance the torc would consider that a valid reason to come to me?"

The king's voice was rapidly decreasing in audibility, and noticeable pauses were beginning to intrude between each word. "Chance does not enter into it, the torc will be there for you, of this much I am certain. From his coronation on, High King Pwyl wore it every day of his life and, although I never wore it, I know it well and will tell you this: it is not by chance that you already wear it about your neck."

Unbidden, Llew's hands flew to touch the heavy gold torc he had worn since defeating Goll One-Eye.

Bran managed a wan smile. "How else would I have known you are not of my line but still, every bit, Boudicca's heir?"

Llew had no words; no one did. Bran held their undivided attention.

"You have filled me with hope and given me a final chance to be of service to all I hold dear. I have no more observations, no more mystic revelations, but what little wisdom I have gained in my long life I now give to you, condensed as far as I can. If it is too much to remember, you may rely on your bard to recall every word. Write it down when you are able, then take what you need and add to it as you can."

He took a long, labored breath before speaking. "With chance you may always hope for the best, but you must plan for the worst. Most men find comfort in believing all is either black or white, but that is seldom true and they only hew to such odd beliefs because they fear and doubt their own decisions. You must be better than that; you must be the master of your own fears and doubts, always striving to find the best shade of gray. Of mercy, deliver enough to maintain your humanity, but not so much that you are judged weak. The perception of weakness in a king or a kingdom, whether true or not, will always have its cost measured in lives. It is not fair, but you must never expect fairness. Despite this, you must always attempt to be fair. Your people will accept much that is not perfect, so long as it is fair. Do not concern yourself with being perfect, or with creating that which is. Perfection is not a natural state for mortals and, as you saw on Avalon, in the long run it is not healthy for us. Know who your true friends are and have faith in them. Rule with wisdom, rule with strength, and do what you must to protect those who rely upon you. Above all, keep your eyes and ears open and question your every thought, yet trust yourself to do what needs doing." Toward the end he was speaking one word at a time, with ever longer pauses in between them.

Waves thudded rhythmically against the bow as the ship rose and fell. A cool salt breeze blew smartly against their faces and whipped across the sail. Bran's eyes rolled up to the azure sky, seasoned with only a sprinkling of small white clouds. High overhead, a pair of sea eagles soared and circled, riding the wind. Bran smiled again and this time there was nothing weak about it. "It is so good," he finally said, "to be back in the world of men," and then he died.

Chapter XIX

Raising the Shield

They arrived back in Rhyl to a scene of nearly overwhelming chaos.

As they approached, they could see the docks were covered in desperate people. Even before they could tie up, there were men crowding each other to get closer to the incoming ship. All of them were shouting out offers for ridiculous quantities of coin in exchange for passage—passage anywhere—if they were in earnest. Anywhere, that is, except Clwyd.

"It looks as though things have gone from bad to worse," remarked Helgar.

"Aye," Llew agreed, "hopefully we have come in time. We need to know more. See that fine fellow in blue directly in front of us? I would like to talk with him before we dock and risk being swamped by refugees."

Helgar grinned. "Easily done." He extended a hook on a pole, ostensibly to grasp the dock and pull them in, but then the

Northman apparently lost his footing during a swell. The hook fell sideways against the man in blue, hooking his clothing and tugging him into the chill waters.

"Oh no, Helgar, what have you done!" cried Llew, in mock alarm. "Haul that poor fellow out at once before he drowns or catches his death of cold."

This was done and in moments the sputtering man was aboard the ship. Vexation for the dunking warred with his sense of relief at being allowed to talk to them. "You must sell me passage for three, I can pay your normal fee one hundred times over, whatever it may be," he pleaded.

"Business after a moment," replied Llew, "first, what news? People had little interest in sea travel just a few days ago."

The man in blue hesitated before saying, "You do not know? Annwyn has commenced a full invasion. Their forces crossed the River Dee three days ago and there are so many of them that they were still crossing it as of yesterday afternoon. King Delwyn has achieved much, but—and no disrespect—this challenge is beyond him. Really, I can double my offer."

"What of Mold?" Llew asked tersely, "does it still stand?"

"We had no word it had fallen as of yesterday, but recall our news is at least a day old. I would say not yet as it is said the King means to offer battle before they get that far. That will slow them, at least somewhat. Once that is resolved, Mold will fall as quickly as the barrow warriors can march upon it, no more than a day later, certainly."

"I see," Llew said gravely, "then we must move now." He half turned to the others. "I am taking Helgar with me. As the next most able sailor, Addfwyn, you are now promoted to captain of this vessel and your charter is to load her with refugees and take her to Aber. Your priority is those whom you think would be least likely to survive walking to Gwynedd. Take as many as the ship will hold, regardless of ability to pay, bearing in mind you will need some capable of acting as your crew. Think of a good name for her while you are at it."

"My lord," Addfwyn protested, "my place is with you and I know little enough of sailing."

"You pledged to serve me and this is the service I currently need from you. As for your skills, it is clear that, other than Helgar, you know more of sailing than the rest of us put together and will get the job done. If nothing else, you will still have the good winds at your back. Your real job, however, is to bring word to Queen Enid and our own emissary—what was his name?"

"Prothos, your highness, it was Lord Prothos. What should I tell them?"

Llew considered before saying, "Tell them what we have done, and what we intend to do. Tell them I have the torc, but do not mention my uncertain parentage. Tell them that the bandit Cai and King Gronw are one and the same. By the time you do, this will all be over. If we succeed then the news is moot, yet should we fail then they need to know, if for no other reason than so they might yet salvage what they can of the situation."

Rather than risk the ship being mobbed at the quay, they contracted with a pair of fishermen to ferry passengers aboard and to take Llew, Helgar, Cymri, Caradog, and the late King Bran, the last wrapped tightly in sailcloth, to shore. A giant of a man, it then took all four of them to carry him to the pasture where the horses were being kept. There was no sign of the farmer that had been keeping them and it was probably good Gower had been guarding the other horses or they might not have been there either. Fortunately, too, the king of all horses had not yet found it necessary to hurt anyone in their defense. As Gower was the only horse that could carry King Bran's body without difficulty, Llew was forced to ride Addfwyn's mount.

"No disrespect intended," said Caradog, "but it is a pity we do not merely need the head." Llew did not comment on that although he had already had a similar thought himself. In a matter of minutes they were retracing their route to the eastern battlefield.

* * *

They arrived the next day to find the armies of Clwyd and Annwyn once again drawn up in the valley below. It was immediately clear this would be no replay of the earlier battle. The forces of Annwyn completely carpeted their end of the valley and more were still marching in. They had simply to engulf Clwyd in all their numbers in order to triumph here.

Llew and his companions reached the top of the hill and found it empty, save for the piles of stone safeguarding the remains of the men who had died there. Llew was mildly surprised. He had half expected King Delwyn to have his command there again. It was difficult finding loose rocks until they realized they could "borrow" from the graves already there. In fairly short order they had piled up enough to create a rude pile shaped vaguely like a throne. They then unwrapped King Bran's body and prepared to situate it on the makeshift throne, facing in the direction of Annwyn, precisely as he had described.

The noise from the massing troops below masked the sound of galloping hooves from Llew until they were very nearly upon them. He turned, expecting riders from Clwyd's forces come to see what they were up to. It was with a shock that he saw the half a dozen riders were not wearing Clwyd's colors. These were men who rode black horses and had covered their entire bodies, including their faces, with thick leather armor. That they carried no identifying pennants or other markings made it clear enough where their loyalties lay. Seeing Llew and company they drew swords and charged.

Helgar reached for his axe and scrambled to meet them, when he felt Llew's hand clasped on his arm. "No, my friend, one thing at a time. Help me with him."

Swearing in frustration, Helgar grabbed one of King Bran's arms while Llew took the other. Together, they half lifted him, half dragged him, to the throne of stone and set him heavily upon it.

Llew had been a bit hazy on what would happen next. Would King Bran's presence drive away all of those sworn to Lord Arawen, or just things that required enchantment, such as the barrow warriors? Would it work quickly or slowly? Would there be a certain delay before it began to be effective? The answers to these questions were suddenly very relevant to the situation at hand!

There was no cover of any sort on the hilltop, save behind the throne itself. "Stay behind the throne and defend Caradog," Llew ordered Cymri as he and Helgar seized up their weapons and mounted their horses. The instant they were in the saddle they both charged straight at the oncoming riders. They had barely begun to build up speed when their foe's horses stopped and began going wild, bucking and rearing, while their riders dropped their weapons and tried to hold on for all they were worth. One failed and was thrown from his saddle, landing heavily on a large stone. The others succeeded in wheeling their recalcitrant steeds and charged back down the hill, although perhaps only because that was the direction the animals insisted on.

Llew glanced at Helgar, then back at Cymri and Caradog, "Scary fellows we be, eh?"

"Aye," Helgar affirmed, "but share credit with King Bran

we should. Look below."

Cymri and Caradog advanced to their position and the four of them regarded the valley below. The vast enemy army was in far worse than a state of disarray. It was in a complete panic. Everywhere the men and creatures were dropping weapons and attempting to flee to the east. Many died as they fell, trampled under the innumerable feet and hooves of their own fellows. The Clwyd commander—and Llew thought he could see King Delwyn's banner in the center front—was not stopping to ask questions. He was advancing at full speed to slaughter the rearmost and pursue the rest.

"There are still too many," remarked Cymri. "They will pay a terrible price in sheer numbers, but their numbers are so great that most will escape back to Annwyn."

"They will not be coming again this season or even next, though," said Llew, thoughtfully. "It will take at least that long to rearm the survivors. Once they have, they still will not be coming this way. They will have to keep to the south and attack through Powys or Gwent before they can come again on foot, at least so long as Bran's aura repels them from this approach."

"Oh no," exclaimed Caradog, "we still have to cover him completely with more stones to make a great cairn. That will take forever!"

This time, Llew heard the galloping hooves in advance, he walked to the south side of the hill and looked down. "Right on cue, Caradog, well done."

Subaltern Ian and two dozen mounted warriors crested the hill.

Sometime later, while his men were still reverently placing stones over King Bran's body, Subaltern Ian asked, "So, Prince

Llew, what will you do for your next trick?"

"Now," Llew announced, "we are going to go rescue a fair damsel."

"Ya," agreed Helgar, "and toss a bandit off a cliff if we are lucky. I think it is my turn."

"Hullo, and what is this?" Caradog asked. The others looked and saw that he had pulled the leather helmet and face guard off of the fallen rider. Llew walked over to take a closer look and the others followed."

"Ugh," said Llew. "Well, I can tell you it is not a barrow warrior. It makes them look almost handsome by comparison. Barrow warriors do not ride horses, either. Even if the horse would put up with it, it is beyond their remaining ability."

Cymri took a quick glance. "It is a Cyhyraeth."

"That might be what it is called, but what is it?" Caradog asked.

"In ancient times there was a tribe of men that feared death far more than any mortal should. So terrible was their fear that, in an effort to evade the ravages of old age, they swore a dark bargain with . . . something. In exchange for this, their minds and bodies would never weaken and fail due to the ravages of age; time would have no power to bring them down. They somehow thought this would make them into immortals. It did not, of course. That is a line not so easily crossed. They did not realize they had only purchased immunity from death by old age, and there are many other ways to die. Worse, although they remain strong, they still age. Ever see what a man would look like, still alive, after thousands of years of aging? Now you have. Given their appearance, the ancient crimes they committed to fulfill their end of the pact, and their cruel, selfish natures, it is hardly surprising that the Lord of Death would include what survives of them in his ranks."

Helgar shuddered with revulsion. "I side with Llew. Even barrow warriors I would rather have than these. I thank the fates that their cursed bargain does not prevent them from dying of a smashed skull."

"What was their end of that bargain?" asked Caradog.

Cymri shook her head slowly from side to side. "We no longer know what price they paid and are glad of that. Whatever it was, it was so blackly evil they can no longer claim a seat at the table of mankind. Indeed, since that time they have ever been killed on sight by all who recognized them, and many who did not. Unfortunately, killing them is not easy to do; they have had a long time to master many skills and will seek to evade death by every means imaginable."

Llew placed one hand on the subaltern's shoulder. "Ian, our time is limited and we must be off at once. Please give King Delwyn my regards and tell him that I look forward to greeting him at Caerleon on my coronation day, whenever that may be, or your father, or you, should it come to that."

Subaltern Ian regarded Llew soberly, then grinned. "I look forward to it, Prince Llew." His expression abruptly changed to one of surprise. "Things have been so grim here that I believe that is the first time in a long time that I have said I was looking forward to something and really meant it! Thank you all for that."

Chapter XX

A Mother's Meeting

As they set up their camp, Caradog remarked, "Tomorrow is twenty-one days, Llew, somehow it seems more like twenty-one years, does it not?"

"In some ways, yes. On the other hand, it has been a rather busy time and that makes the time go by faster," Llew replied, as he tossed another branch onto the fire. "Still and all, we are in here in time to get a good rest tonight, then less than two hours travel in the morning and we will be there."

"So, how are we going to do this tomorrow?" the younger prince asked.

"We," said Llew, with extra emphasis on the word, "are going to leave you with the horses at the ruins of an old castle that I am told is about two miles away from the standing stones that Cai mentioned. The horses are important. You must keep them ready, for we may need to leave in a hurry."

It was clear Caradog wanted to complain at being left

behind with the horses yet again, but he did not. He knew his was an important task, even if it was not the one he would have chosen. Someone had to do it and there was little question that Cymri and Helgar would be of more use should fighting break out at the exchange.

"Cymri and Helgar will hide nearby, but will do nothing until Cai makes his move. If he accepts the torc and releases Bloddeuwedd to us then we will allow him to depart freely with his payment, for now. We will deliver his final payment on another day. Still, I see scant chance of that occurring; he must know that Bloddeuwedd, at the very least, knows him as King Gronw. I cannot imagine that he will forfeit his kingdom willingly to let her come away with me. Whether he does or not, we get Bloddeuwedd, by fair means or foul, then we meet back here and we all ride away, happily ever after."

"I like the happily ever after part," Cymri said. "Can I use that when I compose the ballad?"

"I hope you can," Llew replied earnestly.

Cilgwri came winging in with a single loud caw. Weapons were out and they were all scanning for danger before the bird landed on Llew's shoulder.

"I see him," said Helgar, "it is a rider on the trail to the east. He is not moving, just sitting there on his horse." They all saw him then. Cymri placed one hand above her eyes and squinted. "Is that not Meirion? Cai's lieutenant? Why would he come here alone?"

"Perhaps," Llew suggested, "he wishes to switch sides, but more likely he has some additional instructions for us. I am alarmed he knew which way we were coming from, and how far to ride to find us."

Meirion dismounted and drove a spear into the ground where he stood. He then drew out a streaming piece of cloth and tied it to the top of the upright spear.

"Either way, he seems to want to speak with us," Llew said. "Very well, he is quite a dangerous fellow but I doubt he is a match for all of us. If he wishes to parley we may as well see what he came all this way to say. Caradog, would you mind?"

The prince of Gwynedd sighed resignedly. "No, Llew, I will stay with the horses."

Llew flashed him a quick smile and said, "Good man."

Flanked by Cymri and Helgar, Llew approached within a hundred paces before calling out, "Good evening, Lieutenant, it is a fine evening for a ride, but I do hope you were not planning to ask for hospitality at our fire."

"In truth I was not," Meirion called back, "as you can see, I am only here to speak with you and nothing more. I want your word we will do only that, and that, after we have done so, we will both go our own ways in peace."

"Why would I want to do that?" called Llew. "I would as lief have your head as speak with you."

"My head would tell you nothing you wish to know and bring you nothing you wish to have. Instead I would tell you things which may aid you tomorrow. These are not things Cai would wish you to know, for he and I are done."

Llew looked to his friends, perplexed.

"Do it," urged Cymri. "I know it would be pleasing to lop off his head for his part in all this, but it would gain us little or nothing compared to the potential value of what he might impart to us."

Llew grudgingly acknowledged what she advised with a less than enthusiastic expression and a half nod. "Very well, Meirion. I agree. We will advance to your pennant but I must warn you—"

"I know," Meirion replied. "There will be no tricks and no threat offered. For your part, be sure you leave the boy in camp, where I can see him."

When they were five paces apart, Llew and his comrades stopped again. "Now," said Llew, "I would very much like to hear what this is all about."

Meirion regarded him and replied, "It is what I am here for. I did not have to come to you. I could have just left. Either way, Cai and I will never see each other again."

"So you, the ever-loyal lieutenant, always dutifully following the orders of that pompous bandit, now wish me to believe you have rebelled and parted company? What can you do or say to convince me of such a thing?"

Meirion glanced up towards their encampment. Caradog was watching them but he was so far away it was impossible to tell it was him. It could have been anyone at that range. The lieutenant slowly reached both hands up to his helmet and removed it, shaking out his long brown hair as he did so. Then he looked straight at Llew, defiantly. Llew looked back, not understanding for a moment, although he heard a sudden inrush of breath from Cymri and, a moment later, from Helgar. Confused at what he must be missing he blinked and looked harder. Something clicked and he saw what the others had seen. Meirion was not a man.

"Alright," he eventually said, "you have my full attention."

Meirion scowled. "It is an old tale, a young woman,

unhappy with her fate as heir to a small cantref meets a dashing young man and falls in love. Complications ensue. Her mother forbids her to be with him, he tells her of his secret life as a bandit lord and invites her to join him. She abandons everything to follow him and it is enough. She has the life she prefers, one of freedom and excitement with the man she loves, while at home she is declared dead and the world moves on."

"And what happened to change that?" prompted Llew, already beginning to suspect.

"He—this man she had loved and given up everything for—he kidnapped a younger woman of high birth. It came into his head that if he could win her over, or at least take her for his bride, why, he could declare himself king of her land. He threw over the older woman, told her she could remain only so long as she continued to serve faithfully as his lieutenant."

"He intends to marry Bloddeuwedd?" asked Llew, in a quiet voice. Then, louder, "Bloddeuwedd?" He ground his teeth and thought for a moment. "It is too much! Tomorrow he dies, for I will kill him."

"Wait," shouted Meirion. "Listen to me. There is more to tell. Tomorrow he intends to kill you whether you have the torc or not. I said bandit lord was his *secret* life. You have no way of knowing this but—"

"—but he is actually King Gronw of Penllyn and must kill us to keep that piece of treachery from being at risk of discovery."

Meirion's eyes narrowed. "So you had figured that part out." Her eyes flicked up the hill to where Caradog was standing. "Ah, the boy, of course, he must have gotten a look at him. I imagine he is rather quick of wit."

"He is," said Llew, "but why would you think so?"

"Because he is my son."

The three of them gaped openly at the woman warrior.

Cymri, as usual, recovered first. "That is why you wanted to ensure he stayed up at the camp."

"Indeed, it could only cause complications were he to find out, and I have always sought an uncomplicated life."

Llew was putting it together. "That would mean your mother is—"

"Yes, Queen Enid. I told you I abandoned everything when I left. If I were willing to include a crown in what got left behind why would I scruple over an infant? My mother was declared his guardian, necessary, as I had no husband. It was not as if I left him exposed in the wilderness."

"Who is Caradog's father?" Llew asked softly.

"I think you can figure that one out yourself, Prince Llew. All that matters is that his father was of similar station, a cantref king in his own right. Further, he has rejected the boy and disavowed him completely. Caradog can never inherit that man's lands or titles, nor call on any bonds of blood."

"There is a problem here, Llew," Cymri advised.

"A problem?" Llew echoed, disbelievingly. "I should say there is a problem here."

"It is not the one you are thinking. Caradog is the child of an outlaw, it makes him ineligible for the throne from his mother's side as well."

"So Caradog cannot be king, who is next in line after him?"

Cymri shook her head, "That is open to interpretation,

Llew. There could very well be a war involved in deciding that issue. We cannot afford that right now. Worse, whoever emerged the victor might have no interest in working towards reestablishing the great kingdom."

"A moment," Meirion interjected. "You have been keeping the boy near you. Have you apprenticed him, perhaps made him your shield-bearer?"

"Not really, he wants that, but I did not feel it was feasible for the heir of Gwynedd," Llew replied.

"Do you have a silver coin? Give it to me," Meirion demanded.

"What?" Llew asked. "Whatever for?"

Meirion made an exasperated noise. "I am trying to do you a favor, you and a few others as well. Give me a silver."

"Llew, do it." Cymri urged, her face expressionless.

Wordlessly, Llew searched a coin pouch and held out a single silver coin to Meirion. She snatched it from his hand before he had fully extended his arm. "Very well, Prince of Gwent, I hereby provide you with your apprentice, Caradog of Gwynedd. Accordingly, I name him yours in all ways, to do with as you wish save only the stipulation that you must teach him your craft. I renounce all bonds of blood and family with him and declare them transferred to you. It is fortunate for you we can do this now. In two weeks' time he will turn fourteen and reach his majority and I could not have transferred him without his agreeing to it. By your rules, he would have been ineligible to ever rule. Now he can still claim the throne by virtue of descent from my father."

Llew felt as though he needed to sit down. Instead, Helgar slapped him on the back and nearly rocked him off his feet.

"Congratulations, Llew, a father you are! Who does that make the mother, now?"

"I do not believe Caradog has a mother anymore," Cymri said quietly.

Meirion's eyes flashed and she held up her chin. "He never really did; we have but formalized that. Are we done here?"

"Where will you go now?" Llew asked.

"Does it matter? It will be far from here and we will never meet again."

"Goodbye, Meirion," Llew replied.

* * *

"What do you think?" Llew asked. They had left their horses with Caradog at the remains of an old castle. Before them was a considerable headland overlooking the sea. The path up was confined on both sides by multiple rock faces and sheer drop offs while the circle of standing stones was not visible from where they stood.

"Cilgwri has told you he has eight men hiding near the base of the hill?" Cymri asked. "Since we know none of them is Meirion, and Cai himself will be near the top, I think Helgar and I can prevent them from coming to his aid, beyond that I do not know. It will leave you completely alone with Cai and none to back you up. Bloddeuwedd seems a fragile flower—no disrespect intended—and you cannot rely on her aid."

"I am less concerned with that than I am with the two of you versus eight," Llew replied.

Cymri gave a terse laugh, "I did not say we would attack and defeat them all through skill at arms, only that they would not be coming to assist Cai. My thought is that they are there for another purpose. They will most likely let you pass up without revealing themselves. Then, when you return, they will seek to kill you and recapture Bloddeuwedd if she is with you. The three of us should be able to seriously alter their expected outcome, particularly as they will not know Helgar and I are there until it is too late."

Llew hesitated, "I have seen you with your sword these past two weeks. I must confess, in all our time together before that, I never suspected you possessed any skill at all with one, let alone that you might approach a level of prowess at arms comparable to that of my own and my other closest friends. Is there anything you would tell me about that?"

"Why Llew," Cymri exclaimed, "you said other closest friends! I am deeply touched, truly."

Llew flushed. "You know what I mean."

"You think Taliesin, chief of all bards, would ever have permitted his only daughter to travel as a wandering bard were she unable to defend herself to his standards? Is that not the fabled Fragaroc, his own sword, I see upon your baldric?"

Llew nodded curtly and made a wry expression, acknowledging the point.

"At any rate, Llew, we can discuss this at some other time and place if you still wish. For now we have more pressing concerns. Give Helgar and me half an hour to find a place where we can position ourselves, ready to descend on Cai's minions when you return. I would say less time than that but stealth is not precisely this one's main strength," she added, her eyes on Helgar.

"Nor should it be," agreed Helgar.

The hike to the standing stones was a substantial one, but

Llew took his time. He had no intention of arriving tired and out of breath. At last he came upon a collection of a dozen stones, each one a couple of heads taller than a man and just a bit wider than he could spread his arms. They were relatively thin from front to back, none of them being deeper than his arm. Their gray weathered surfaces gave no clue as to what purpose they had originally been erected for. They were not really in a circle or any other discernible pattern and they rested on an open relatively flat area that was perhaps fifty paces wide and a hundred or more long that sloped up to the bottom of a cliff face on the landward side and down to a cliff that rose nearly vertical from the waves far below. Clearly, the tide was in. He strode out boldly into the clear area. There was nowhere for Cai to be hiding anywhere close as the nearest stones were on edge to him and offered no hiding place.

He listened carefully and was rewarded by sounds so faint no one would imagine he could hear them. Behind one of the stones at the highest point near the cliff face he could hear the creak of leather from a boot with weight upon it. Had the waves on the rocks below not been making a fair amount of noise, he might have been able to hear breathing, not that it really mattered.

Making sure he could get to quick cover behind one of the stones should Cai appear with a bow, he cupped his hands before his mouth and called out. "Hide and seek, Cai? Really? Given the limited hiding places, you have picked a very poor place to play."

Cai stepped out from behind the stone Llew had already identified. Llew made to move in that direction, but Cai abruptly held up a wicked looking dirk, then reached behind the stone . . . and pulled out Bloddeuwedd. Llew could feel his heart pounding with relief. His greatest fear was that she had already been harmed or even killed or that Cai would not bring her. Despite three weeks of captivity, she looked good, surprisingly good. It did not appear she had been made to suffer privation, at any rate. Certainly she was rather pale and frightened at the moment, but that was understandable.

Make the exchange and get her out of here, Llew thought to himself. *Cai thinks he has already won the day with his men below ready to ambush me, but in that he is mistaken. His overconfidence will be his undoing.*

Chapter XXI

An Evil Thrust

Unsmiling, Cai called out, "So, Llew, you come empty-handed? I told you my price for a princess and you have failed to meet it. Now I will exact a different price—one you will find far more dear."

Quickly drawing back his collar, Llew exposed the golden torc at his throat. "Perhaps I have had it all along, Cai."

The prince of Gwynedd started to say more but was forestalled by Cai's raised hand. "No, do not pretend to offer me your own frippery in place of Math's Torc. Know you there are quite a few tales circulating about the great hero of Gwent. Some even mention that you wear the torc you took from Goll One-Eye, war chief of the Picts."

Llew inwardly cursed himself. Why had he ever mentioned his torc's provenance to anyone? "Yes, Cai, and that torc, the one I took from him, is the torc you seek. It chose to come to me in that fashion."

Cai sneered at this. "Persist in this stupidity and I will grow angry, young prince, I warn you. Yet I am a forgiving sort and even I hesitate to spill fair Bloddeuwedd's blood upon the ground of this remote place as if it were no more than wine from a broken flagon—at least not while I might still realize some profit from this. The tales also say you wear the fabled blade, Fragaroc. Give it to me and she is yours, whole and unharmed and as you see her."

"Would that you asked for anything else," replied Llew, "for Fragaroc is not mine to give. It belongs to another and that is nothing less than the truth."

"Do not toy with me!" shouted Cai. He yanked Bloddeuwedd up harshly, pulling her head back by the hair with one hand and laying his naked blade upon her bare throat. "You know me well enough to know I will do this."

"You seem to have lost your faithful lieutenant, Cai. There would be no one to prevent me from delivering Fragaroc to your neck should you do so!" returned Lew.

"Aye, we would dance then, but I do not know that even Fragaroc would bring you victory, indeed, I would like very much to find out as I weary of you and I greatly favor my odds." He lowered his voice then, "But this lovely one would be beyond caring. Give me the sword and I give you my word, on all that is sacred or heinous, the most horrendous curses to befall me should I ever be forsworn, that I will let her come to you now of her own free will, as whole in mind and body as the day I took her."

"Rather, you would strike me down with my own sword the instant you held it," accused Llew.

Cai gave a grim smile. "The thought had crossed my mind, but I will go this far. I will send her to you now—if you but pledge to leave Fragaroc upon that stone beside which you stand. You may then depart with her immediately. I will even promise to come not one step closer, and to touch neither Fragaroc nor my own blades, until nightfall."

Llew considered the words, looking for the hidden catch that might undo him. Could he leave Taliesin's sword? It had not been a gift, only a loan. Then he thought again, what, he wondered, would Taliesin do? Phrased in that way, the answer came to him at once. Taliesin would not hesitate. He would rescue their plans to reforge the great kingdom of Tethera and avert the coming doom that was Annwyn. What use was a sword, any sword, if all Tethera were to become a windswept ruin?

"Decide now, boy-who-would-be-king. This opportunity, and her life, will soon be beyond your reach."

"Enough! I will agree and so pledge to your terms, but first," said Llew, "I will hear your oath . . . and it must be clad in cold steel."

Cai smiled. Then the smile faded and he swore his oath. The marrow in Llew's bones ran cold as he heard what Cai swore by, and of the penalties should he fail to uphold it. Cai finished and pushed Bloddeuwedd roughly down the slope towards Llew. She stumbled on the rough terrain and caught herself, then, as she came close, stumbled again. Llew stepped forward and caught her in a fierce hug.

She seized him tightly in return and pressed her cheek against his. "Thank all the powers that be that you have come! We must away at once! He dares not break his oath but he still means to kill you before tomorrow's dawn."

"Aye," said Llew, "but I promised to leave him my sword atop this great rock and so I shall."

Meaning to break the blade before letting Cai possess it,

Llew drew Fragaroc and held it over the stone, point down, while gripping it with both hands. From a distance, he heard Cai cry out in dismay. Then he brought the enchanted blade down with all his strength.

Amazingly, it did not snap. Instead, the bulk of the blade buried itself in the living stone. Only the hilt and a few inches of blade projected from the top. *There must*, thought Llew, *be some tiny fault or crack and the enchanted blade is strong enough to force a path where no other could have.*

Cai's laughter carried to him. "Thought to cheat me, did you? Take your lovely bride and go, but be comforted. The one drawing forth that sword will be the next high king of Tethera."

The prince glowered at the gloating bandit lord. "If it is so easy to prophesy then know that cantref king was your limit. You will never be a true king, let alone high king, Gronw."

Without waiting to see Cai's reaction to being revealed, he took Bloddeuwedd by the arm and turned to make his way down the slope to the cliff top trail. He never saw Cai reach down into the grass at his feet and take up something hidden there. His first intimation of doom was Bloddeuwedd pulling away from him and screaming out, "Now my love! Aim true!"

Llew had only begun to turn when he felt the shock. It staggered him several paces and his head rocked forward, giving him a full view of the jagged spearhead and two feet of haft that protruded from just below the right side of his rib cage. It jutted forth from his armor and was covered in the slick redness of blood—his blood, he realized remotely.

He fell heavily onto his right side trying to grasp the spear that ran through him. It was not until then that the pain began to hit. He tried to scream but taking in the breath to do so was so incredibly agonizing that he nearly blacked out completely.

Desperately needing breath, he was forced to resort to small rapid gasps, each one creating its own microcosm of pure distilled pain.

There were words being spoken but Llew could not immediately understand them.

"Cai, my love, my husband, finish him!"

"Alas, my dear Bloddeuwedd, I have already thrown Celtchar's Spear. Now I may approach no closer until nightfall, lest the nameless ones by which I pledged find I have broken my vow. I will not forfeit myself to them. Not to worry, my dear queen, this has its advantages as well. In this way, I can still cause him some pain.

"So, Llew, all your great plans have come to this: a slow death in a lonely place, betrayed by your one true love. Does it feel good? It does to me. Know that Bloddeuwedd and I married in secret more than a week ago. I am king of Gwynedd and will soon proclaim it. In time, I expect to be high king of all Tethera. Will it not be wonderful to have the old place all back together again?"

Llew tried to say something. His lips moved haltingly, but the words were not discernible.

"What was that?" inquired Cai. "Are you asking how I can hope to do this? Or are you asking how I will avoid falling prey to the Lord of Annwyn? Silly fellow! I have not pledged myself to his service nor are we in opposition to each other. The Lord of Death is my ally. Who do think provided the long lost Spear of Celtchar that you have become so close to? Interesting is it not? It always hits and it always kills, yet you are wearing armor that cannot be penetrated so look what happened. The armor failed in that it was penetrated, yet the spear also failed in that, while it hit, it did not kill. Well, not immediately, but I expect that will soon be a moot point.

"Now I need only send your head to Lord Arawen, pickled in brine, and he shall provide me with the resources I need to complete my victory."

"Enough, Cai," shouted Bloddeuwedd, "I do not love him, I do not even like him, but I have no wish to see him suffer. Put him out of his misery; this is pointless."

"Cause and effect, it is your own fault, my dear. By calling to me you gave him just enough warning that he was able to begin to turn around. The effect is that I was slightly off target—only slightly. If not for that enchanted armor of his, it would not have made a difference; even a scratch would have killed him instantly.

"I could come use my sword, or even my dirk, but I shall not. The price for being forsworn is not one I wish to pay, nor do I need to. He will be dead soon enough. If you want the job finished more quickly, it cannot be by my hand."

"Then I shall finish him myself," she promised grimly, and started forward, apparently to grab the end of the spear protruding from Llew's back.

Somehow, the shock of her betrayal, freely admitted, overwhelmed even the physical pain of Llew's universe and galvanized what remained of him. He rocked himself to his left, continuing his rapid shallow breathing, and got his right foot under him. Then he grasped the bloody spear by the haft to keep it still, reached deep inside himself and seized all the will he could find, funneled it all into his right leg, and staggered to an almost upright position as he pushed away from the ground. Bloddeuwedd, already reaching for the spear's haft, gave a small shriek and jumped back from him as he did so.

"Cai! He is up, he will get away!"

"Not to worry, my dear, just stay well clear. He cannot go

far and he has nowhere to go."

That resonated in the cathedral of pain that was Llew's mind. Where could he go? Mortally wounded, it dawned on him that all the things he had meant to do would now go undone! Surely there were others who would continue on without him? Afaggdu had often told him that no single man was irreplaceable. Now, in his despair, Llew could not make himself believe that. His failure would have consequences for all.

These thoughts and others flickered through his mind in a moment until one came to him in the form of a realization that did not pass; all that remained for him was to reach out for whatever he could accomplish before his life spilled out completely. There was no way to help his friends, no way to hurt his enemies. Failing that, what part of their victory could he prevent? Attempting to keep to his feet, he let himself stagger on down the slope. This worked, insofar as it helped him to stay upright a bit longer, but it was hardly likely to achieve anything. His enemy was behind him—and Bloddeuwedd? Whatever she was, she was behind him as well, in every way imaginable. The cliff top was coming up rapidly and there he would be stopped, unable to go any further. Unless . . . .

Llew staggered on, gaining speed. Cai had erred in revealing that he needed Llew's head to present to Lord Arawen of Annwyn. It lay within Llew's fading abilities to deny him that, at least. At last perceiving what he intended, Cai shouted down to Bloddeuwedd, "Stop him!"

That was not something she was equipped to do, either physically or mentally.

With a last push, Llew reached the top of the cliff. Far below him, rocks were pounded by the same waves endlessly striking the cliff at its base. Leaning forward while still moving, he put what remaining strength he had into pushing off with his legs.

He fairly sprang off the cliff but gravity seized him in its grasp at once, and the rocks and surf below came rushing up to meet him.

Holding his legs together, he held his arms straight out and away from his sides as he half fell, half dived. Reflexes kicked in and he flailed at the air, desperately seeking a nonexistent grasp on it. He continued to fall but, after a long moment, he flailed harder and with more purpose, and his rate of descent actually seemed to slow. Perhaps, he thought dimly to himself, this was what everyone felt as they were falling such a great distance. Yet it drove him to greater effort, despite the waves of smothering, all-encompassing pain that redoubled from his right side with each stroke of his arms.

Those same arms had begun to feel curiously light and long, but Llew was far past curiosity. He clenched his feet and let out an enormously loud cry, one that resounded from the cliffs, an indivisible blend of mortal agony and the torment of total betrayal.

The water was coming up fast. Instinctively, he sharply angled his wings and went into a long sloping glide that became flat just above the wave tops. Then, ever so slowly, ever so painfully, he began to periodically flap his powerful wings, slowly gaining altitude as he fled the place where he had been so terribly hurt. As he went, he gave one last cry of anguish from his great hooked beak.

From far above, Cai and Bloddeuwedd watched him go. Neither had eyes for the small black bird following him.

Chapter XXII

In Caradog's Defense

Caradog waited in the ruins of the ancient fortress where the others had left him. For the fourteenth time that day, he questioned his need to be there. Gower could as easily guard the other four horses as well as he could. Truth be told, Caradog admitted to himself, Gower could probably handle anything that turned up with more authority than he himself could.

It was not his fault that his growth was late in coming. He knew this, but it rankled, nonetheless. Within weeks of his fourteenth birthday, most still took him to be several years younger, whereas he knew that Llew, even before his eleventh year, had already been as tall as most grown men—and with the strength to match, no less! No, there was nothing at all fair about the process of growing up. At least arms training should help him considerably. He wondered again, not for the first time, what sort of transformation this trainer of Llew's, one Afaggdu by name, could work on him.

Caught up in his thoughts, he did not notice Crug and Glo

stand up, intent on something behind him. It was not until they began making low growls that he looked up and, standing as they were, right in front of him, his first confused reaction was one of fright. Had they somehow decided to turn on him? He had not raised them from pups and had no feel for how deep their loyalties to him were. He had been their master for scarcely more than two weeks. As one, they sprang in his direction and all he could think to do was cower.

They passed over him and viciously tore into the bandit that had been approaching unseen from behind. The man had used a low wall as cover while he crept up, and it had fully obscured the hounds from his vision. While Crug hamstrung him, Glo leapt straight for his throat and dragged him down. Caradog gaped and then movement in his peripheral vision alerted him to another man charging at him from the right.

In addition to not noticing the dogs, this one had apparently been so unimpressed by Caradog that he had not even bothered to draw a weapon. He simply attempted to seize the young prince with both hands. Caradog ducked under them and sprinted past him, leaping for a crumbling wall. He pulled himself to the top before he saw there was no place to go. A large stone came loose from its aged mortar and he grabbed it, lifting it up with both hands while he pivoted back toward his attacker. Just as this second attacker climbed to be within arm's reach, it was the work of a moment to hurl the stone down. His pursuer was far too close to dodge it.

The sound it made on impact sickened Caradog, but he was confident that this man would pose no further threat. The bandit fell quite heavily and lay unmoving. In similar fashion, the first assailant was no longer putting up even a token resistance as the dogs continued to savage him. A meaty thunk sounded as an arrow appeared in Glo's side. She made one half-hearted attempt to bite at it, then collapsed where she stood.

"No!" Caradog breathed. He looked up in time to see a second arrow pass close enough to his left ear that he felt the motion of its passage. Two bowmen were just beyond the ruins of the gatehouse and each was already notching another arrow. Caradog froze, there was no cover from them on his ledge and it was too high to jump from. At the least, he would almost certainly hurt himself too badly to run.

But there was nothing else for it, Caradog prepared to jump and hope for the best when, with a furious growl, Crug abandoned his first adversary. Suddenly neither bowman had his attention fixed on Caradog any longer. Both had their eyes focused fully on the furious Crug, almost a blur as he closed the distance to the men that had hurt his pack mate. Yet the remaining hound was not going to make it in time, both men were already raising their bows to aim. That same focus on one threat made them oblivious to the other.

Neither man saw nor heard Gower before he reached them, coming in at an angle from the rear. Both of them flew a good twenty feet on impact with the charging warhorse. Then the horse and the hound leaped upon the fallen men, teeth bared. The young prince looked away almost at once when he realized that neither bandit would ever again be a threat.

Half an hour later, after dragging the dead men off to one side of what might once have been an old moat, Caradog was busily engaged in digging a grave for Glo—the tears had slowed him down considerably at the start—when Helgar came running up. The Northman's face was bruised and showed several small cuts and splits. He was also limping and his left arm and leg were slicked with fresh blood.

Each of them eyed the other for a moment. Then Helgar glanced towards the boots of the dead men and his eyes widened. "Four? Very good on you! So many I got also, but not so cleanly as you."

Caradog blinked, trying to understand for a moment. "Oh, no, only one, the others were Gower and the dogs." He looked towards Glo, now lying motionless beside the grave he was digging. "Each of us got one."

Helgar noticed the dog himself then. "Ah, I see," he said quietly. "Remember her, you should. But keep in your mind she did what she was born to do. She would do no differently if she could do it over. Here, let us get her covered up; the hole is deep enough and we can more quickly pile rocks on it to protect her than by digging it deeper. We have no time for more than this and, in any case, she was a war dog; she would understand that."

Caradog wiped his remaining tears on his sleeve. He was ashamed that Helgar must have seen them but the Northman did not mention them. In less than a minute the two of them, working together, had laid Glo to rest and refilled the shallow grave, then took another two minutes to pile enough stones on it as they judged would be sufficient.

"Helgar," Caradog said abruptly, "where are Cymri and Llew? And Bloddeuwedd?"

Helgar scowled. I do not know where Cymri or Llew are. I waited in ambush with Cymri—we were waiting for Llew to come back down from the mountain, maybe with Bloddeuwedd. Instead this one that must be Cai came down with Bloddeuwedd. The eight men they had left below came with horses for them and I kept waiting, not sure what to do. I thought maybe Cymri would signal to attack, or Llew would come down and then I would attack them."

"So what did happen?" asked Caradog.

Helgar shook his head. "They helped Bloddeuwedd mount,

treating her with great respect. She even rode off some distance away and yelled at Cai to hurry up. Then they rode off together. I do not think she was a prisoner at all."

Caradog felt sick in his stomach. "We have never been terribly close but I find that very hard to believe—maybe she was tricking him?" He tried to convince himself that might be the case but failed. After a moment, he gave voice to what concerned him even more than the prospect of his cousin being in league with the enemy. "Do you think they might have killed him up there and stolen the torc?"

Helgar shook his head, lips pressed tightly together, and Caradog thought to wonder if the big man wanted to cry as well. "I do not know. Four men ran off to do some bidding of Cai's and that left only four. I decide I have to go check on Llew but they were in the way. Sure I was that Cymri and I could take the four men that remained. I did not wait for her signal. I attacked. Cymri never appeared so some excitement was had. Then I ran up the mountain."

"And?" prompted Caradog, impatiently.

"I found the standing stones. Llew was not there but his sword was stuck in a big rock. It is stuck really hard because I tried to pull it out and I could not. But here is the part that is most bad. There was a trail made of blood, much blood, maybe so much blood a man could not live through losing it. It ran right down to the cliff over the sea."

Caradog was stricken. "And you took time to help me bury a dog?" he accused.

"You needed a moment to think," protested Helgar. "Maybe I did, too."

Caradog had no argument there.

"What I am thinking is that I need to track down Cai and take care of him. He cannot have your cousin and, if he has Llew's torc, he should not have that, but, more than anything, we must know what happened up there and those two know."

"I will not accept that Llew is dead before I see his body," declared Caradog. "I refuse. Yet it sounds as though he desperately needs help, we must make every attempt to find him as quickly as possible."

"That falls on you, young shield-bearer. I am thinking if you can but find Cymri or Llew, you might also find the other and you can do that far better than can I. Just as I can take care of Cai much better. You get along well with Gower and, if anyone can lead the way to Llew, it is him. Also, I can show you precisely where Cymri was last and it may be that Gower can track her. He has done such things before."

"I think we should let Cai go while one of us seeks Cymri and the other seeks Llew," offered Caradog.

Helgar shook his head in the negative. "No. One way or another Cai is the center of this and I will have him and your cousin as well. She is either a prisoner or a fiend and, either way, leaving her with Cai is not something Llew would allow. You take two horses and Gower, and Crug, of course. I will take two horses. If possible, I will return here and you can do the same. Otherwise, go east into Gwynedd and seek your grandmother so that she may do what she sees fit."

"You could be right; I cannot say it is not what Llew would do. Good hunting to you, Jarl Helgar," Caradog said gravely.

"And to you as well, Prince Caradog," Helgar replied.

Chapter XXIII

The Wounded Bird

Night fell like a black cloak drawn across the land as the light fled into the west. Noting little of it, the great eagle flew on, his entire world a red haze of anguish. Darkness fell and he flapped on, riding the winds so that he need exert himself only when it was needful. The anguish in his thoughts warred with the physical agony, although neither dispelled the other in any way.

Each beat of his wings felt as though he were being cleaved by a liquid fire that spilled and ran though his entire being in waves. Nevertheless, when the pain of his thoughts became more than he could bear, he welcomed the pain of his wound.

Every word continued to resonate in what remained of his mind. "Cai, my love, my husband, finish him!" the sweet voice had called. The eagle flinched from his own thoughts and gave another great stroke of his wings.

"I do not love him, I do not even like him . . . put him out of his misery," the same voice had later said. Another great flap, another great wave of pain, and he rose marginally higher above the treetops that he passed over.

Although perhaps not the cruelest, the final blow had fallen. "Then I shall finish him myself!" she had declared. Fire flowed through his every fiber as he flapped twice in quick succession, although he did not need the elevation.

Came the fall of night on the second day he could fly no further, sinking until he was forced to alight high in an oak so great that it might have rivaled even the king of the Fae in age. In ages past it had stood proudly upon a plain, now it was nestled into a great bog. The pain of his body had dulled until he felt he was a single great glowing coal of agony, but without the additional distraction of his labored flight it was insufficient to distract from his own black thoughts. Perforce, he sank ever deeper into them and the world beyond faded from any possible importance to him

Blood, both clotted and fresh, as well as suppurated flesh, dripped down the spear that still impaled him, falling from the barbed point through the branches to the ground below. A day later, a passing black bird caught the smell of carrion and hove in to investigate. It did not take it long to ascertain the source. Upon perceiving the wounded eagle, all unmoving high up within the oak, it immediately launched itself to the east. It returned, many hours later, in the company of a second black bird. Both landed beneath the tree.

Where the second black bird had landed on the ground beneath the oak, a human figure now stood. As it changed, the smell of the putrefying tissue smelled much different to the human than to the bird, it was far less interesting, far more unpleasant. "Gah, phew," it said. "We have come none too soon, the rot has set in and, shape-shifter or not, he will not last long now."

The figure looked up into the tree and saw no hope of helping the eagle where it sat, high in the upper branches. "The problem, Cilgwri, is that I cannot begin to heal him until I change him back. I cannot change him back until I can induce him to come down. I cannot induce him to come down until I can engage his mind to begin the healing of his crushed spirit. And engaging his mind gets more difficult each hour; he has been an eagle so long that his mind is vanishing away while we stand here. It is becoming that of an actual eagle, rather than a man."

From the base of the tree, a harp began to play. Words floated up to accompany it. If the giant eagle could hear it, there was no sign.

> In a dark bog—still alive, perched on oak,
> The frogs croak, will he survive?
> Life ebbs, though his friends arrive;
> Selfish choice, he will not revive.

The dying eagle shifted slightly on its perch, the long end of the spear knocking slightly upon the branch, but it did not otherwise give any acknowledgment it had heard.

> In aerie that is no safe place, Llew dies.
> 'Neath gray skies void of grace;
> Yet evil proceeds apace,
> Concede life now? Such disgrace.

At this the eagle, opened its eyes and glared down at the figure below. It gave a sharp cry that was quickly absorbed by the marsh's damp. Scarcely pausing, the harper began another verse.

> On his throne, Arawen has won, he crows,
> For the prince goes, undone;
> His foe gone, Death now has none,
> A quick end for all, such fun!

The eagle gave a great cry of mingled pain and defiance, and then it launched itself at its tormentor, talons spread wide. At the last moment, it saw the harper's bright red hair. Memories fought to the surface from beneath an ocean of liquid pain. No time left to completely pull out of its short dive, the raptor still tried, flipping aside and coming to a hard landing on the turf beside its former target.

The harper made a final riff and there was no eagle. Only a dying young man, motionless on the ground, a great spear still thrust through his body. All unmindful of the stench of the rotting flesh, the figure swiftly bent over him, first laying a hand to his face, then to the wound.

"Oh Llew, Llew, how can this be? It is not possible. You will not die; this we will not allow! I will call on such aid as I may, my blood for yours if it must be. How could I have missed this? Why did I not plan for it?" Fury came then, "Whatever the cost, the price they pay will be still higher—this I so swear!"

And then, in a quiet voice, tinged with despair, "Such wounds, such rot, can any power heal them? I fear the answer, what help can there be for such? No, I will find a way, somehow. There is always a way for the willing and the determined."

From the shadows around the great oak there was movement. Cilgwri flew up like an arrow shot from a bow, cawing all the while, then flew north and east towards the coast. The harper looked up from Llew at the enormous wolves that came padding out to surround the two of them, then smiled.

Chapter XXIV

On Betrayals

"Llew, my drott, you must waken and heal." Llew considered keeping his eyes shut. If he did, perhaps Helgar would let him die peacefully. Then it came to him, despite everything, to wonder. Could it really be Helgar? How had he come here? And where was here? Llew cracked an eye and saw that he was lying on rough ground, with his Northman friend standing before him a few paces away. All he could see of their surroundings was swirling mists, roiling in darkness. His side still ached but, compared with the agony he had long endured, it was as nothing.

"Helgar, how came you here?"

"You know how I came here, Llew. Betrayed I was, by one I held dear. My own uncle, who taught me the ways of the spear, and of how to sail a ship, he killed my father and many others. He caused me and my brothers to flee to the wilderness where we were taken by Picts and my brothers sacrificed in savage rituals—burned alive while I could but listen. You can see I have curled into a ball I have, and I shall never emerge."

"Now just a minute—" Llew objected. But Helgar was gone and another figure stepped forward out of the mists.

Llew strained his eyes to see until he could make out the other's features. "Llewellyn? How come you here? I thought you safely back in Caerleon."

"There was a betrayal, Llew. Every man and woman on my ship—many of whom had served me, cared for me, and guarded me for all of my life—all killed because of Dylan's betrayal. He was to keep my crew and retainers alive and capture all of us for Moriganna. Instead he thought that too easy a fate for me; he let the Picts slaughter most of us. He had already told Lord Arawen of Annwyn when and where to find us, hoping the Lord of Death would kill me on the spot. That betrayal was not directly a betrayal of me, but it took the lives of a great many that were near and dear to me."

Llew considered that. He had seldom thought of how close many of her companions on that ill-fated voyage must have been to her, and how badly their deaths must have hurt her. She had always been a bit on the somber side since he had first known her. It also explained how so many barrow warriors had managed to ambush them a year earlier in the hinterlands of Clwyd—what many would consider to truly be the middle of nowhere—yet there was a problem. "Wait, how is it that you know this?" he asked.

She continued without answering his question, "It slashed open wounds across my soul, Llew. I retreated into myself and was never of any use to anyone ever again."

Embarrassment infused his face. "That is not true and we both know it! Are you implying that I—" but, like Helgar, she was gone.

Another woman emerged from the mists, but Llew did not know her. She wore fine clothing of green and white. Her hair was a rich shade of chestnut brown, cut shorter than that of most women, yet her beauty was every bit the equal of Moriganna's or Bloddeuwedd's. She was older than Llewellyn, younger than Moriganna, but more could not be said for she had a look of wisdom, mingled with sorrow, in her eyes that somehow made it impossible to judge her age. The mists lightened and Llew heard birdsong as she came toward him. She stopped where Helgar and Llewellyn had stood and regarded him solemnly, then her expression softened, and a gentle smile came upon it. It conveyed such a feeling of warmth and affection that he was at a loss for words.

"Why, Lleu," she said, in a voice that was so perfect he wondered if it was not the result of some enchantment upon his ears, "no words of greeting for your mother?"

Stunned, it was a moment before he could speak. "My mother is dead," he whispered.

She lifted one eyebrow as she gazed on him. "Am I? Perhaps I am, it is difficult to tell at the moment."

Llew tried to speak again and she gently shushed him. "No, Lleu, now is not the time; I sense I am here for a purpose and have very little time. You were betrayed by one you were completely enamored with. You know now she never cared for you at all. Many would think that would make it easier for you, but we both know it does not. Intellectually, perhaps, it should, yet we do not love with our thoughts. We love with our emotions. We support and strengthen those dear to us with our emotions, not with our thoughts. It is a double-edged sword. We are also vulnerable to emotions, our own as well as those we care about. There is no impenetrable suit of armor we may don to protect us from these save an attitude of savage indifference. To maintain such an attitude contradicts every reason for being alive. You have many that love you, more than most, in fact. Further, if you wallow in your self-pity overlong it is they that will suffer, and they will suffer far more than you will."

"You have great things to do, my son. Know that I love you and am very proud of you, but this is no time to quit. I was betrayed by those closest to me. Although my hearing is far better even than your own, it only took a sleeping poison in a cup from one I trusted and I never heard them coming. Then I had to flee and it was hard for I would have preferred to die, but I had things yet to do. If I can recover from that, then so can you from this. As your mother and your queen, I order it. Bend all your will to recovery, for everyone is waiting on you. Now I must go. It hurts and I do not wish to, but I will do it because it is necessary." So saying, she turned to go.

"Mother," he called, finding his voice at last "who betrayed you and why did you flee?"

She paused then and looked back over her shoulder, "Revenge is a luxury and, as such, a distraction. Save it for later. I was told my only son was murdered by those closest to me and his body thrown into the sea. They spread blood on me while I lay in drugged sleep—they knew full well how sensitive my hearing. Before I even awoke, they had already claimed I was the villain. I did not flee then. I fled when my own husband would have killed me for the deed. But do not think too badly of your father; his mind was broken by this, as it was meant to be. The grand architect was my own father. It was he that had the deed done and the blame thrust upon me. So many betrayals . . . and yet I did not surrender."

Llew gaped at her.

"Hardships come and hardships go, Lleu. The only way to counter them is to go on so you may yet outweigh them with the good. You will never do that if you give up just because the present does not seem good." Then she was gone.

Llew blinked. Was she alive or was she not? Was that even really her? And why had she called him Lleu, as the Fae had?

Caradog stuck his head out of the mist. "For what it is worth, Llew, you are very fortunate. My own mother betrayed me when she abandoned me for her own selfish reasons. Of course, I do not know that yet, but you are going to have to be the one to tell me someday. Even had you not adopted me, it will be your responsibility to make sure I do not take this news so badly that it crushes my spirit." And then he was gone.

Llew blinked twice in quick succession.

Abruptly, Caradog stuck his head back out of the mist again and said, "Oh, and I am supposed to tell you that you should probably wake up now, at least for a moment."

Chapter XXV

A Moment in Nowhere

Llew awoke. He knew he was awake because the crushing pain of his wound was back, even if not as strong as it had been before. Someone had managed to remove the spear without killing him outright. He could see that it was gone, and little else, for he also could not move, save to wearily blink his eyes.

A man's voice spoke then, unnaturally deep and melodious. "He is waking now. You said you had another task once he was out of immediate danger. Now would be a good time to attend to it if you are quick. We will not fail you. He is dear to us as well and now, more than ever, he is as one of us and we are kindred in a way that trumps all bonds of blood.

"You asked how long? The healing itself will only take a single season, but then we will have much to do to restore him fully to his previous condition—and there is also the training you wanted. I cannot say with surety but if, as you said, he must be ready to fight when he leaves . . . I would say we will need one year and one day. As for you . . . the tide is very high and the very sea of time surges before the coming storm; the swells rushing in have risen until each seven waves now span an entire generation. I can give you anything but time, for even you cannot reach the reefs to pass behind them as they are now. You must return within a single hour. If you cannot be certain of that, then I would humbly submit you should not leave the kingdom.

"Do not worry, although the storm approaches quickly, our calculations hold. Our forces will muster at the gates and be ready to march when it arrives."

There was no reply, but a head moved close to Llew's, although he could make out no features. There was a quick kiss on his brow and the head withdrew and was gone, all without a word spoken. Something wet ran down his cheek to his lips. With a momentous effort he managed to intercept it by extending his tongue. It was salty; a tear? It had to be. But who had shed it? Cymri? His mother? Would either not have said something?

Darkness fell over him again and then the dreams came and did not stop. He ran along forest branches, nimbly leaping from tree to tree, endlessly thrilled at the speed and freedom. He was a great stag galloping through a forest of impossible shades of green. When great beasts sought to hunt he became one of them, exulting in leaping over obstacles and feeling the pine needle trails beneath his paws, smelling his prey as it fled. And the smells! So strong and wonderful were they that he could close his eyes and still see all around himself, both above and below—not just as it was—but as it had been for hours earlier. Sometimes he and his companions had feathers, then they soared above the land for hours or, in a smaller form, performed aerial acrobatics that were unadulterated bliss. Most of all, regardless of what form he traveled in, he knew, somehow, that those he ran with, flew with, or swam with, were as his brothers and sisters; there were so many of them and he loved them all!

* * *

Llew awoke slowly, lying on a pony fur, with another laid over him as a blanket. He blinked and looked about blearily. He was in a boggy glade beneath a great oak tree. A small fire burned not far away and a figure was tending it. It was then he must have made some noise for it turned and looked at him. "Llew, you are awake! Do not move yet. I have just brewed a cup of tea and Cymri said you were to drink it before you tried to move."

Llew struggled to focus but he already recognized the voice. "Caradog? Whatever are you doing here? You are supposed to be at the ruins and keeping an eye on our mounts." Something large and disgustingly wet, both smooth and soft, ran up the side of his face. "Ack, Gower! Leave off you big galoot! Cease, stop!"

He managed to pull his face back far enough to regard the happy horse. "And what are *you* doing here?"

Caradog came over then, carrying a metal cup of tea. "He is the one who led me to you. Go easy on him, he is just glad to see you. We were worried you might be dead."

"Wait, what?" asked Llew, confused. He then noted Crug was lying next to him, awake but just thumping his tail rhythmically upon the pony hide. Cilgwri cawed from his perch on one of the oak's lower limbs.

"Cymri was already here when Gower and I found you. She said Cilgwri led her here but that you were not here, just more blood and an awful stench. Then you were here and where you were in between she could not say. She built a fire over the blood to burn away the stench and tried to make you comfortable. It is evident you have been injured and somehow made whole. Your armor is a frightful mess and I do not know how you survived the injury you took."

"Where is Cymri?" Llew asked.

"She took your armor and said she was going to try to get it cleaned and repaired. She said it might take awhile and not to look for her before tomorrow. Take the tea."

Llew did and sipped. It was too hot but it somehow helped settle him, letting him better orient himself on the situation at hand. "Why did you think I might be dead before you even found my armor," he inquired mildly.

"Helgar found your sword, Fragaroc, stuck in a boulder amidst the standing stones on Pyn y Gogarth and there was a lot of blood. It almost made us think Cai killed you, and that your body was tossed over the cliff into the sea."

Llew hesitated. "That sounds familiar," he admitted, although I am a bit uncertain as to why I am still alive." Unbidden, his fingers sought the region below his right ribs. There was no pain but he could feel a terrible scar. With a feeling of profound unease, his hand rose and felt of the golden torc, still circling his neck. Beneath the blanket it was all he was wearing. Ignoring the proffered tea he cast his eyes about for his clothing and armor and then he saw it. A bit taller than he was, with a point that was a triple barbed head of gleaming sharpness, it was casually leaning against the great oak's trunk. Llew felt his soul shrivel up within him and the echoes of remembered pain came flooding back. If it was the Spear of Celtchar, and he knew in his heart that it was, it had been meticulously cleaned of his blood.

He heart skipped as he remembered something else and a leaden weight seemed to fall across his spirit. He had to force himself to ask the next question. "What news of Bloddeuwedd?"

Caradog licked his lips nervously before speaking. "Llew, Helgar saw her return down the mountain in the company of King Gronw—Cai. By her actions and bearing he became convinced she is in league with him."

"I seem to recall learning that," Llew said heavily. "I also seem to recall that they are married and have thrown their fortunes together."

Caradog froze. "Llew, I am so sorry—" he began.

"Nay, do not be overly concerned for my part, Caradog. Surprisingly, just as the hole in my side has healed with unexpected rapidity, so, too, has the hole in my heart. I do worry about you, however."

"Me?" asked Caradog.

Llew lifted his face to establish eye contact with the younger prince. "Recall what King Bran said. For what she has done there can be no mercy, it is not even an option. I know she is your cousin but we are both to be kings and we know this is the way it must be. If, in time, you wish to talk about it, I would be glad to listen."

Caradog nodded, then swallowed. "Thank you, Llew."

A thought came to Llew then. "Caradog, what of Helgar?"

"Llew, I tried to dissuade him but he has gone after Cai. He is convinced we cannot let him escape and thought he could tell us what had become of you."

Llew went cold inside. "He went by himself? Nay, if his mind was made up, you could not have stopped him. Cai must surely think I am dead, even though he must have watched me fly away."

"Fly . . . away?" Caradog asked, worry writ large across his face.

"Never mind," said Llew.

Caradog frowned but appeared to drop it for the moment.

"If Cai thinks you are dead he could be anywhere. He may even have gone back to his cantref."

"No," Llew said slowly. "I believe I called him Gronw at one point on the cliffs. When he considers that he will know I had ample opportunity to betray—er, reveal—his little secret. He cannot risk going back to things as they were. It is not even an option, even if he were willing and able to keep Bloddeuwedd a secret. He can only go forward and for that he needs something, probably more troops, to install himself as king of Gwynedd. Lord Arawen has pledged to give him that something in exchange for my head. So long as he believes I am dead he has little choice, he will have to range down the coast seeking my body."

Caradog picked up on the logic. "Because he will be slowed by his search, Helgar will likely catch up to him, if he has not already."

"Aye," replied Llew, "and I fear that meeting. Helgar is a very scary fellow, but then so is Cai . . . and he cheats."

Llew considered a final time, drained the cup of tea and passed it back to Caradog. "I cannot delay, it may be too late already," he said, as he made to stand.

"Llew, no!" cried Caradog. "You are freshly injured, even if it has healed over somehow."

"No, Caradog," said Llew, thinking back on his dreams. "I believe I may be healed, both in body and in mind."

"Well, you have no armor, mine will not fit you, and the only weapons here are my own and I doubt they will suit you either."

Llew picked up the spear from where it leaned against the tree. He hefted it and found it had an odd balance. Seeing that barbed head up close again required him to keep a tight rein on the dread it invoked in his heart. "I believe I do have a weapon and, as for armor, I am not sure I could carry it with me, anyway. Take care of Gower while I am gone," he said, as he walked out from under the oak tree's canopy.

Caradog looked aggrieved. "You are leaving Gower? Listen to yourself, Llew. Please, I beg you, lie back down, get some rest until Cymri returns."

Llew glanced sideways to Caradog. "Rest? I think I would prefer to go flying." He let the Spear of Celtchar begin to fall from his hand, then caught it in a huge talon as his mighty wings launched him skyward. He had eyes only for where he was going but, had he looked down, his superior avian vision would have clearly seen Caradog, head turned up to the sky, his open mouth forming a perfect circle.

Chapter XXVI

Better to Give Than Receive

Llew reached the coast in less than half an hour. At Pyn y Gogarth he turned to fly east along the shore. Despite the height, he found he was able to see the ground very nearly as though he were standing on it. An eagle's sight was a wondrous thing. Looking down at the mountain he could clearly see the standing stones on the cliff overlooking the sea. He could even see Fragaroc, rising out of the stone near the center. Had he lips he would have smiled. So, Cai had been unable to withdraw the blade.

It seemed likely that he would be able to succeed where Cai had failed, even if he had to call on the power of the torc to become a great bear or some such. He wanted to retrieve it then and there but did not feel he could spare the time, besides which, he had no place to carry it. The spear clasped in his talons was all he could manage at present.

Rising up to over half a mile above the ground, he began scanning the terrain below. East of Pyn y Gogarth, there was a broad swath of sandy beach that extended for miles, yet nothing was upon it save seaweed and driftwood. At one point there were the remains of a fishing village, but it looked to have been abandoned for many years. Past the beach was another headland, smaller than Gogarth. It was there, very near the water's edge, that he saw another collection of standing stones. Two men were there as well, facing each other and perhaps fifty paces apart. One had a sword, the other an axe.

Llew struggled to fly faster and was soon able to perceive that one was Cai and the other Helgar. Three men lay on the ground near Helgar, dead or unconscious. Of Bloddeuwedd there was no sign. Of much more concern was that he could see Helgar was barely able to stand. There was much blood on him and he was obviously wounded. Cai, on the other hand, appeared to be fresh and uninjured; apparently he had waited for the skirmish between Helgar and the other men to end before deciding to take part. He was advancing slowly, in no special hurry, and talking. That was hardly surprising, Llew thought to himself, given the man's penchant for taunting fallen foes.

Flying at top speed, Llew drew closer, but it seemed he would be too late.

Realizing that, he used the great strength of his legs and talons to spin the spear end-over-end as he released it on a trajectory that would let it fall between Cai and Helgar. With a near perfect center balance, an odd thing for a throwing spear, it fell away, still spinning and remaining perpendicular to his path.

Instantly pumping his great wings for all he was worth, he plunged in to a power dive for that same point, midway between Cai and Helgar. As he dived, Llew could feel a warmth about his neck and realized the torc was changing his body, ever so slightly, away from that of an eagle to something even better adapted to the task at hand. His speed seemed to become faster than thought and, had he time to think, he would have been frightened, for nothing lives that can exceed the speed of a diving raptor. Even the freely falling spear, only slightly slowed by its spinning, was left far behind and above.

The ground rushed at him and instinct warred with intent as, at the last possible moment, he finally performed a short loop to kill much of his speed, then angled his wings to slow his impact. The sudden air resistance felt as though he had nearly ripped them out of his shoulders but his claws spread to land and, as they touched the ground, he changed.

Cai regarded him with complete surprise. It was the first time Llew had ever seen him so. The bandit king recovered in an instant and his lips curled back. "Alive? Yet weaponless? I have a quick remedy for the first!"

Llew hardly heard him. He was listening for something else entirely. When he heard it, he risked a quick glance up, then raised one hand, palm open, high above his head and closed it as the midpoint of the spinning Spear of Celtchar slapped into it with bruising force. Cai paled and stepped back when Llew whipped the haft about and couched the spear at his foe.

Llew gave a Cai a slight smile more foreboding than any scowl. "Oh, Cai, had you forgotten? You gave me a weapon yourself and here it is!" Llew tilted his head to one side in an almost avian manner and regarded his old adversary. "It may be too fine a weapon for me, and I know Lord Arawen gave it to you. Perhaps it is time for me to return it?" Llew hefted the spear as if to throw it.

"No! Wait, Llew, Your Majesty, I am king of Gwynedd now. I will pledge both it and myself to you—by vows that you know I will not dare break! Is not rebuilding the great kingdom more important than simple revenge? The fate of all Tetherans, perhaps all men everywhere, depends on it, you have said so!"

"I have said many things, Cai. I never realized you were listening. Apparently you were, but you only recall what you hear when it suits you." Llew hefted the spear again and Cai took a fearful step backwards.

Llew considered. His fury had passed as quickly as it had come. Seeing the man he so hated, now fearful and cowering before him, had extinguished it like a bucket of cold water. He could not draw pleasure from this, much as he might want to; it was too much like something his enemies would do. He should either kill the man, capture him, or let him go. Needlessly taunting and frightening him before doing one of those things was just a form of punishment; even Moriganna—had it really been Moriganna?—had told him that punishing something that could not learn was just evil.

As for Cai's offer to pledge himself and Gwynedd to a new great kingdom? Llew considered that for only an instant. Moriganna had certainly once said something to the effect of, "With friends like these, who needs enemies?" It fully applied in this case. A great kingdom, built of such weak bricks, would never truly be great and must surely fail, sooner, rather than later.

Celtchar's Spear was smooth in his grip, allowing him to easily feel the sweat between it and his palm. Should he throw? The spear could not miss and always killed—well, almost always. Cai had no impenetrable armor to complicate things. The question was whether Llew should kill a man attempting to surrender to him, regardless of how expedient it was, and regardless of how much the man deeply deserved it.

In his dream, his mother had told him that revenge was a luxury, but was this just revenge? Bran had cautioned him against too much mercy. Was it more merciful to kill Cai now, or to execute him later? Afaggdu had told him that, when a man closed to fighting range, he no longer had any right to expect quarter.

Would it be too much of a stretch to apply that here?

Cai seemed to sense Llew's uncertainty and started to say something, but then there came a labored groan from Helgar. Llew spared a glance behind him for his friend. Helgar had slumped to his knees and clearly needed aid—this had to end now! He returned his attention to Cai, but the villain had taken full advantage of the distraction and darted behind a large standing stone that completely hid him from view.

"It is not much of a surrender if you run away just a few seconds later, Cai. You say you are king of Gwynedd by dint of having married Bloddeuwedd. I would ask you when the coronation was, but I do not believe there has been one. Further, she colluded with you in her own kidnapping, and also in your attempt to commit regicide on me. That makes her an outlaw and she cannot be in the line of succession. No, Cai, you are not now, nor will you ever be, king of Gwynedd . . . but your son will!"

Llew drew back and threw the Spear of Celtchar with all of his might, despite the fact that Cai was no longer visible. The spear flashed through the afternoon light like a lightning bolt and made a noise like thunder when it struck the large stone in its center. Llew shielded his eyes from the tiny pieces of rock sent flying and, when the dust and debris from the impact had cleared, he blinked in disbelief. The spear had passed completely through the rock itself, creating a circular hole wide enough for Llew to stick his entire arm through, had he chosen to do so. He had really rather expected the unerring spear would fly around the stone, not through it.

Cautiously, for he was now unarmed, Llew walked to the boulder and carefully peered around it. Cai lay upon the ground, transfixed by the spear, and very, very dead. Scarcely able to believe his tormentor would scheme against him no more, the prince of Gwent seized the spear in his right hand and withdrew it. He turned to go, then realized that, save for the golden torc, he was still quite naked. He turned again and his gaze fell on Cai's clothing and armor. Reaching down, he grasped the dead man by the neck with his left hand and felt the torc again grow warm upon his neck as the muscles of his legs, back, and arm twisted and reshaped themselves for additional strength. He had no difficulty dragging Cai's body with him back to Helgar, who was now lying prone upon the turf, apparently unconscious.

Fortune favored him again when he found that none of Helgar's wounds were life threatening, nor had they done any permanent damage except for inevitable scarring. That was hardly a problem. Llew knew Helgar took great pride in his scars, regarding each one as either a badge of honor, a reminder of some special memory, or both. He glanced down at his own new scar, still bright red below his ribs. That one, he was certain, would never be either of those—not so far as he was concerned.

It was not until he had the worst of Helgar's injuries attended to that a question came to him. Where was Bloddeuwedd?

* * *

From their rude camp further up the headland, Bloddeuwedd watched Llew and Cai's last meeting. Its conclusion convinced her she had lingered too long. It was time to go. *Where* was less important than making sure she was no longer *here*. She turned to gather what she would need and discovered she was not alone.

"Who are you?" she exclaimed.

"Just someone who considers you a living stain upon the land. Someone who despairs that anyone could do what you have done. Someone who will see that you never do anything like it again," came the answer.

Fingers played lightly over a harp. Bloddeuwedd, emboldened by the lack of any overt threat, opened her mouth to order the other to stand aside, then found she could not speak. Her eyes grew large and wide, then larger still, until they dominated a face where there were no longer any other features save a small, sharp beak.

"Did you think I would kill you?" the harper asked the large white bird, although it could no longer understand the words. "Perhaps it would be kinder but I will not. For what you have done, I condemn you to never show your face again by the light of day. All other birds will hate you and persecute you wherever they may find you. Fear not, however, you will still keep your name. I shall see to it that Bloddeuwedd, flower-face, shall evermore be another name for owl."

Chapter XXVII

Wings in the Wind

After he had finished ministering to Helgar as best he could, and dressed himself in such of Cai's things as were still usable, Llew took to the air again. He quickly found where the bandit king and his men had camped while they searched along the coast for his body. He landed and was gratified to see that he still wore the clothing and armor he had been wearing when he had changed into eagle form. He quickly inventoried the little camp to see what he and Helgar might use. In doing this, he found certain things there that must have belonged to Bloddeuwedd as well. The flurry of emotion this triggered sent him back into the sky but, although he ranged high above the area for some time, even an eagle's sight found no trace of her.

He waited until the next day, when Helgar was doing considerably better, before temporarily taking his leave. Helgar's healing had gotten a significant boost because Llew had no fear of using the healing chant over his friend, especially when the two were alone in the wilderness. Arriving back at the great oak where Caradog was camped, he landed and changed. Cymri was back and had his armor, freshly cleaned and repaired, even the damage from the spear had been repaired.

"Beware," Llew told her, "Addfwyn will think you are after his job."

"I think his post is quite secure for I am not nearly so ambitious as that," she replied with a smile. "I was just fortunate enough to find a village that still had enough people to support a blacksmith. Llew, it is so very good to see you hale and whole—we were so very worried. Helgar probably thinks I abandoned him. He must have been terribly disappointed when he never got the signal to attack those bandits. The truth is that something came over me, a terrible feeling of despair. I think it might have been when the Spear of Celtchar struck you. I can barely describe it except as I already have. I raced to find a way up to where you were, unobserved by Cai and his men, even though it meant climbing some very sheer rock faces. I never got to the top, before I could, something told me to head to the east and then to the south and I did, without even taking the time to seek my horse.

It was the next day when Cilgwri found me and he was frantic that I should follow him. We arrived and it was the strangest thing—did Caradog tell you? Your armor and other clothing was laying on the ground, as though it had just been tossed to one side, and it was a disaster, caked with filth and stench and that gaping hole both front and aft in your hauberk. You were absent, there was just a stench of dried blood and rotting flesh. I cautiously explored about, sick with anticipation of what I might find, yet when I circled back about, there you were, laid out upon the ground and apparently all unwounded."

"Um," managed Llew, coloring. "So I was just lying on the moss beneath the tree with, ah, all of my armor and clothing tossed to one side?"

"Yes, and you were between a pair of pony hides. I cannot imagine where you found them."

"Oh," Llew said, relieved, "wherever they came from, it is

good that they were here."

"Certainly it was," responded Cymri, "but it is yet another mystery. Such as why, although I checked you very thoroughly, I could find no trace of any wounds, just that big scar where the hole in your armor was."

"Oh," said Llew, his face gone crimson again.

"I simply did not know what to think then. You had certainly had no time to receive and heal from such a terrible wound in a mere two days' time. Yet even your moustache says you did have that much time."

"My what?" Llew's fingers flew to his face and there it was, he could feel it. He unmistakably had a Tetheran style moustache stretched over his mouth and running down to his jaw line on either side. Two days earlier he had been clean-shaven, unwilling to let what hair he had grow out while there was not yet enough of it make a proper showing.

"Though but two days have passed for us, it seems as if two years might have passed for you," Cymri said. "Could you have been taken into a Fae tumulus? It makes little sense but it is the only thing that makes any."

"Nay," he said thoughtfully, running his fingers down the right side of his moustache. "It was not two years, merely a year and a day. And it was no Fae mound. I do not know what it was but it was not that."

He glanced at Caradog, who had not yet said a thing and was just staring at him. "And how are you doing, my young shield-bearer?"

Caradog tried to say something but it was unintelligible.

Looking at both of them in quick succession, Cymri said,

"I think you have awed him all over again. He saw you fly away as a great eagle and return as one. Do not be over worried. He is young and in time he will likely recover and be twice as talkative as we are used to. Yet even I must ask the question. Have you any explanation for flitting about the way you do now?"

Llew regarded her and shrugged one shoulder. "It is the torc. I do not know how, but it senses my need or desire and changes me."

"As it did for High King Math and no other, before or since," she said quietly. She looked up at him then, eyes shining. "It is said that with his torc he could change himself into any natural beast of the field or wood, sky or sea, and that he was able to do so only because the gods themselves favored him so. Not even Boudicca or Mathonwy, or the twelve of their line after Math himself, could use it so. That you are so favored brings me renewed hope that we shall either shatter or fulfill the prophecy."

"Which prophecy?" Llew asked, "There are so many."

"The one that all Tetherans quote when what they mean to say is 'never'."

"The great kingdom of Tethera shall not be restored until Pwyl's heir sits upon his throne?" Caradog asked excitedly, finding his tongue again at last.

"Pwyl died and left no heir," objected Llew. "That is why it means 'never' to most folk. Even if there was an heir, no one would accept one of Pwyl's line, not after what he did. That is why my father does not seek to restore the great kingdom of Tethera and instead seeks to create a new one in its place."

"Semantics," Caradog said flatly.

"Semantics are everything when dealing with prophecy," insisted Cymri.

Caradog shook his head in disagreement. "We do not need semantics. King Bran had the sight and he said that Llew was Boudicca's heir. If Pwyl had no surviving offspring of his own then that alone would make Llew his rightful heir. The torc is but more proof of that. Llew has proven it is undeniably Math's Torc and therefore that it is also Boudicca's Torc, the Torc of Tethera."

Llew shook his head in confusion. "But are we missing something? Some crucial piece in our logic that will tumble the whole structure? Enough! We must return to Helgar and make sure he is still recovering."

Cymri gestured to the sky. "Go ahead, Llew. You told us where to find him and we will be there by midday tomorrow. I dare say with Gower and Crug we are safe enough for such a short trip.

* * *

Llew landed amongst the standing stones on Pyn y Gogarth. The place held unpleasant memories for him and he reflected on that for a moment. He had settled Cai, and that was strangely satisfying, but he had not been able to locate Bloddeuwedd. Oddly, he did not know if that was a blessing or not. He did not like her running loose in the world after the trouble she had created, but neither did he relish taking her back to Gwynedd to face a headsman's axe.

He put the thought aside. This was not a day for considering death. It was a day he would much rather use for appreciating life.

He walked to Fragaroc, the hilt still rising from the same stone into which he had driven it. As he grasped it, he tensed his muscles. If neither Cai nor even Helgar had been able to withdraw the blade then it seemed likely this might require some shape-shifting to get the needed strength. Still, he gave it an experimental tug and, to his surprise, he pulled it out easily. The prince of Gwent gave the sword a suspicious glance. "Have you and the torc been talking?" he asked.

He started to chuckle, then considered. Perhaps the sword was aware of who was grasping it and capable of deciding if they should draw it. The torc had changed him into an eagle when he was falling and saved his life. It certainly had been a clever thing to do but he had neither ordered nor suggested it. He also suspected its shape-changing power had kept him alive far longer than he should have lived with the Spear of Celtchar in his side. And the spear itself . . . had it failed to kill him instantly because of Moriganna's enchanted armor, or because it had chosen not to? Hafgan had said even stones had some basic level of awareness. Even if a stone's state of awareness was insignificant compared to that of a living creature, a question persisted. Could enchanted items somehow be much more like living creatures than a stone? If so, just how aware were they?

Llew shook his head and sheathed Fragaroc. That was a thought for later, for he already had enough mysteries to sort through. Now was not the time for any of them.

The air came in gusts, brisk and invigorating; it blew in from the sea with a strong tang of salt and made endless ripples in the long grass. The sky was cloudless—an impossible shade of blue—while the sea itself was bluer still, just rough enough to give every wave a whitecap.

Now it was time to fly. With a joyous cry he threw himself into the sky as he spread his wings and caught the wind.

Author's Notes

This is more of a ramble and if it seems to you to lack cohesion and a unifying theme . . . well then, you are correct.

In case anyone missed it, *The Torc of Tethera* has a wee bit more violence in it, and perhaps even some borderline naughty bits, when contrasted against the previous volume. Am I caving to reader demands in the modern world? Hardly, but our protagonist is growing up and these things happen.

In this volume, we also venture into *The Mabinogi* itself. Please don't think that exempts you from reading it for yourselves. I have taken such enormous license with it that these books won't even make a decent set of Cliff notes.

For those who insist that Llew and Lleu sound exactly the same and are only spelled differently—I request that they go back to circa 700 A.D. (on an alternate timeline no less, where magic is real, and Boudicca won) and come back with proof that such was the case. Yes, Virginia, authors can cheat.

Finally, if you find anachronisms, maybe they aren't what you think they are. The astute reader may have noticed references to time travel in this volume.

Carp pie anyone?

Michael Laird
Eastchester, New York

Social Levels in Tethera

Tethera is a society with a landed warrior aristocracy. Female warriors do exist but are surpassingly rare. Also, at all levels, land inheritances go to the appointed heir, almost always a male when possible. In the past, inheritances were split amongst the male progeny but this led to inherited lands becoming too small to support a warrior and the practice was stopped during the reign of High King Mathonwy.

Warriors hold land which is worked for them by the peasantry. These are not vassals, serfs, or slaves, they are fellow tribe members.

Taxes and military service are still a fact of life but their ruler's power over them is never considered absolute.

Above the level of simple warriors are lords, which is also a common title that could be used by anyone of that level or above. As this is also a military rank, it is very rare to find a lady without a lord, although it can happen, especially if the lady in question is also an able warrior.

Above the lords are the cantref kings and queens. These are monarchs, although not in the way we are often used to thinking of such. Their primary concern is in administering their cantrefs. Cantrefs are holdings usually comprised of anywhere from fifteen to fifty villages, although even these numbers are not firmly established. These rulers are considered royalty, if a lesser sort, and can be addressed as Lord or Lady, King or Queen, and might also be referred to as 'my lord,' or 'my lady', or 'your highness,' or even 'your majesty.' Their offspring, called princes and princesses, might also be referred to as any of these save for 'your majesty." Daughters are almost never appointed as heirs unless they have no living brothers.

Generally, there are kings and queens, once called great kings and great queens, who rule kingdoms, sometimes called great kingdoms, of as few as seven or as many as twenty-five cantrefs. For them the term 'your royal majesty' could also be used.

With the creation of the great kingdom of Tethera, an additional layer was added, that of High King (or High Queen, as in High Queen Boudicca's case). Proper honorifics included any and all from 'my lord' and up, with the caveat that these are pronounced with a more formal inflection which we indicate in print by ensuring that they are capitalized (i.e. My Lord, Your Highness, Your Majesty, Your Royal Majesty).

About the Author

The author thinks it a bit silly to write about himself from a third person point of view and believes he will soon cease doing so. Before doing so, he would like to point out that it seems a bit early for a bio as he is quite certain he is still not even halfway done with providing content for it.

I've lived all over the world and worked in a large number of jobs ranging from lifeguard, appliance salesman, rifle range instructor, intercontinental ballistic missile crew commander, assistant professor at the University of South Carolina, war planner, and captain in special ops. More recently, I have primarily worked as a contractor/consultant in fields pertaining to software development.

The Forged Prince was my first published work of fiction.

I live with my wife, Linda, in Westchester County, New York. Between us we have four grown children and expect that this may eventually lead to grandchildren (even though we are obviously much too young to be grandparents). Currently we are between dogs.

Please feel welcome to visit my site at: http://lairdmichael.com

I can also be twittered (what a word!) with @King_of_Tethera